D0870375

THE
PARTY

BOOKS BY TRÍONA WALSH

The Snowstorm

THE
PARTY

TRÍONA WALSH

bookouture

Published by Bookouture in 2023

An imprint of Storyfire Ltd.
Carmelite House
50 Victoria Embankment
London EC4Y oDZ

www.bookouture.com

Copyright © Tríona Walsh, 2023

Tríona Walsh has asserted her right to be identified as the author of this work.

All rights reserved. No part of this publication may be reproduced, stored in any retrieval system, or transmitted, in any form or by any means, electronic, mechanical, photocopying, recording or otherwise, without the prior written permission of the publishers.

ISBN: 978-1-83790-503-4
eBook ISBN: 978-1-83790-502-7

This book is a work of fiction. Names, characters, businesses, organizations, places and events other than those clearly in the public domain, are either the product of the author's imagination or are used fictitiously. Any resemblance to actual persons, living or dead, events or locales is entirely coincidental.

For my favourite parents

PROLOGUE

Panting and dizzy, Lizzie felt her knees weaken, leaden, just as she needed them most. Lizzie felt Claire's feet begin to drag.

'Stay with me, Mam, stay with me,' she cried into Claire's ear.

'Lizzie,' she whispered back.

Lizzie gave in to the hot tears that had been begging to start. Already nearly blinded by the night, they blurred what little vision she had left. The trees closed in around them.

Everything conspiring to obscure a fallen branch on the forest floor.

They tumbled. Lizzie gasped as the air slammed out of her lungs. Flat on her back she stared up at the overhead branches, seeing a tiny gap among the treetops. A star, just visible, twinkled at her. Mocking her. Lizzie made a wish. *Let us get out of here alive.* Summoning her last reserves, she pushed herself over, pain searing through her wounded arm. Lizzie stretched out, feeling for her mother. Listening for her. She crawled towards Claire's pained mumbles, feeling the forest floor squelch and ooze through her fingers.

She found her mother in a heap, put her hands under her arms and dragged her up against a large tree; using touch and smell to find a way in the all-consuming dark. Lizzie leant back against the damp trunk and hugged her mother to her. 'So s-s-sorry,' Claire said, quieter still. Holding her, Lizzie traced her fingertips down Claire's arm to her wrist. Felt the faint, slow, thump, thump, thump of her pulse. So weak.

If they didn't get to a hospital soon, she knew Claire would die. Lizzie let her tears flow unchecked. Silently.

She heaved her mother up again, getting little help from her, her chest shaking with her noiseless tears.

A sound. Nearby.

The crack and clunk of metal. The shotgun being reloaded.

1

THREE DAYS PREVIOUSLY

Friday 2 p.m.

Lizzie kicked the rucksack at her feet, loaded with a handful of books and a few changes of clothes. All of which she'd read or worn a million times in the six months she'd been here at St Brigid's Rehab Farm. As she wiped sweat off her brow and tucked behind her ears the few strands of her long black hair that weren't already sticking to her face, she wished she'd packed a sun hat. But six months ago in the depths of a bitter winter she'd packed her bag in a hurry.

Lizzie looked down the long driveway again. There was no sign of anyone other than the centre's cat, a ginger tom, who watched her lazily from the shade.

She let out a long sigh. Her stay here hadn't been easy. But she'd done the work. Lizzie was going home, clean. Well, she wasn't going home exactly. If her mother ever got here they'd be heading west for the long weekend.

There was a rumble in the distance and Lizzie looked up. A vehicle was coming. Lizzie's stomach twisted into a knot. She hadn't slept well for days. Worried about this reunion.

The car slowed. And stopped. A driver, eyes hidden behind shades, paid her no attention. The back door slid open. Dressed in a blue T-shirt, jeans and hiking boots – incongruously paired with a fancy updo and full face of make-up – Claire, Lizzie's mother, clambered out of the vehicle.

'Hi, Mam,' said Lizzie, testing a small smile.

'Hi, Lizzie.' Claire's face remained neutral, a mask hiding how she was feeling. Still cautious after everything. Lizzie couldn't blame her. Driving drunk had been the final straw that had landed Lizzie in here. Such a dangerous and idiotic thing to do. And, unforgivably, she'd done it with her brother Liam in the car. Mercifully he hadn't been seriously hurt, escaping with a nasty gash near his chin. But even a tiny scratch was too much. Claire hadn't been able to look at her after that. Their barely hanging in there family, already half destroyed, and Lizzie had done this. Claire had driven her straight to St Brigid's. They'd agreed no visits. Limited emails. They needed a break from each other.

'Who threw the confetti?' asked Lizzie as some coloured dots drifted by her. She tried to hide the note of suspicion in her voice.

'Just the staff at the guesthouse. And before you ask, they did witness duty too. We didn't secretly have a big wedding and not tell you.'

'I know...' said Lizzie, but she didn't really. She wouldn't have invited her pre-rehab self to anything. So maybe Claire hadn't invited her the wedding. *The wedding.* It felt surreal, but as she'd packed up her meagre possessions this morning and had her last ramble around the farm, her mother had been getting married in Dublin – to a guy Lizzie had never met.

'So, do I get to meet him, Prince Charming?'

'Of course.' Claire turned to the car and nodded. A grey-blond floppy-haired head appeared out the car door. A very large man, also dressed for the outdoors rather than a wedding, followed it. He beamed at Lizzie and thrust a hand in her direction.

'Hello there, Elizabeth! George Butler, pleased to meet you. You can call me...' and then he stopped. The smile slipped from his face. The three of them knew what he'd been about to say. *'You can call me Dad.'* A silly joke, an off-the-cuff ice-breaker from a mother's unfamiliar new husband. Innocent enough for another family. But not this one.

Poor George stood there, mortified.

'Don't worry about it,' Lizzie said. Reaching out and taking his hand. 'It's good to meet you.'

George smiled down at her.

'It's good to meet you too. Your mother's told me all about you.'

'That's a shame,' she said. George belly-laughed but Lizzie only managed a weak smile. It wasn't really a joke.

But it was good to finally meet George. Lizzie had heard very little about her mother's new husband. She'd even thought it was a joke when Claire had dropped the bombshell that she was getting remarried. There'd been a brief mention of meeting someone when Claire had emailed Lizzie about how Liam was doing. Claire had told her that she'd met a man in a Facebook support group for young widows and widowers. (*We're hardly 'young' though*, Claire had written. *I'm 45, not 25, and he's 54. But it's all relative, I guess.*) He was from Mayo and had a daughter the same age as Lizzie. That was it. But it hadn't just been the speed of it that had shocked Lizzie. How the romance had gone from first meeting to wedding in the six months she'd been in St Brigid's. It was also because of everything that had happened before. Five years ago. With Dad. After all of *that* she couldn't comprehend how Claire could be this spontaneous, this devil-may-care.

George grabbed Lizzie's bag and took it around to the boot. Lizzie took steps towards the car. Found herself closer to Claire.

Simultaneously, they realised most reunited mothers and daughters would have hugged by now. Lizzie leaned in. Claire did the same. Stiff and formal, there was enough space between them for a parade to march through.

'Come on,' said Claire. 'We've a long drive ahead. Your brother's in the very back.'

'In you hop!' George said, letting Lizzie get into the back beside her sibling. Beside Liam. From the frying pan into the fire. Just like Claire, or maybe even more so, this was a reunion she'd had sleepless nights over.

He sat there, bulky headphones on. Lizzie's breath caught. He'd grown so much since she'd seen him. She hadn't expected that. He'd turned eighteen while she was gone. He looked like a man now, and very much like one man in particular. Their dad. The black hair, the blue eyes, they were the same. Liam's jaw was stronger, more like how Declan's had been. She only hoped he was still the sweet and gentle boy he'd always been, and that he hadn't grown into Declan's personality as well. She could think of nothing more awful.

She sat down on the bench seat and pulled the seatbelt across her. Liam stared out the window. Didn't acknowledge her. The light caught the white line that ran along part of his jaw. Not so red or swollen now. Faded. Lizzie hoped like the memory of that night. Liam's pointed silence didn't suggest it had.

As the miles passed, Liam made no attempt to talk to her. He didn't even look at her. He rolled the window down at one point to let a fly out, but never turned in her direction. Lizzie caught Claire a few times, sneaking glances back at them. Lizzie turned away. The green fields and sheep, the small towns and villages slipped by. Lizzie was rocked into calmness by the movement of the car.

As the mobile signal wavered Liam began to pay more attention to those around him in the car.

'What happened to civilisation?' he muttered.

'We left it back there,' said Lizzie, 'about fifty years down the road.'

He looked at her, finally, but didn't laugh. Then went back to staring out the window.

Twenty minutes out from the last village – one pub and a shut post office – they pulled into the side of the road. Everyone disgorged from the minivan, into the late afternoon's heat, stretching out limbs and shaking off the stiffness from the long journey.

'Down the end of that boreen there,' said George, pointing across the road at a bumpy-looking lane, 'we'll find the entrance to my humble abode.'

Everyone looked over. There was a lane alright. But far more compelling were the trees on either side of it. Crowding up to the very edge of walls that stretched for miles in either direction. Dense, thick, overshadowing everything, dominating every inch of the landscape. And even on this super-hot summer's day, this forest looked murky and cool.

George handed out bags from the back of the minivan then went to the driver's window. He handed the man a wad of cash.

'Back here, one p.m. on Tuesday,' he said to him. 'We've no mobile signal out here, so can't be contacted in the meantime. We've flights from Knock Airport Tuesday afternoon which we can't miss, so we need you here, then. Okay?'

As the man nodded and started the minivan, Lizzie and Liam looked down at their phones. True enough, the bars were completely greyed out.

'Feck,' said Liam, a cloud passing across his face.

Lizzie was less upset. There was no one waiting for her text or social media post.

She looked up and saw George's animated face grinning like a five-year-old at the pair of them.

'Okay, come on, gang. Let's walk!'

2

'This is mental,' grumbled Liam, trudging on, batting away low branches. 'Who builds a house in the middle of the woods?'

Lizzie side-eyed him. Claire and George were up ahead, so he wasn't talking to them. But he wasn't talking to her either, his mumblings clearly just for his own ears. Lizzie decided to reply anyway.

'I think,' she said, slow and tentative, 'that the woods came after. We passed the remains of gate pillars back there. They must've been the start of a driveway once. I don't think this place has been properly looked after for a long time.'

Liam looked at her, scowling, but said nothing. Lizzie filled the silence.

'Did George ever tell you anything about the house?'

Liam shook his head.

'Nothing?' said Lizzie, forcing conversation on him.

'I think Mam said it's a wrecked cottage, maybe. Something like that.'

'Okay, I see.'

Lizzie swatted away a cloud of midges and peered through

the trees looking for any sign of this house. They were following a winding compacted earth path. Totally surrounded, hemmed in on all sides. Occasional fallen trees, their trunks moss covered, lay settled on the forest floor. There were rustles in the undergrowth and flurries in the branches above them. Lizzie wrinkled her nose at the damp rotting mulch smell they were kicking up as they walked. This place was entirely, unapologetically, wild.

She looked back at Liam.

'How've you been doing?' Relieved she'd gotten some words out of him, Lizzie kept going. 'Mam kept me informed. A bit. I'm glad the accident didn't stop you finishing school.'

'The accident? Is that what we're calling it? I thought it was you driving drunk with me in the car and we hit a wall? It's not like we tripped, Lizzie.'

'I'm sor—'

'Oh, please don't.'

'I need to tell you that I'm sorry, Liam. I need to show you. And Mam.'

Liam looked at her. Shook his head.

'Really, Lizzie. Just leave it.'

He pulled his headphones on again. She shouldn't have pushed it.

'Everyone okay?' Claire called out from further down the path. Holding George's hand, Claire was standing in one of the few patches of sun that managed to dapple through the dense forest canopy. The sunlight sparkled and danced on her face and Lizzie thought her mother looked radiant. Transformed, unrecognisable, in her happiness.

'Liam?' Claire cried, louder this time. Lizzie turned around. Liam had stopped, and was staring back the way they'd come. At his mother's second cry he'd spun around, pushing his headphones off his ears. Looking like a five-year-old caught in the treat cupboard.

'Planning your escape?' whispered Lizzie as he caught up with her.

'Something like that,' he muttered, then kept walking, falling into step next to Claire and George.

'Are Lizzie and I Hansel and Gretel?' Liam asked Claire, who smiled, rolling her eyes affectionately. Lizzie looked away. The change of tone, the lightness in his voice when talking to their mother, hurt.

'Behave, Liam,' Claire chuckled.

'Is the plan to dump us here while you and George go to a five-star hotel? This place has total evil fairy-tale energy, Mam. You could have warned me, I'd have brought more breadcrumbs.'

'Don't worry, young man,' George said, 'no one's getting abandoned!'

Liam turned to his new stepfather.

'We might get lost though, no? I mean, there isn't even a proper driveway.' He looked around him.

'A sturdy four-by-four can make it through,' replied George.

'Why are we walking, then?'

'Because it's fun! And also, I don't actually own one of those big gas-guzzling environmental nightmares!'

'Wouldn't one of them be a bit essential though, no? Around here?' said Lizzie. 'Like, how do you even get the shopping in?'

George laughed.

'I have an old quad and its trailer. And if I need anything bigger there's a farmer I've an arrangement with. He ferries in my supplies in *his* big gas-guzzling environmental nightmare!' George pointed to a few track marks in the path. 'Look, he's been by, dropping off what we need for the weekend. Good, good.'

'Couldn't he have waited for us?' said Liam. 'It's such a trek, and having to carry our bags on our backs like pack mules. It's too hot for this, even in here.'

'But don't you see the charm?' George said. 'I've grown to rather like that if you want to get to the house you have to do it on nature's terms, not man's. I respect it! It reminds me that we aren't the ones in control. It's good to be kept humble, don't you think?'

'Er, if you say so,' replied Liam.

'But I understand, it is a bit... unconventional. We've been renovating the house since my father inherited it and it's so bloody expensive. There's always something urgent and essential that needs doing. The priority has been getting it liveable again.' George looked around, peering up with a frown at the tall trees. 'We've rather ignored out here. But, if nothing else, all the trees and lack of driveway keep people away! No need for fences.'

George took Claire's hand, and they strode on ahead. Liam looked at Lizzie.

'Fences or no fences, I'm not sure he has to worry about people bothering him,' said Liam.

'Perhaps not.' Lizzie smiled. 'He's a bit over the top.'

'Yeah.'

Liam looked behind him.

'So, what do you think – have we been walking thirty-five minutes now? Forty? Does that sound right to you?' he asked.

'I haven't been keeping track. Why are you asking?'

Lizzie peered at her brother through narrowed eyes. Why the interest in how long it was taking them? Was he planning a – not so fast – getaway?

'Seriously, you're not thinking of bailing, are you?'

'What?' Liam looked at her.

'You're so interested in how long this is taking, it sounds like you're making plans.'

'I'm not going to bail. I wouldn't do that to Mam.'

Lizzie felt the sting. They all knew who the troublemaker was. Who might do that.

Lizzie wasn't sure she was so keen to talk to Liam if that's what he might say. She let him walk on ahead.

She saw Claire had stopped and was crouching down, holding her phone over a patch of small blue flowers. Lizzie went over to her.

'Taking photos?'

Claire looked up.

'No, using my gardening app – I'm identifying plants.'

'Is it working? Don't you need signal for that?'

'Yes, but I downloaded the app database before we left. I thought signal might be dodgy.'

'Smart.'

Lizzie looked around. An awkward silence settled between them. She took a deep breath.

'George is very at home in the wilds, isn't he?'

'Absolutely,' said Claire standing up. 'He's a big boy scout.'

'He really loves this place,' Lizzie said.

'He does,' Claire smiled.

'I hope he loves you as much.'

'You don't need to worry, Lizzie, he does.' They started down the path again. 'We're older, and our love probably looks a bit quiet to you. But love doesn't have to be all drama and grand gestures.'

It was left unspoken who had been all about drama and grand gestures. Declan. Including one, final, grand gesture to top them all.

'You got married very quickly, that's not old and boring.'

Claire looked at Lizzie as they walked but didn't reply. Lizzie felt the old discomfort, the itchiness in her skin whenever her mother went quiet.

'I learnt a pretty tough lesson that knowing someone a life-time doesn't guarantee you a happy ending.'

'I'm sorry, Mam, I didn't mean...' she began but Claire shook her head.

She looked back at Lizzie. 'Don't worry, I know what I'm doing.'

They caught up with George. The path out of the woods started to widen. The four of them followed it until, through the gaps in the trees, the grass of a lawn and the first hint of man's influence on the landscape – some greys of stone against the greens and browns of the woods – began to come into focus.

'Welcome,' cried George, as they emerged from the trees, 'to Butler Hall!'

'Bloody hell,' gasped Lizzie, her jaw dropping.

3

Lizzie stood there, speechless. As did Claire and Liam, their jaws similarly slack.

'This is *your house*?' she finally managed.

This was no tumbledown cottage. No run-down ramshackle abode. Instead, sitting here in the clearing, deep in the wild wood – near magically – was an enormous, grand, stately home. Uncomfortably squeezed onto a plot of land far, far too small for it, this house was three floors high, had a four-granite-column portico in front of a large, glossy black front door, fronted by wide stone steps.

'Yup.' George grinned. 'This is the place.'

Lizzie let her rucksack fall to the ground. She put her hand to her forehead to shield her eyes and looked up to the roof and down again. The summer sun, high in the sky, cast little shadow. Lizzie felt it scorch her skin.

'She's a stunner, no?' said George, his grin even wider, if that was possible.

'Liam told me it was a run-down old cottage!'

George laughed.

'Well, I was a bit vague about the details.' He turned and

looked at Claire, eyes shining. 'I had to be sure you loved me for me and not my house,' he chuckled.

'George Butler, you old fool, of course I love you for yourself... though I might love you a bit more now.' Claire laughed, and put her arm around George's back, cuddling into him. 'It makes a lovely change from your poky apartment in Dublin, I'll say that.'

'Are you rich?' asked Liam with all the tact of a five-year-old.

'If only!'

'Is that one of those "I'm not rich, I've only a couple of million in the bank" kinda not rich?' Liam continued.

George laughed again.

'No, I'm afraid not. It's a "not rich", not rich kind of thing. The money left the family a long time ago. Around the time the house was burnt down in the 1920s. That's why it's taken decades to begin to rebuild. I run corporate hunting weekends here and do estate management consultancy around the country. That brings in enough to chip away at renovations. But sadly, no, not a secret billionaire!'

Lizzie looked back at the forest from where they'd just emerged. For all the house's stunning grandeur, it was surrounded, crowded, by the woods. What must it look like from above? Lizzie wondered. She pictured a birds-eye view – miles and miles of forest, with this mansion at its epicentre, a needle at the centre of a leafy haystack. At the side of the house it looked like the trees might come within metres of the walls. It all unsettled Lizzie.

'Who'd like to see inside?' George said, looking at the three of them. 'And let's see if Freya is here yet. Her plane would have landed a couple of hours ago. She might have beaten us here.'

Lizzie remembered Claire mentioning George's daughter.

But she hadn't mentioned she was going to be here. Her heart sank.

George took Claire's hands and led her up the steps towards the door.

'I think this might actually be Downton Abbey,' said Liam, following them.

'It's incredible,' said Lizzie, bringing up the rear. 'Those trees are making me super claustrophobic, though. They're intimidating.'

Liam looked over his shoulder at the woods.

'You need to chill, Lizzie. They're just trees.'

They followed Claire and George up the steps and into the house.

'Wow,' said Lizzie, amazed for a second time, reflecting an identical wonderment on her mother and brother's faces. Like children who'd stumbled accidentally into Aladdin's cave. The three of them looked around them, drinking it all in. The hall floor was tiled in white and black, and the walls were half panelled in a dark wood. Old paintings were dotted around the place. It was cool again, in here, like the woods. The heat outside forgotten. They stopped, the echo of their feet quietening.

'Oh!' exclaimed George, pointing to a crystal vase full of woodland flowers on a dark wooden hall table. 'She's home!'

A heavy wooden door on the left of the hall opened fully and a light, happy voice chimed.

'She certainly is.'

A petite girl, with loose flowing blonde hair, wearing cream yoga pants and a floaty beige top – a look that screamed contrived hippy to Lizzie – stepped into the hall.

'Freya! My darling!' George opened his arms and the girl ran into her father's embrace.

Claire slipped back to Lizzie and Liam.

'She went travelling and has been in the States for the last two, three years. Hasn't been home in all that time because of her visa,' she said, whispering. 'They're very close. Her mother died a long time ago, when she was only small, so it's just been the two of them.'

'I see,' said Lizzie.

'She's twenty-three, like you, Lizzie. You might find things in common.' Lizzie suppressed a snort, reminded herself to be New Lizzie. Her mother didn't sound like she was being sarcastic, but it was hard to imagine she was being serious. This girl, with tiny braids with silver cuffs in her long blonde hair didn't feel like some kindred spirit. *Is she a failure and addict too?* Lizzie was tempted to ask.

George turned to them, his arm around Freya's shoulder, the pair of them grinning ear to ear.

'Freya, this is Claire, and her kids – Elizabeth and Liam.'

Freya stepped forward.

'Hi, everyone!' She gave a little wave. 'It's super lovely to meet you all.'

Claire offered her hand to Freya. 'It's really good to finally meet you in person, and not on a computer screen.'

'You too, Claire,' said Freya, ignoring the hand and instead gathering her new stepmother in for a hug.

Lizzie held her breath. This apple-cheeked girl had the energy of someone about to say, 'Can I call you Mum?' Lizzie, for all her complicated relationship with Claire, was in no mood to hear that. But it didn't come. She exhaled.

'It's really wonderful to have you here, Freya,' said Claire. 'But, I think I feel a bit guilty.'

'Guilty?' asked George, frowning.

'I mean, won't you have trouble getting back into the US? Your dad told me that you hadn't been home in so long because you'd overstayed your visa. That if you left you couldn't return. I can't help but feel bad if you've done that, just for us. Obviously, we're over the moon to see you, but such a sacrifice... are we worth it, George?' Claire looked worried.

'Don't fret, Claire, my dear. It's Butler Hall that's responsible. It's what brought her home. Isn't it, Freya? No one can ever stay away from here...'

Freya smiled indulgently at her father.

'You're so thoughtful, Claire. But don't worry. It was time.'

George guided Freya in Lizzie's direction.

'This is Elizabeth.'

'Elizabeth, it's lovely to meet you,' Freya said, kissing the air close to Lizzie's left and right cheeks.

'It's just Lizzie, really,' she replied. Lizzie should have corrected George sooner. He'd been calling her Elizabeth since they'd picked her up. There was only one person who'd called her Elizabeth and he was dead.

'Ah, okay, *Lizzie* it is then,' said Freya, a gentle smile on her face.

'And this is Liam.' George moved on. Lizzie watched her brother hold his new stepsister's hand a little too long. God, teenage boys were the worst. Thankfully Freya seemed too distracted to notice.

'What do you think of our home?' she asked.

'Simply stunning,' said Claire.

'She's a beauty, isn't she?' George seemed to grow even larger as he absorbed their amazement at the house. 'Still so much work to do though.' He walked over to a door off to the left of the hall. Opened it. They all gathered round and peered in. Inside was a shell of a room. Half plastered. A gap like a missing front tooth in the chimney breast where the fireplace should be. The floorboards were a jumble of old and new, patched together. Everyone wandered in and looked around, their footsteps echoing all the way to the rafters two floors above. Following the echoes they looked up and could see the room above through the missing ceiling, it, too, equally bare and pared back.

'We only have the main reception rooms over on the other side of the house finished to a standard Freya and I like, but bit by bit we're getting there!'

'Speaking of which,' said Freya, 'come into the drawing room, Daddy. I brought you a present from America.'

'Oh, lucky me,' said George, rubbing his hands and smiling. 'What is it?'

'Come on and I'll show you.'

They all trooped out of the unfinished room and followed Freya across the hall. She opened the door into the drawing room. Lizzie took in the high-ceilinged room, with oak floorboards and large windows hung with thick, flowing burgundy curtains. A red patterned rug covered most of the floor. On it sat two cream brocade sofas with wooden legs and silk throws.

And on one of the sofas sat a very handsome, blonde young man.

He stood up.

George looked at the stranger, his smile stalled. He looked back at his daughter.

'Freya?' he said.

She crossed the room and linked arms with the young man.

'Daddy, Claire... I've a bit of a surprise for you.'

4

'A surprise?' said George, confused. Looking from his daughter
to the young man and back again.

'You see, you're not the only couple on honeymoon this
week! Daddy, everyone, this is Hudson Gore. Hudson, this is
my father, George Butler. And his new wife, Claire.'

George's mouth flapped, opening and closing, wordless.

'What?' he finally managed, dumbfounded.

'We wanted it to be a surprise,' replied Freya.

'That it is,' George spluttered.

Claire opened her arms.

'Congratulations, guys! I'd say welcome to the family,
Hudson, but I suspect you beat me to it, you might want to
welcome me!' Hudson's shoulders relaxed and he laughed as he
hugged Claire. George took a reluctant step forward.

Hudson put out his hand.

'I'm very pleased to meet you, sir. And, em, I hope you'll
forgive me for not asking your permission first. And springing
this on you. Freya promised you wouldn't mind. Everything was
so rushed in the end. So we could be here... so Freya could come
home...' The words came tumbling out, his American accent

soft and languorous even in its haste. His accent conjured pictures of second homes, private schools and Ivy League colleges.

'Well, that explains why she was able to travel,' whispered Lizzie to Liam. 'She'll get a green card being married to this guy.'

'Cool,' said Liam with little interest. He slipped his headphones back on his head and sat on one of the sofas. Lizzie drifted over to the windows. Behind her George sounded like he was already rallying.

'Oh, well, goodness, welcome to the family!' she heard him say. She looked over her shoulder and watched George pull Hudson into a bear hug. The two men, similar in height, and both fair-haired, half merged, like a time-lapse photo of young to old. Lizzie smiled to herself – Freya might just have done the classic and married a man like her darling Daddy.

Lizzie stared back out at the trees. Not quite as close as they seemed at first glance outside, they were still closer than seemed wise. If it wasn't for the tall windows, this room would have been quite dark. A rabbit darted from the forest edge and hovered nervously for a moment, nose twitching in the air. It made Lizzie think of Hudson, quivering anxiously.

'What do you think of Butler Hall?' A voice in her ear made Lizzie jump.

She turned and looked into the sea-blue eyes of Freya. Lizzie stepped to her left a little, the girl felt too close.

'Sorry, I didn't mean to startle you,' said Freya, smiling.

'No, don't worry. I was distracted by a rabbit there.' Lizzie pointed and Freya looked out the window, but the creature had slipped back into the forest.

'It's gone,' said Lizzie, instantly feeling stupid stating the obvious. She looked back at Freya. 'What do I think of Butler Hall? It's like nowhere else I've ever been.'

Freya beamed.

'It *is* like nowhere else, isn't it? I don't think I realised quite how unique it was until I went away.'

'Did you grow up here?'

'Oh yes. Daddy has the small apartment in Dublin, but we spent all our time down here. It was just the best. Like, the house was a wreck, but the forest, the closeness to nature, it's always been glorious. I'll sound kooky when I say this, but it was a mother to me when Mum died.' Freya stepped closer to the window and pulled it open. The soundtrack of the woods meandered in. The rustling of wind in the trees. Birdsong. And the absence of other sounds. No traffic, no bustle of modern life.

Freya lowered her voice. Gestured to the woods outside.

'I think... I think we're all connected to this earth. I know, that's such a hippy thing to say, but Hudson agrees with me.' Freya looked over at her new husband with a dreamy grin on her face. 'And Daddy understands. He feels it too. When I was a child he'd forget about me, when he was engrossed in restoring the house. I'd go out for the day, and if I got tired, I'd just sleep on the forest floor. When I got hungry I knew what berries and mushrooms I could eat safely. All the deer and birds, the badgers and the foxes, they were eyes following me, making sure I was safe. I was never afraid out there, on my own. There was no big bad wolf waiting to gobble me up.'

'You sound like a Disney character,' Lizzie said, laughing uncomfortably at Freya's intensity. 'Did you sing to the woodland creatures and did they help you with your chores?'

Freya rested back against the windowsill and frowned.

'Ah, I'm sorry. I was only messing,' Lizzie mumbled. She might be intense but Lizzie could see where Freya got it from. George seemed just as evangelical. These two loved this place, that was clear. 'Our walk through the woods was amazing. I can see how growing up here could have been magical.'

Freya called to Hudson who was still being interrogated by George.

'Our children, darling, can't you see them running around out there, playing hide and seek with each other? Getting happily lost?' Hudson took her interjection as an opportunity to escape from George. He trotted over.

'Definitely, sweetheart.' He put his arm around her waist and his puppy-dog eyes stared down at her.

'And please let's have more than one,' said Freya. 'As glorious as it was to grow up here, I was lonely at times. I'd have loved to have a brother. Or a sister.' She looked at Lizzie, a shy smile on her face. 'It's a shame our parents didn't meet ten years sooner.'

'Well, my father wasn't dead then. So, it would have been complicated.'

'Oh, I'm sorry. How stupid of me.' Pinpricks of embarrassment dotted her cheeks.

'Lizzie!' snapped Claire, who'd been within earshot. She walked over and joined them. 'Freya, I'm sorry, Lizzie can forget her tact sometimes.'

'Thanks, Mam. Any other of my failings you want to apologise for?'

'Lizzie, please don't start...' Claire's voice wavered.

Lizzie took a deep breath. She felt Freya's delicate fingers rest gently on her forearm.

'I don't know the circumstances. But I understand how hard it is to lose a parent. The grief never ends.'

Lizzie nodded but said nothing. Freya was wrong. For Lizzie her grief over Declan had ended. Pretty quickly. When the truth began to reveal itself. They'd only arrived home from meeting with the Gardaí – who'd told them they'd keep searching for Declan's body – when Claire had gotten the call from the company accountant. Telling her what he'd discovered. It gradually became clear what her father had been up to. Robbing Peter to pay Paul. Dodgy deals. Risks and lies. Destroying their lives in secret. Lizzie's grief had given way to rage. Liam and Claire hadn't been able to cope with her like that. A ball of fury. She hadn't been able to cope with herself. It's why she'd started drinking too much and taking drugs. Sleeping with awful men. Going so far off the rails that she thundered off course, demolishing everything in her path. Still, five years later she wanted to say to Freya – *'I'm not grieving. I'm apoplectic. He killed himself, you see. He killed himself rather than face up to what he did. Betrayed us. Destroyed everything. Not just our finances but our memories of him.'*

She looked back at Freya.

'Freya, thank you.' She took a deep breath. 'I'm sorry, this whole area isn't my greatest strength. Sorry, Mam.' Humility. Acceptance. Forgiveness. St Brigid's had drummed into her the new path she had to take.

'Right, everyone!' George, planted in the centre of the room, beckoned them all back to him. 'I expect everyone might appreciate a chance to go to their rooms and freshen up after our trek. It'll be dinner time in not too long, I suspect, from the delicious smells that have been wafting in to us from the kitchen. Looks like we must thank you, Freya darling; you've been busy while waiting for us. What a great girl you are!'

Freya looked at Claire, a conspiratorial smirk passing between them.

'What's this?' asked George, a confused but amused look on his face as he glanced from his new wife to his daughter.

'Well, darling,' began Claire, taking a few steps toward the drawing room door. 'It seems today has one more little surprise in store for you... give me a moment...' She grinned and winked at her husband and slipped out of the room.

George looked at Freya. She smiled but said nothing. He looked back at the oak-panelled door, a happy frown on his face.

'I wonder what it is...'

A moment later Claire returned.

She beckoned someone in. A dark-haired woman stepped into the room behind her.

George froze. His face dropped, going deathly pale.

5

Lizzie stared at George. What on earth was wrong? Her mother couldn't see his face as George had stepped beyond her, closer to the stranger. Liam and Hudson too were at the wrong angle to see the reaction. Only Lizzie, and maybe Freya, could have caught the bolt of shock on his face.

'Sweetie,' said Claire, oblivious to her new husband's shock. 'You've just been brilliant, I love you so much. And bringing us all here to stay at Butler Hall is just going to be the best start to our honeymoon. So special. Even more special now we've seen the place.' Everyone laughed. Lizzie watched George force a mirthless smile onto his face. 'I know we're all going to relax and chill out and have a great time and I thought, wouldn't it be extra special if I hired someone, to come in and look after us?"

Claire half-turned to the woman beside her. She set her hands like a gameshow hostess showing off the prizes to be won.

'This is Mia Casey, she's from Mayo too, and she is a trained chef. She is going to cook for us during our entire stay and just spoil us. We won't have to lift a finger. This is my wedding present to you.' Claire clapped her hands like an excited child.

Lizzie watched George stare at the cook. He turned around

to Claire, the forced grin still on his face, not that Claire seemed to notice its unnaturalness. He gathered her into him.

'Thank you, darling, so thoughtful,' Lizzie heard him whisper into her ear.

One arm still around Claire's shoulder, he put his hand out to the cook.

'Pleased to meet you... I'm sorry, I didn't catch it, what did you say your name was?'

'Mia Casey,' she said.

'Okay. I see.' He shook her hand but quickly dropped it.

'Thank you again,' he said to Claire. 'Such a lovely surprise.'

Claire beamed up at him.

He then looked around the room,

'Come on, everyone, let's get you all sorted upstairs. Then we can come down later to enjoy my wedding present.'

They all trooped after George, following him out of the room and up the polished wooden stairs to the second floor. Lizzie saw him glance through the banisters at the departing cook as she disappeared back into the kitchen. But by the time he stopped in the centre of the landing, he seemed himself again. His good cheer reasserted. *What the hell had that been about?* thought Lizzie.

'This is the main bathroom,' George opened a door, revealing a large, white-porcelain and panelled bathroom. 'I'm afraid this old house doesn't have en suites so we're all sharing. Everyone will need a bit of patience. But the hot water is reliable, so there should be enough for everyone each day. As long as no one lingers too long in the shower. It'll probably gurgle and the pipes will make all sorts of noises, but don't worry!'

'Freya, you two are in your room, obviously. Liam, you're over there,' George pointed to the first door to the left at the top of the stairs. 'And, Lizzie, you, my dear, are over there.' He indicated the door across the other side of the landing. 'For our newcomers, the bedrooms aren't entirely renovated yet, so please don't be disappointed. But they're clean and all in one piece, don't worry.'

Lizzie watched the relaxed George as he spoke. Could she have imagined that moment with the cook? She was definitely feeling overstimulated by all the new people and places after six months in St Brigid's. Was that all it was? He certainly seemed fine now.

George looked at Claire. 'Right so. I think we're going to freshen up before dinner.' Claire nodded. He lifted his and Claire's bags and everyone dispersed.

Lizzie opened the door to her room. The door handle of Lizzie's room rattled in her hand. She was greeted by a large room, plain but comfortable. Nothing like the grandeur of downstairs as George had warned. No four-poster beds nor antiques.

Lizzie walked over and sat down on the large brass metal bed. It was the best thing in the room. Instantly enveloped in plump white linen and eiderdown, Lizzie felt like she was being consumed by a cloud. Her whole body relaxed. Doors out on the landing opened and closed. People heading for the bathroom. Getting ready for dinner.

She heard a gentle knock on her door.

'Lizzie?' a quiet voice called from the other side. Reluctantly Lizzie hauled herself off the bed. She went over, opened the door a crack.

It was Freya. A tentative smile on her face.

'Can I come in a moment?' she asked.

'Sure,' said Lizzie standing back. She'd rather be left alone in these precious people-free moments. But Freya looked like she'd something on her mind. She stopped in the centre of the room and looked about the place.

'I hope you'll find it comfortable in here. I think the bedrooms are next on the list...'

'It's lovely. Don't worry.'

'Good.'

Lizzie stood there, waiting for Freya to say what she'd come to say. She didn't think her comfort was what had prompted the visit.

'I think I might have put my foot in it there, downstairs. I want to apologise.'

Lizzie waved away her words.

'You've nothing to say sorry for.'

'No. I do. Daddy just popped into my room and filled me in on your family... history. I'm mortified.'

'Honestly, Freya, don't give it another thought.'

Freya nodded, and took a few steps towards the door. She stopped again and looked back at Lizzie.

'What was he like?' she asked. 'I mean, before it all went wrong.'

Lizzie frowned. 'Why do you want to know?'

'Ah... I was just thinking it might be nice to hear about him in better times. Nice for you, I mean. To think about that.'

'That's... that's very thoughtful of you,' said Lizzie. She closed her eyes, and took a breath in. Those particular memories she'd locked away. Hadn't let herself think about. 'He was... he was fun.' Lizzie opened her eyes again. A sad smile on her face. 'He was fun. A joker. Never in the kitchen at parties! He'd be right there, in the centre of everything. You couldn't miss him. He knew everyone's name, never forgot a face. I don't remember him ever being downbeat. But I guess he must have been sometimes. He made my mam laugh... it's been good to see her smile again with your dad. He spoilt me rotten, which I never realised. Until after. He and Liam never totally clicked. But not in a bad way, you know, just I think Dad would have liked him to be more like him. I don't think they really understood each other. I, on the other hand, thought he was superman, that he could do anything. And he did too. I don't think he meant to destroy the business. He messed up, scrambled to fix it when it went wrong. And he got in too deep. Made some awful choices.'

She shrugged. 'But, he was a good dad. Well. Until he wasn't.'

'You should let yourself remember those good times more. I don't think it's a bad thing.'

Lizzie nodded.

'Maybe you're right. But it's hard. Very hard.'

'I can imagine... Look, I'll leave you in peace now. And, again, I'm truly sorry for being so insensitive.' Freya slipped out of the room.

Lizzie stood still for a moment, the ghost of Declan at her shoulder. Then, like a shiver, she shook it off, dragged herself back to the moment. She looked around the room. It was stuffy in here. She went over to one of the sash windows, pulling the bottom half up with a tug and a squeak. Resting her elbows on the sill, Lizzie pushed away the past and stared out.

Lizzie glanced down at the paved terrace below. There was a long table set with silverware and china. There were two scarlet sprays of flowers displayed on it, and candles, not lit yet, running its length. Cream ribbons were tied to the backs of all the chairs and strings of fairy lights were strung all around the terrace. Lizzie could already imagine the soft glow of them and the candles when it finally got dark. Red rose petals were scattered about the table and from this height they looked like little hearts.

Her eye was drawn from the table to the trees. There was movement in the woods. Someone was in there. She leant further out the window. Squinting.

It was Liam.

What was he doing down there? Why wasn't he up in his room like the rest of them getting ready for dinner? Instead, he was standing there, stock-still, staring into the thick of the woods. He crouched down on his hunkers, still looking straight ahead. Like he was searching the trees for something.

Lizzie leant out the window.

'Liam, what you doing?' she yelled.

Liam nearly jumped out of his skin. Knocked off balance with the fright, he fell backwards on his rear onto the terrace. His phone, which he'd been holding, skittered from his hands, stopping a little way away from him.

He looked up at her with a scowl. 'Jeez, Lizzie. Don't do that.'

'Sorry.'

He pushed himself up off the ground, and stood.

'What were you doing?' she repeated. She opened her mouth to continue, to make a joke, but she stopped herself. Things weren't like how they'd been before between them.

'I wasn't doing anything. Just looking for signal.' He waved his phone at her.

Liam shook his head and headed for the house, disappearing from view without another word. Lizzie stood back from the window and shrugged. From the landing the click of the lock on the bathroom door sounded, and she looked towards her door. She'd try and get in there before anyone else nabbed it.

Lizzie grabbed her backpack from the dresser. She had a nice yellow cotton dress she could wear once she'd freshened up. She could hang it in the bathroom while she showered, so the steam would help the wrinkles fall out. She searched for it through the bag, but instead her fingers found one of the books she'd packed. She pulled it out, looked at the tatty paperback. In a crazy moment she'd grabbed it from her room as she'd gathered her things for St Brigid's. She leant back against the end of the bed and stared at it. Declan's ghost lingered.

The book had the musty smell that old books got. The page edges were browning ever so slightly. She turned it over in her hands, brushing imaginary dust from it. The illustration on the cover was of four children and a dog, hiding in a wood as an old-fashioned car pulled up. *Five Get Into Trouble*. She remembered how Declan used to read to her. Imbued with those good memories Freya had asked about. Lizzie smiled as she remembered how he'd done all the voices. Even for the girls. They'd giggle when he did Anne's voice, all silly and high-pitched. Her smile faded. Claire would probably remember the book too. A little differently though, Lizzie realised. As a child her mother offered to read to her too. But Lizzie had only ever wanted her dad to read to her. She remembered Claire's hurt face as she said, 'I can do boy voices just as well as your dad can do the girl voices,' and Lizzie and her dad had just rolled their eyes behind her back.

It was only now, clean and sober, and an adult, she could see how Declan shouldn't have done that. The disrespect he'd shown Claire. The disrespect he'd taught Lizzie.

She closed the book.

She shouldn't have brought it. She shouldn't have listened to Freya, well intentioned as she was. It wasn't healing remembering Declan. It was just another way to punish herself now she couldn't drink or take drugs. She gripped the book, her face contorted with disgust and self-loathing, then flung it, launching it across the room with all her strength. The book hit the far wall with a quiet thump and fell to the floor.

6

Lizzie pulled on the yellow dress. It was nearly 7 p.m. but it was still warm. She grabbed a light pink scarf from her bag for later in case it cooled down. With one last quick look at herself in the dresser mirror, tucking her dark hair behind her ears, she had to admit she looked okay. Lizzie had stopped looking at herself in mirrors for a long time, repelled by the way her black hair had hung lank to her shoulders, as dull as her emotions. Her skin pale and grey where it wasn't raw with clusters of red, angry spots. Now, her hair shone and her skin glowed. The gaunt look she'd become accustomed to had been lost, left somewhere behind the gates of St Brigid's. It was a relief.

She opened her door. It was quiet on the landing. She'd heard everyone else's footsteps on the stairs already. She'd be the last one down.

With a quiet nod at the red-faced and busy cook, Lizzie slipped through the kitchen and out the back door. She stepped onto the terrace where everyone else was gathered. The air was filled with lively chatting and laughter. Music floated out from open double doors at the back of the house. The terrace, still bright in the evening despite the trees blocking any direct sun, was further illuminated by the twinkling of the criss-cross of fairy lights.

Freya and Hudson, in each other's arms, swayed to the music's mellow beat. Hudson occasionally whispering in Freya's ear, eliciting quiet giggles from her. George was expounding animatedly on some topic, directing his enthusiasm at Liam, all the while with an arm around Claire's shoulder. Lizzie watched her mother smile up at him. Her eyes gleaming. Lizzie looked away. She wandered over to the table where a bottle was chilling in a bucket. And despite so much warmth in the evening, Lizzie felt her insides go as cold as the ice. She stared at the bottle. While reassured that she wasn't feeling an urge to grab it and drink, it was still like running into an ex-lover unexpectedly – you may not love them any more, but it still hurt.

'It's safe, don't worry,' called over Claire. 'Non-alcoholic.'

'Thanks,' Lizzie called back. Her insides unclenching a little.

Claire slipped out from under George's arm and came over to her.

'There's no alcohol anywhere in the house,' she said as she lifted the dripping bottle out of the bucket and poured two glasses. 'We didn't want to risk a scene,' she muttered under her breath.

'There wouldn't have been a scene,' said Lizzie, counting to ten in her head.

'Well. I didn't want to take any chances.'

'Mam, I'm straight out of six months of rehab. Give me some credit. You'll have to start trusting me again sometime.'

'Trust is like a bank, Lizzie.'

'Oh God, not this.' Lizzie rolled her eyes. Claire's 'trust is like a bank' spiel, she'd heard it many times before.

Ignoring her, Claire continued.

'I can only dispense the amount of trust that has been deposited. You build up your "savings", and I'll be able to start trusting you again.'

'I don't think that's actually how banks work, Mam.'

Claire fixed her a look.

'You know exactly what I mean...' Claire handed her a glass. Taking it, Lizzie eyed her mother over the rim. Claire turned and walked back over to George. Lizzie sighed. She had to admit her line of credit with her mother was deservedly bad. She took a sip of her drink. Felt the harmless bubbles burst on her tongue. She looked at the glass. There wasn't a non-alcoholic drink yet that hadn't depressed her a little. No one drank alcohol because they were thirsty. And she couldn't help but feel bad. On her wedding day Claire couldn't raise a glass of real champagne to celebrate. Because of her. Another sacrifice, another compromise due to troubled burdensome Lizzie.

Mia emerged from the kitchen carrying two large, heavy-looking jugs of water. Liam trotted over to her, taking them and bringing them to the table. Lizzie heard Mia's quiet words of thanks.

'You can all come over now and take a seat, dinner is ready,' Mia announced to the group. With happy murmurs of assent, everyone made their way to the table and sat. After several trips in and out, Mia had laid a feast in front of them, its aromas bringing new glorious notes to the idyll.

'Thank you so much, Mia. This all looks wonderful,' said Claire, smiling up at the cook.

'Yes, thank you,' agreed George, surveying the spread.

Lizzie studied George but this time he didn't give Mia a second look.

'If you need me,' she said at the kitchen door, 'just call.' She slipped back into the house, leaving them to their dinner.

'Come on then, everyone!' said George, with gusto. 'Let's enjoy our wedding breakfast!' He picked up a dish, filled to the brim with buttery asparagus, and passed it to Claire. He then grabbed a plate with slices of beef, pink at the centre, and handed them to Liam. Quickly the food was moving round, everyone loading up their plates. 'Veggie for us,' trilled Freya as she dished up a spiced chickpea and feta dish for herself and Hudson. 'Smells delicious,' said Claire, smiling at them. Chat and laughter followed and as the sun set, the strings of lights, like regimented fireflies, sparkled against the darkening sky. Surrounding them, casting a soft and soothing glow on them all. Mia reappeared, moving quietly, unobtrusively taking empty plates, replacing cutlery. While the sun had gone the heat remained. A warmth that felt a little like it came from this new family, gathered around the table. Lizzie felt a yearning, to find some way to press fast forward to when she'd be readmitted to this club. She stole a sideways glance at Claire sitting next to her at the table. They were so close, physically, but the spaces they occupied... there might as well have been miles between them. Maybe this weekend would help. Once they got used to each other again and Claire could see that Lizzie was herself again. Lizzie heard a fluttering above her and looked up to the lights above their heads. A moth, the kind with a thick body, hairy, dusty beige fragile wings, battered itself against one of the small twinkling lights. Lizzie wrinkled her nose.

George stood and held his glass of non-alcoholic champagne aloft. He looked around the table at everybody.

'Today is my wedding day and typically – even though this hasn't been a typical wedding day – you have speeches. So, I want to say a few words.'

Hear, hear rippled around the table.

'Look at this beautiful place.' George turned and waved a hand around. 'Standing here since 1790. My family built this house. Bought up all the land for miles. They were a colourful bunch, liked a party and a gamble. But good sorts too. Indeed, the family's finest hour was when good old John Butler, a man who loved to put a few bob on the horses, used all his winnings, back in the 1840s, to feed all the tenants on the Butler estate during the potato famine. No one died of hunger on our land. We are very proud of that. But the family has been dogged by bad luck and declining fortunes ever since. And more recently, I felt I too was part of that bad luck. As you all know, I lost my dear Grace nearly twenty years ago. She was strong and funny and my anchor. I have been adrift ever since. That is, until six months ago when I met this amazing woman, Claire O'Shea. I never thought I'd meet another woman as smart and clever and strong as Grace, but I was wrong. And now, looking around me... looking at these beautiful people at my table, how lucky am I? My darling Freya, my light, now so happy with Hudson. We are overjoyed to welcome you to the family, Hudson. Be good to this girl of mine!'

'I will.' Hudson smiled, raising his glass.

'Liam, Lizzie,' George turned to them, 'I always wanted a large family, a troop of Butlers to enjoy this place with me. I feel in you two I have belatedly gotten my wish. Thank you.' He turned to Claire, looked down at her, tears in the corners of his eyes. 'And to you, you sweet, lovely woman, thank you for taking a chance on a crazy coot like myself. I have never been happier.' George raised his glass and a cheer went up from around the table. Claire stood and hugged him. Wiping tears from her own eyes.

'So, everyone,' said George, his arm around Claire. 'We're here for a long weekend, until Claire and I fly off to Mauritius for a couple of weeks. I want you all to relax and have a lovely time. I can't wait to get to know you all properly.'

There was a quiet rustle from the woods behind them. Freya looked over Lizzie's shoulder in the direction of the noise.

Liam's head shot around. Freya's face softened and she gasped a quiet 'oh'. Everyone turned and looked.

A tiny fawn, brown with white spots, its pointy tail raised and its spindly legs knobbly at the knees and looking so delicate they didn't look capable of keeping it upright, had wandered out of the trees. Its large dark eyes, framed with lashes they'd all have died for, stared back at them, just as surprised and taken with them as they were with it.

'Oh goodness,' whispered Claire. 'What a beautiful little creature.'

Its nose twitched and it dipped its head down, to nibble some grass. But it didn't take its eyes off them as it did so. Everyone around the table held their breath, no one moved a muscle. Rapt attention bestowed on this baby of the woods. There then came another noise, louder this time. A larger, more wary face appeared. A doe took a half step out from the cover of the trees. It bleated quietly to its baby, who turned and trotted on wobbly legs back to her watchful side. They turned and disappeared into the safety of the woods. Lizzie felt a hand on hers and looked down. Claire, still watching the departing pair, had rested her hand on her daughter's. Claire squeezed it gently, and Lizzie, her own eyes dark and dark-lashed like the fawn's, felt them fill. With her free hand she brushed away the unexpected tears, but left the other where it was.

'So special,' George murmured, the volume turned down on his normal bombast, but the love of this place, the joy he felt in this environment, only shone more brightly from his eyes, and oozed from every pore. He looked away from the trees to his new wife. Smiled when he saw mother and daughter's hands touching. 'This place... this is a healing place,' he said, his own eyes filling with more joyous tears. Shining in the lingering summer light.

. . .

Mia placed two pots of hot coffee on the table, next to a glorious pavlova, tumbling with summer berries, ripe and bursting, scattered wantonly on top, bleeding their vibrant red juices onto their bed of whipped cream and meringue.

'One last thing,' she said, skipping back into the kitchen. She returned a moment later, carefully carrying a cake on a platter. Two generous tiers, it was decorated in white icing with white and red piped flowers. Mia set it down on the table in front of them.

'You can't have a wedding party without a wedding cake,' she said.

'Oh, Mia, thank you, what a surprise,' said Claire. There was a chorus of thank yous which morphed into gentle laughter. Claire, puzzled, looked at the cake again. On top of it, there stood a bride and groom figure. And a second bride and groom.

'For all of you,' smiled Mia, looking from Freya and Hudson to George and Claire. 'I had a set spare in my kit, so I thought "why not" and added them.'

'Aw, thank you, Mia,' said Claire. Freya reached a hand up and squeezed Mia's arm, adding her own thanks.

'You're welcome. And congratulations, both of you,' she said and withdrew back to the kitchen with a shy smile. Lizzie watched one of the lights from the kitchen go out.

'Wow, this looks amazing,' said George. 'Which do people want? Cake or pavlova?'

'Why not a bit of both?' said Claire.

'Fine idea!' replied George, picking up the knife and plunging it first into the voluminous cream and meringue dessert. It sank in up to the hilt. Claire gathered bowls and put them next to it. 'Who wants what?' George cried, and was greeted with delighted replies from everyone. Lizzie laughed as she joined in. She had to admit to herself that she was having a good time. It had been so long she didn't really remember when things had been this relaxed, this happy, with her family. She looked at George and his silliness, slopping collapsing pavlova into bowls, Claire laughing as she tried to catch it all. Freya and Hudson, cuddling and laughing too, people she'd only known for hours, but whose happy faces were now awakening long sleeping parts of her, parts she'd deliberately quietened. Drugged and subdued. And Liam, her darling little brother. Her reliable, sensitive little brother who deserved all the best things in life. His face was lit up, beaming, happy. Lizzie, who had thought her mother was crazy, had lost her sense taking up with this eccentric man, was beginning to think that her mother was right. As usual. Knew best. As usual. Lizzie felt that treacherous emotion – hope – catch, and flicker and take flight in her belly. The happy chaos was loud and raucous, drowning out nature's noises around them.

'Here you go!' declared George as he handed Lizzie her dessert.

'Thank you,' she replied. He smiled down at her, but then paused. He turned and squinted into the dark woods before shaking his head and looking back at Lizzie, the smile returned.

'Who's next?' he boomed.

Then Lizzie heard it too. Whatever had distracted George. She looked over her shoulder, her spoon halfway to her mouth. Peered into the darkness. There was a rustle. Not as gentle as the deer from earlier. Harsher, rougher.

A shape, dark and barely distinguishable from the forest's darkness, moved.

Then emerged.

It was a person.

Lizzie's heart froze.

'My,' they said. 'Doesn't this look cosy.'

Lizzie dropped her spoon. Claire screamed.

George leapt up.

'Who the hell are you?' he roared.

Lizzie gripped the arms of her chair. Forced herself to

stand. Everything around her swirled, the edges of her vision blurry, like those bad trips after bad pills.

She opened her mouth. And spoke. Hoarse and croaky, her mouth suddenly desert-dry.

'*Dad?*'

7

For years after he died Lizzie would think she'd seen him. Pushing a trolley in the frozen food aisle of Tesco. In the middle of Grafton Street, looking at the Christmas display in the window of Brown Thomas. One time, when she came back from the toilets in an old man pub in Kerry she had, for a split second, thought it was him taking a pint of Guinness off the barman. But she'd rubbed her eyes and the spell had broken. It hadn't been him. It hadn't been her dad. It hadn't been him in Tesco, or on Grafton Street either. In fact, when 'he'd' turned around that time, the man in front of Brown Thomas had been twenty years too old. Looked nothing like him at all. Her therapist had assured her this was common among people who had lost someone. Not to worry, it was normal.

But. Here, now. Standing there in semi-darkness, the light from the terrace half-illuminating him, was the impossible.

Her father. Declan O'Shea.

Dead these past five years.

'How... what...?' Lizzie stammered.

George put himself between Claire and this stranger.

'"Dad"?' George said. 'What? Who the hell are you?' He glared at Declan, his voice rock hard.

Declan stepped closer, fully entering the radius of soft light that moments before had held only the happy diners in its warm embrace. Lizzie looked at everyone's faces. George, Freya and Hudson, confused. Liam sat bolt upright, an expression on his face Lizzie remembered from his childhood, one he wore when waiting, sitting strapped into a roller coaster car or ghost train ride – in anticipation, a nauseous mix of horror and delight. And beside her, shaking, a pale and horrified Claire.

Declan looked at George with a smile, a smile that hadn't a care in the world.

'The name's Declan O'Shea.' He thrust out his hand at George who looked at it as if it was diseased. 'Your new wife's original husband. You might have heard I was dead.'

Hudson stood.

'No,' said Freya, reaching up and grabbing his arm, but he shook his head.

She let go and he circled the table, placed himself beside George.

'I don't know who you are, sir, but you're upsetting people.'

'Ha, a Yank to the rescue! Nice,' said Declan, looking Hudson up and down. 'Don't worry, kid, I'm not going to hurt anyone.'

'I know you're not,' he replied, staring Declan in the eye. 'I won't let you.'

Declan turned away from him.

Hudson grabbed his shoulder, turned Declan back around.

'Don't you turn away from me,' Hudson snapped, his voice low and controlled, but the anger palpable.

Declan glanced at Hudson's hand, still on his shoulder.

'First thing you can do is take your hand off me, kid,' Declan said slowly. 'And then you can stay out of this. It's none of your business. Whoever you are.'

Hudson stepped in. George grabbed his arm.

'It's okay. Go back to Freya. We're okay.'

Hudson looked reluctant.

'Come on, this won't help,' said George in a low, soothing tone. He moved Hudson back, Freya doing her bit, reaching out for her husband. Unsure, Hudson gave in and went back to her.

Declan watched him go, then glanced down at Claire.

'Hey there, Claire-bear,' he said, smiling. 'You're looking well.' He then looked at Lizzie and winked at Liam.

'Hey, kids, Daddy's home.'

'But... you're dead!' Lizzie blurted out. She was still standing, paralysed, rooted to the spot. Transfixed by this apparition that looked like her dead father. This evil spirit conjured up in the darkest corners of the woods.

'Reports of my death have been greatly exaggerated, sweetheart,' he said, smirking.

'There was an inquest. Witnesses.' A small voice came from Lizzie's right. Claire was speaking. Her voice was so altered that if Lizzie wasn't looking right at her, she wouldn't have known it was her.

'Ah yes, well, as it happens – I was that witness. I provided the statement about "the man" going into the water. How he seemed to surrender to the currents and went under without a struggle. I rang the Gardaí too, in fact. And, as I was "out of the country" – handily – when the inquest was meant to happen, they were happy to use my sworn written account of events instead.'

George looked down at Claire.

'Was there no body?'

She shook her head. 'No, but they said... the coastguard said that spot was notorious.' Each word came out slow, as if she was learning a new language and these sounds were unfamiliar on her tongue. 'Bodies went out, never came back. They said.' Claire looked up at George, as if pleading with a hanging judge.

'He was depressed. He'd been talking about ending it all... the business was collapsing, *we* were collapsing. Someone saw him go into the sea and be dragged out, go under... there was no reason to doubt...'

She turned in her seat and stared at Declan.

'No reason to doubt at all...'

Declan looked down the table at Lizzie, who was still standing next to her chair, rooted to the spot. He headed in her direction, touching her shoulder and pecking her cheek as he passed. Lizzie recoiled as if scorched by a branding iron. She put her hand to her face, half-expecting she'd be able to feel blisters swell there. He stopped at the end of the table. Lizzie, and everyone, watched as he pulled out the last empty chair and sat down. He turned to Liam, sat to his left, and patted the young man's hand.

'Good to see you, son.'

Liam nodded mutely at his father. He looked to Lizzie now like how he'd been at the end of those childhood fairground rides, green and nauseous, sorry he'd gone on them. Confused that he'd ever been excited in the first place.

'I didn't invite you to join us,' said George.

'I know, rude.' Declan sat forward and grabbed a bottle of champagne from an ice bucket. He took Lizzie's glass, filled it and took a long, slow, sip. Then looked at the glass.

'Not much of a kick.'

'What is going on?' Lizzie heard herself say.

Her father looked up at her.

'Why don't you sit down? Everyone should sit down.' He nodded at George and Claire at the other end of the table. 'I'm not going anywhere soon, not after that bloody awful hike anyway.'

'Daddy,' Freya turned to George. 'Shouldn't we call the Gardaí? Get him out of here? I don't feel safe.'

'As I said already, I'm not here to hurt anyone.' Declan

rolled his eyes. 'You and your *daddy* will be fine. No need to be so dramatic.'

'I don't think you're in any position to lecture anyone on being dramatic,' spat Freya. 'You're a dead man! Here! What the hell? And how many laws have you broken? This is terrifying. Who does this and thinks it's okay?'

Lizzie looked from Freya to her father. She was definitely scared too. Terrified.

'Calm down,' Declan said. 'Seriously. And, Elizabeth, please sit down, you're making me uncomfortable, looming over me there.'

Lizzie sat. Not because her father had asked her to, but because she could feel her legs begin to shake. She didn't think she could hold herself up any longer. She sank into her seat and stared at Declan. He was older, his face lined. His black hair was greying at the temples. But he looked well. Wherever he'd been, life had been kinder to him than it had been to the family he'd abandoned.

Lizzie looked at Claire. Her mother appeared dazed, like she was having an out-of-body experience.

'So,' said George, 'it seems you took the coward's way out of your troubles, leaving the mess you made behind for Claire to pick up. Have you any clue of the devastation you left behind? Do you?' He growled at Declan, his finger jabbing the air. 'You don't look like you've been suffering too much either. Whatever provisions you put in place for yourself, you look like you planned that well. Which begs the question – why come back? What's with this resurrection? What do you want?'

Declan leaned forward in his seat, reaching out a hand for the pavlova and a spare bowl. He cut himself a large slice and slopped the cream and meringue and fruit into it. Scarlet berry juice dripped across the table as he lifted the bowl to him. The moth from earlier, exhausted, fell to the table, landing in Lizzie's bowl. Its fat, hairy body spent in its futile efforts.

Declan sank a spoon into his dessert but stopped. He looked at the wedding cake. He stretched out a hand and snatched one of the grooms from the top. He looked puzzled at the doubles. He rolled the little figure around in his fingers. Spinning it round and round. He looked at everyone, an audience gripped by fear and terror and disbelief. He snapped the groom in half.

'What do I want?' He dropped the broken figure on the table and smiled. 'I want my family back.'

8

'What?' George stopped a moment then laughed. Threw his head back as the gales of laughter rumbled from his belly. 'You, my good man, are funny.'

'I made a big mistake.'

'I'll say,' said George, wiping tears from his eyes. He turned to Claire. 'What did you ever see in this clown?'

Claire, the colour beginning to return to her cheeks, shook her head. 'I have no idea.'

Lizzie looked at her father. She too was coming round from the bombshell of her father's reappearance. There was now a stampede of new emotions clamouring to be heard. Anger was barging its way to the top of the queue.

'You made a mistake,' she parroted back at him. 'You want us back?'

'I know that I will need to make amends, my sweetheart.' He reached out his hand to touch hers. She snatched it away. She didn't need to be burned again. 'I understand that you might be confused. You have to understand that I wasn't thinking straight. I was desperate. I realise now that I was foolish. I would understand if you were cross with me.'

Lizzie stared at him open-mouthed.

'Cross?' It came as a whisper first. '*Cross?*' The second time louder, quicker, her anger bubbling up and boiling over like milk left too long on a hotplate. 'I'm not cross at you, I'm furious!' she roared, slamming the table with her open palms. The glasses and dessert bowls rocked and clanked as they shook. She reared up, her chair flying back.

'Do you have any clue what we've been through? What "your death",' she put air quotes around the words, her face contorted, 'did to us? Do you know what you left behind? You destroyed us. Annihilated us. You coward. You lying, spineless, selfish coward. You want to waltz back in here – on Mam's wedding day of all days – and take up where you left off? Have you even said sorry?'

Lizzie snatched up her dessert bowl and flung it at Declan. Ducking swiftly, the bowl flew by him and smashed against a stone pillar beyond the garden table. Smithereens of ceramic splintered and scattered. The animals of the wood went quiet again.

'Lizzie! Stop it!' Claire jumped up and ran to her side. She took her by the shoulders. Lizzie shook her off.

'Don't tell me what to do,' she snapped at her mother. 'This... this... monster... he deserves to know what he did to us all. Look at him! Sitting there, smug, says he wants us back? Something has gone wrong in his new life, I'm sure that's why he's here, why he crawled out from under whatever lying bastard rock he's been hiding under.' She turned back to her father. Hot tears streaming down her face.

'You destroyed me. Do you understand? I was your little girl, your sweetheart. We were a team. And then... then... and it was a lie?' She gulped and shook, tears mangling her voice, snot unleashed and a despair beginning that felt as vast as the universe, with no outer edge, expanding, too much for her brain to comprehend. Claire touched her again, this time with tender hands, but again Lizzie shook her off. There was no space for anything in her now except this devastation.

'You see this?' said Claire, voice ice-cold. Lizzie felt her mother stay close. 'We weren't a movie, Declan, left on pause. You can't walk in here, hit play, and think things will just resume.'

'I didn't think it would be that simple, but I wanted to try.'

Lizzie watched her mother pick up the toppled chair, and move it close to her.

'You're in shock,' her mother whispered to her. Lizzie felt her head nod, but it didn't feel like she'd done it, she felt like a puppet, controlled by someone else. Claire guided her down. Lizzie sat, compliant as a child.

Claire turned to Declan. Lizzie listened to her speak.

'I think you've different reasons for coming back. I don't think you missed us. You certainly don't look like you've been pining. I think you've seen how well I've been doing, bringing our business back from the brink. You'd have been able to see the official filings online, seen how significant the turnaround has been. You're back because the money is back.'

'I have seen how well you've been doing, true. But not because I want a cut but because I was keeping an eye on you all, from afar, hoping you were all okay. I knew within weeks I shouldn't have done what I did. But I felt I couldn't come back. That I was in too deep. It was some consolation when I saw that you'd saved the business. I remembered the girl I married when I saw how well things were going. The smart, go-getter who convinced me to take those risks and start up. I've been impressed.

'Perhaps,' Declan laughed, 'I should have faked my death sooner.'

'Christ.' Claire shook her head. 'You're here now because of the money and that's it.'

'I'm here because of this chump.' Declan pointed at George.

'I saw the engagement announcement in the paper. For some reason I thought you wouldn't move on. We'd been together since we were fifteen. We were Claire-bear and Dec. I thought you'd always be there. I realised I had to do something. So I've been trailing you all day. I tried to make it to the hotel before the ceremony, but you'd been and gone. I came west and I found the guy who drove you out here. I got him to take me too. I couldn't believe it when he abandoned me by the tumbledown stone gate. I got lost in those damned woods a few times. But here I am now. And that's the truth.'

'The truth? You wouldn't recognise the truth if it smacked you in the face. How on earth do you think I'd go back to you? After everything? Look at them.' She pointed to the shuddering Lizzie and the dumbfounded Liam. 'Look what you did to us.'

Declan, for the first time, looked less sure. Lizzie, through blurred eyes, watched her father look at her and then her brother with something that possessed a hint of shame.

'Okay. I guess it's not as simple as I'd hoped.' He held his hands up. 'I think it'll take some time. I know I messed up. And I know I will have to face the consequences – though, I'm hoping when you come round that you might facilitate me with one last... issue. I was thinking I might need to plead amnesia, to untangle myself from all of this. If you can keep schtum I think I might get away with it. I will tell them that when I walked out to sea I hit my head on a rock, something like that...'

'You definitely hit your head. You're out of your mind if you think I have any interest in any of this. I'm with George, you are legally dead. This is my life now and I'm finally happy. How could you, how could you now, do this to me? It's like you're destroying my life one more time. How could you do this to your kids? Again. You're a selfish, evil man. I can't believe I ever was fooled, ever loved you.'

'Obviously, you don't need to make up your mind immediately.'

Claire rounded the table and stood right in front of Declan. She stared at him, saying nothing. Then, in one swift movement she smacked him across the face.

'Oof,' exclaimed Declan, holding his reddening cheek.

'Claire!' George jumped up, his chair scraping across the stone as he pushed it back. He raced to the end of the table.

'Don't worry,' said Declan as George dragged her away. 'I deserved that.'

'I think, perhaps, we need to talk about this, privately.' George looked at everyone around the table. 'Hudson, Liam, can you two stay here and keep an eye on our guest?'

'Of course,' replied Hudson. Liam looked over at him and nodded. He still hadn't said a word. 'Everyone else, let's head to the kitchen.'

Freya and Lizzie stood and trooped after George. Lizzie paused and looked over her shoulder.

Hudson had gotten up and begun pacing the terrace. Put himself between the kitchen door and Declan.

At the table she saw Liam turn to their father. It looked like he was saying something.

'Lizzie, come on.' Claire beckoned her in. She looked at her mother and then back at the table. Liam was now back to staring straight ahead. Lizzie stepped into the house.

George was leaning against the kitchen island. Claire went to him and let him put his arm around her. Like her husband outside, Freya began pacing.

'I'm so sorry, George,' said Claire, crying quietly. 'How on earth... just how...'

'Hush, darling, hush. There was no way for you to know.'

'I think it's time to call the Gardaí,' said Freya.

'Actually, that's one of the reasons I wanted to bring you three in here. We have a bit of a problem.'

'What? What's wrong?' asked Freya.

'We've... we've no phone. One of last winter's storms took

out a few of the trees which took down the line. I wasn't too upset at the time, I hardly used it and you know how I love to get away from it all...'

'You're joking,' Freya replied.

'And no mobile signal either,' muttered Claire. They all looked out the window at the dark forest.

'We have no way of getting help,' said George.

9

'No phone?' said Lizzie. 'At all?'

George shook his head.

'I'm sorry.'

Lizzie looked from one to the other.

'Is there nothing we can do? At all?'

'What about the quad bike, Daddy?' said Freya. 'One of us go get the Gardaí?'

George shook his head.

'Not a runner.'

'Why not?'

'Because it's an unreliable piece of crap, darling. It would probably break down in the middle of the trees, in the pitch black, leaving whoever went stranded. And even if it didn't, riding it at night? That's just asking to run into a tree and be killed. It's far too dangerous.'

'We have to do something,' said Lizzie. 'I can't look at him. I can't bear him to be here. Mam, don't you agree?'

'Yes, it's awful. Just horrific.'

'At first light I will go myself to the police,' said George, looking at Lizzie. 'I promise you that. Or even, to hell with the police, I can give him the option to just scarper, get rid of him. I'll drive him out myself on the quad.'

'So, what then? He just stays here tonight? Joins the party?' Lizzie threw her hands up.

George looked down at Claire.

'Darling, is he dangerous?'

'No,' she said. 'He's just a monumental dickhead.'

'I think then, the only option, unfortunately, is to let him stay until the morning.'

'Oh God,' groaned Lizzie.

'I'm not going back out there to sit around the table and play happy families,' said Claire.

'I wouldn't ask you to do that, darling,' said George. 'I think the party mood is rather dampened now, don't you?' He looked up at the kitchen clock. It was 11 p.m. 'I suspect after such a long day, and this happening, we might all be agreeable to heading off to bed. What do you think?'

'Perhaps,' said Claire. 'Lizzie?'

Lizzie could see the three left outside. They weren't talking. She agreed with her mother, certainly she wasn't going back out there. But could they all just head off to bed? Simple as that?

'Where would he go?' she asked.

'We could put him in one of the attic bedrooms?' suggested George, looking at Freya.

'The cook is in one of them already.'

'Oh God, Mia. Of course she's here too,' said Claire, running a hand through her hair. She looked up at the ceiling, as if she could see up to the cook's attic room. 'What am I going to tell her? She mightn't have seen him arrive if she'd already headed upstairs, but we can't leave her in the dark, not completely anyway.'

'You don't need to tell her anything. I'll go talk to her,' said George, pulling away from Claire.

'No, no,' said Claire, taking his hand and pulling him back.

'I hired her, I'll go talk to her. She's my responsibility. And we can't put him up there near her. I know I said he isn't violent, but I don't think it'd be right for him to be in such close proximity to her either. Especially as we'll all be in the other part of the house, far away if she were to need us.'

'There's the sofa in the drawing room?' suggested Freya.

'Yes. That's good enough for him,' said Claire.

'Alright, that's agreed,' said George.

'I'll go talk to Mia.' Claire pulled away from the group and headed out of a door in the corner of the kitchen, right next to the door to the pantry, that Lizzie hadn't noticed before. She glimpsed a narrow wooden staircase, and the sound of Claire's feet on the wooden treads echoed down to them as she went.

'Back staircase,' said George, following Lizzie's gaze. 'Up to the attic servants' quarters. Nice rooms up there, though, if a bit small.'

'I see. Well, I agree with my mother, he's not going up there. The sofa even sounds too good for him if you ask me, but I don't think we have much choice.'

'No, Lizzie, I'm afraid we don't. But, on the plus side, it's summer and the sun rises around five thirty. I'll go the second there's enough light for it to be safe.'

'Thanks, George.'

Freya walked around from the sink.

'I'll go get a pillow and a blanket. Just get that set up so there's no opportunity for any delays.'

'Okay, thanks, my dear.' George kissed the top of his daughter's head as she passed by. Freya smiled up at him. Lizzie looked away. They didn't mean to make things worse, they were just doing what came naturally to them, but this demonstration of a healthy – ideal even – father–daughter relationship was a slap in her face right now.

Freya headed out of the kitchen. It was just Lizzie and George now. A silence settled between them. Virtual strangers, their relationship not quite worked out yet, they weren't ready for this. An implication of the situation dawned on Lizzie. She looked at her new stepfather. This big man, broad and solid as the oaks and horse chestnut trees that populated his own private forest. This ebullient would-be squire.

'George?' she began, not sure how to broach this.

'Yes?' he said, his head slightly cocked, curious at her tone.

Lizzie paused. Now wasn't really the time.

'No, sorry, it's nothing.' She half turned away.

'It doesn't feel like nothing, dear. Don't be worried about sharing whatever's on your mind.'

Lizzie looked back at him.

'Go on...' he encouraged her. Lizzie took a deep breath. She would rather say this to George than her mother.

'It's just that...' She snatched a quick glance up at his face. His expression open. 'Just with *him* reappearing. Like, not being dead... doesn't it mean they're still married? My mum and dad. Your wedding, this morning – is it even valid any more?'

George looked at her and his shoulders slumped.

'Oh,' he said, crestfallen.

'Sorry, I shouldn't have said anything. God. I can't believe he's done this. When you think he's found all the ways he can hurt us, he finds some all-new ones.'

George rallied, resting one of his large hands on her shoulder. Steadying her. Looked at her with an overflow of gentleness in his eyes.

'Oh, don't say sorry, you poor girl. None of this is your fault. None at all.'

They heard Claire's feet on the stairs.

'Don't mention this to your mum, okay?'

Lizzie nodded.

Claire came back into the kitchen.

'I gave her half the story, and she hadn't seen him show up so she seemed to believe me. I think anything is more believable than the truth.' Claire stopped at the window and shook her head. 'This is all... something else.'

'Why don't you go on up to bed now, Lizzie,' said George. 'You must be shattered. Let your mother and me deal with this.'

'Okay, thanks,' Lizzie said. She looked out the window, one last time, at her father.

'The sooner you go to bed,' said George as she turned towards the door, 'the sooner all this will seem just like a very bad dream.'

10

Lizzie lay on her bed. The white bright room of earlier had flipped like a photo negative and was now entirely black. The only reminder of its pale charm was a moonlight pall that glowed ghost-like from the windows. Lizzie had left them open and the shutters folded back. It was near 2 a.m. but it was still warm. She lay there with the covers pushed aside. The sounds of the night drifted in, a natural white-noise machine. Not that it helped her sleep. She was wide awake. Instead she listened to the nocturnal animals, busy like shift workers with the business of living at night. A symphony of crackles and cries, snuffling and swoops played out. The discordant call of foxes – city-girl Lizzie was happy to be able to identify something in the wild-ness – floated in on the air. Occasional whooshes by the window, fluttering shadow arcs cast fleetingly across her bedspread, hinted at bats hunting insects.

Lizzie wanted a drink. She'd hoped to not be tested quite so soon after leaving St Brigid's. She knew real life would be harder than the cosseted confines of rehab. But one day? It was a joke.

By now, in the past, she'd already be milling into something.

Preferably alcohol, but she'd have been happy with a spliff, or pills. She'd never been fussy. Whatever had been quickest. That confident feeling from earlier, when she'd been confronted by what she thought was alcoholic champagne – it felt a lot less sure under her feet right now. But at least all she was doing was thinking about it. She picked up her phone. No signal. She couldn't call her sponsor. She took a deep breath. What had they told her in St Brigid's? These urges should only last fifteen to thirty minutes; if she could manage to not give in, it should pass. She took another deep breath. Five years ago her father's death had knocked her off course, set her adrift. She'd only been righted these past six months. His rebirth couldn't do the same. She couldn't let it.

'I am stronger than this and it will pass. I am stronger than this and it will pass,' she muttered the mantra rehab had taught her, staring at the dark, crackled ceiling above her. She sighed.

Lizzie sat up and swung her legs over to the edge of the bed, still repeating the words to herself. She was giving up trying to sleep. Knowing he was down there, in this house, it was too much. She'd never relax. As if mocking her, a shaft of moonlight spotlighted the Famous Five book she'd thrown across the room that afternoon. Splayed open, pages crumpled, it sat there on the floor. Lizzie jumped out of bed and hurried across the room. She snatched it up and went straight to the window. With effort she hauled the window up, opened as much as it could. She took the book and flung it out, a strange bird, graceless in flight.

'Fuck you!' she roared after it as it disappeared into the darkness.

In the treetops, in the distance, a ghostly creature stared at her. Its face, a blanched skull, glowered. Lizzie felt her pulse quicken. Then it was moving, gliding through the air, coming at her. Screaming.

Screeching in the night. Heading straight for her.

Lizzie screamed and fell back, stumbling. Tumbling to the floor.

At the window the ivory underbelly of the spectre swooped up and was gone.

Lizzie's terrified brain unfroze.

An owl. Just a barn owl. *Scréachóg reilige*, the Irish name she'd learned in school, came back to her. *The graveyard screecher.* Probably where the stories of the banshee had come from. Lizzie had never heard one before, but she could see now why it might have given rise to that myth. Her pulse still racing, she crept back to the window and looked up to where it had disappeared. She could see in the moonlight that one of the panes of glass in the attic window above her was broken. A moment later the pale, skull-like face of the bird reappeared and with a quiver was in the air again, disappearing into the night, its screaming cry calling in the distance.

'Sweet Jesus,' Lizzie breathed. She definitely had no chance of sleep now. She looked around her. What to do? Perhaps a glass of milk might help. Lizzie walked to the door and opened it a crack. Had her scream disturbed anyone? She opened the door fully and stepped out. She heard nothing but quiet snores and creaking pipes.

'I am stronger than this and it will pass,' she repeated mindlessly to herself as she tiptoed down the wooden stairs. Self-soothing. The shadows of the night were worse here, inside the house. Even less light was available, and if not for a small lamp left on in the hallway below she would have risked walking into something and hurting herself.

She stopped at the drawing room door. It was slightly ajar. She could see through the gap that the sofa was empty. A pair of shoes were sitting on the floor beside it, and the green fleece blanket Freya had retrieved was cast back, as if someone had been sleeping but had gotten up. Lizzie looked about the hallway. The door to the kitchen was also open a touch. And the light was on. She padded down the corridor and peered in.

Sitting at the island, with a faraway look on his face, was her father. He was sipping on a glass of amber liquid. Lizzie spied a slightly dusty, thick-based crystal decanter on the counter beside him. Its bulbous stopper lolled on its side next to it.

She felt a dart of adrenaline throughout her body at the sight of it, half-full of whiskey. She repeated, 'I am stronger than this and it will pass' to herself, again.

She stepped into the kitchen.

Declan turned and looked at her, unperturbed.

'Was that you screaming a minute ago?' he asked, as if they always met in the kitchen at 2 a.m.

Lizzie nodded.

'Nightmare?'

'Something like that,' she mumbled.

Lizzie looked at the whiskey again. Declan followed her gaze.

'Want some?'

Lizzie shook her head violently.

'No. No. In fact there wasn't meant to be any alcohol in the house. Mam said.'

'Might explain why it was hidden at the very back of the cabinet behind a bunch of vases.'

Lizzie nodded.

Declan lifted the decanter.

'You sure?'

'Absolutely.' Lizzie crossed to the fridge and took out the milk. She searched the unfamiliar kitchen cupboards for a glass, finally finding one and filling it. She felt her father's eyes on her the whole time. As her eyes avoided the whiskey, his eyes stayed on her, on her every movement.

'I'm sorry,' he said.

Lizzie looked up and stared at him. She stayed silent.

'You said I hadn't apologised. Earlier. And you were right, I hadn't. So...'

'Right.'

'...I just want...'

Lizzie could see a lot of his bravado of earlier was gone. In front of her was more the man she remembered. While Declan O'Shea had always been a larger than life individual, with a ready smile and handshake and joke, she'd seen the quieter man. The thoughtful side of him. This was the man she'd missed, whose absence she'd replaced with drugs and alcohol and bad choices.

'It's too late. An apology might have worked five years ago. But – you've no idea – too much damage has been done, we can't be put back together.'

'I'd like to try.'

'We'd rather you didn't. Your timing is ridiculous. You somehow managed to pick the exact moment when we're all finally happy again.' Lizzie knew that wasn't quite true, but she'd been on the way to happy. And she wanted to stay on that road. His reappearance was already threatening to take her off course.

Declan sighed. 'I didn't think it would be easy. But this wasn't my plan. It wasn't meant to go like this.'

'What? Faking your death and leaving your family to cope with the emotional and financial fallout didn't go how you'd planned? No shit, Dad.'

Declan glared at her but said nothing. He lifted the glass to his lips and sipped his drink.

'Where've you been?'

'Where've I been?'

'Yeah, all this time? Where've you been hiding?'

'Ah. Well, initially I stayed in Ireland, but it was too risky. Ireland's too small, I'd have run into someone who knew me eventually. So I went to England. London. I disappeared among the millions there.'

'I see,' said Lizzie. 'And how did you live?'

'I'd put some cash aside. For those purposes.' Declan didn't look her in the eye.

'Right. So, while we were having trouble putting food on the table after you fecked off, you were living off stolen cash? Jesus, Dad. Can you hear yourself?'

'I wasn't thinking straight, Lizzie. And honestly, it was only meant to be temporary. I never intended staying away so long.'

'You should have stayed away permanently. I think Mam is right and you're back because of the money.'

He shook his head.

'No, I was serious. I want her back. I want you guys back. That's why I'm here now, because of him.'

'George?'

'Yeah, that pseudo upper-class twit. What on earth does your mother see in him exactly?'

'That pseudo upper-class twit is a nice man. A decent man. Do you even know what that is?'

'Oh, knock it off, Lizzie!' Declan snapped at her, his voice raised. 'Knock it off.' The words echoed off the walls and bounced around the room.

Lizzie stared back at him. She felt tears threaten. Felt annoyed at herself for that reaction. She took in a gulp of air.

'Please go,' she whispered.

'Don't worry,' said Declan as he stood. He lifted the decanter and topped up his glass. Leaving it back down, the hefty cut crystal vessel chimed like a dull tuning fork against the island's granite worktop. 'I'm tired of this conversation. I'm going back to bed.'

'I mean go. Leave this place. Leave us alone. When George wakes you in three hours and gives you a choice. Go with him. Leave us.'

Declan stopped at the door. Turned and looked at her.

'Ah, I see. Well, sorry, darling, I'm not leaving here till I've won your mother – and you guys – back. I'm going nowhere.'

He flicked off the light switch, plunging Lizzie and the room into darkness, and walked out, not bothering to shut the door behind him. Lizzie sat there in the shadows. She didn't stir. Only her tears, which she let go now that he was gone, moved as they ran down her face.

A slice of moonlight lit up the whiskey he'd left behind.

11

Lizzie stood up and reached out her hand.

She would pour it out. Quickly.

She stopped though, hand in mid-air. There was a sound from the hall. Declan was coming back. Probably to retrieve the decanter. She rubbed away the tear stains from her face. She didn't want to give him that satisfaction.

The door slowly opened. Lizzie stood stock-still, mouth firmly shut. He could apologise, he could extend the olive branch.

But the light didn't go back on. And the person who crept into the kitchen, moving as quietly as they could, wasn't her dad. Cloaked in shadows, it was someone else. Someone carrying something in their hand.

Liam.

Jeans pulled on, and his bed shirt half tucked in, his hair was messed up as if he'd been lying down. From the gentle pad of his feet on the kitchen floor tiles, he mustn't have shoes on. Lizzie did nothing to alert him to her presence in the shadows. She just stood there, watching him.

Liam headed to the back door. Opened it and slipped out.

Lizzie got up and went to the window. Watched him as he headed straight for the woods. The night swallowed him whole in moments.

What was he up to? Then her heart sank. Had he followed her example? Going down the road she had, self-medicating to deal with the pain. She'd never forgive herself.

She stood there and looked back at the clock every few minutes. Eventually, after fifteen torturous minutes, she saw his indistinct form emerging from the gloom. He appeared to be wiping his hands on his trousers, rubbing something off them. Lizzie leaned closer to the window. What was he at?

He pushed open the back door. Lizzie inhaled deeply, checking for the telltale aroma of illicit substances. But there was nothing but the fresh scent of a summer's night and a hint of the coming dew. Liam, looking neither left nor right, headed straight for the kitchen door.

'What are you doing?' Lizzie asked.

'Christ!' Liam yelled. He swung around. He grabbed his chest. 'Lizzie! Bloody hell! What are you doing there!'

'I couldn't sleep,' said Lizzie.

'That's no excuse to punish anyone else... my heart...' He let go of his bed shirt and even in the darkness Lizzie could see the dirty marks his hand had left behind.

'What were you doing out there?'

'Nothing. I couldn't sleep either, I was just getting some fresh air. That's all.'

'What were you really doing?'

'I was really getting some fresh air,' he sneered.

'Were you doing drugs?'

'What?' Liam's eyebrows flew up and he glared at her. 'Drugs? After the state of you the last few years? I'm not that stupid.'

'Then what were you doing?'

He shook his head and said nothing more.

'Why are your hands dirty?'

Liam looked down at his hands then stuffed them in his jeans pockets.

'They're not.'

'You left a mark on your shirt.'

He looked down.

'I slipped.'

'Right.'

'Lizzie, what I do is none of your business. Leave me alone.' Liam's gaze fell on the whiskey decanter on the counter. He whipped around, mouth agape.

'Oh my God, Lizzie. Are you drinking? We only just picked you up! Jesus! Accusing me of doing drugs and you're at it again.'

'I am not at it again!' It was Lizzie's turn to be defensive.

'What else are you doing? Here in the dark with this?' Liam grabbed the whiskey and started pouring it down the sink. 'Where'd you get this?'

The heady smell of alcohol wafted into the air as it glugged down the drain. Lizzie shuddered. They said smell was the most evocative sense. Lizzie was instantly seated in the front row of the largest cinema screen, watching all her worst moments play out in front of her.

'I wouldn't do that to you and Mam, I promise,' she said, eyes closed, trying to calm down. 'I have changed, Liam.'

'Then where'd it come from?' he said. But it was a question, not an accusation. He was calmer too. Giving her a chance.

'It's Dad's.'

With a sonorous thump, he set the now empty decanter down on the draining board.

'Dad's?' he said in a small, sad voice. Like a dart, the mention of their father deflated his outrage. He shook his head. He stared at the empty decanter. He looked back at Lizzie.

'Can you believe it's him?'

Lizzie shook her head. 'No, not really. It's so insane.'

'It is.' He nodded. They were both silent for a moment until Liam spoke again.

'You know, I actually used to hope this would happen. That he'd just reappear, that he had actually hit his head and lost his memory and would eventually come back to us. But now it's happened, it's not what I thought it would be.'

'No,' said Lizzie sadly.

'He's not a nice man, is he?'

'I'm afraid not, Liam.' She came around the island. She wanted to wrap her arms around him. Gather him in, inhale his boyness. Even though he was eighteen, to her she imagined he still smelt of dinosaurs and baked beans and footballs. She reckoned he always would. But she held back. He didn't want her reassurances. She hadn't earned that right back, yet.

'Come on, let's go back to bed,' she said instead. 'Something tells me we're going to need all our energy for tomorrow. He says he's going nowhere, and I believe him.'

'Oh feck,' said Liam.

They left the kitchen and walked down the hall in silence, pausing at the door to the drawing room. It was shut now but gentle snores vibrated from within. Lizzie shook her head as they began to climb the stairs. On the landing they parted without another word.

Lizzie slipped back into bed and lay there. Still exhausted. Still awake.

She tossed and turned. Feeling further away from sleep, if anything, after the encounter with her father. But it couldn't stay away forever. Gradually it found her. And as she gladly surrendered, sleep's grip firmer now for its absence, she thought, in that middle place as she drifted off, that she heard a door open. And footsteps on the stairs.

12

Lizzie hoped she'd slept more than it felt like she had. She'd woken on and off, her subconscious mind anxious for the morning. She'd watched the light scale its chromatic steps from dark to bright, the sun in summer mode rising early by 5.30 a.m. to make the most of the day. The little brass clock by her bedside ticked away the minutes. Lizzie lay there on her side. Waiting. Waiting for George's step.

At 5.35 a.m. she heard the sound of a heavy bedroom door opening. She sat up and went to her own door. She opened it just as George passed. He stopped. He was fully dressed, wearing his tough hiking trousers, his waterproof gilet, ready for a trip through the woods.

'Thanks, George,' Lizzie said quietly, holding on to her door.

George smiled gently at her.

'Don't worry,' he whispered back. 'I'll have him gone in double quick time. Don't you worry.' George reached up and touched Lizzie's cheek. She'd seen him do this to Freya. A simple show of fatherly affection. Something Declan might have done once too. But never again. Lizzie felt the lump in her throat.

'If you need any help...' she said. George shook his head.

'Thank you, Lizzie. I think it will go quite straightforwardly. He can either go back to being disappeared or we pay a visit to the Gardaí. Either way, he's gone.'

Lizzie nodded. Hoped it would be that easy. Declan had seemed pretty determined last night. George took a step towards the stairs.

'Oh, George,' she said. He stopped and looked back at her. 'I'm sorry... sorry about what I said last night, about the wedding...'

George screwed up his eyes and waved away her words.

'No, no, don't apologise, young lady. You were just upset, worried. Like the rest of us. Your mother and I would have realised the same thing soon enough. And we don't need to be married to love each other, that can't be taken away from us.'

Lizzie felt relieved at his kind words. George smiled one more time and then began to descend the stairs. Lizzie retreated back into her room. She left her door ajar though. She wanted to listen to what happened. She wanted to make sure George was okay. He was a much bigger man than her father, but he was nearly ten years older. She also wanted to hear her father's voice as he was put in his place, told he was being removed. She wanted to hear the rev of the quad bike as George presented him with his taxi out of here.

She lay back down on her bed, the noises floating up from below. She heard the drawing room door being opened. George's footsteps on the wooden floor. And then the creak of another door. No voices floated up. Then the sounds became more distant, further away. Was he really going that easily? Without a word? Perhaps he'd had time to think and realised it was better this way. Lizzie got up again and went to the window that overlooked the terrace. She ignored the sight of the book she'd flung out the window last night, which she could see now had landed in a concrete planter, flattening a few bright pink dahlias.

She looked out, looking for George and her dad.

Then came rapid footsteps on the stairs. They sounded like George's. Lizzie moved quickly to her door and pulled it open. Just in time to see George rush past, heading for his room. Lizzie crossed the landing, floating as lightly as she could. She stopped outside George and Claire's room, put an ear to the crack of the slightly ajar door.

'He's not downstairs,' Lizzie heard George say.

'What? Are you sure?' her mother replied.

'Maybe he saw sense and took off in the night?' George suggested.

'I hope so.'

Lizzie straightened up. No. He hadn't seen sense. The Declan O'Shea she'd spoken to only three hours ago in the dark kitchen was going nowhere. Lizzie pushed open their bedroom door. George was standing at the foot of a large, four-poster bed. Claire sat at the end of the bed, dressed in a pink T-shirt and loose pyjama bottoms. They both turned to look at her.

'I talked to my father at 2 a.m., he had no intention of going anywhere.'

'What were you doing, talking to him at 2 a.m.? I thought we'd all gone to bed.' Claire looked up at her, the familiar guarded distance in her eyes. That moment, not long before Declan had reappeared, where their hands had touched. It felt like she'd imagined it.

'I couldn't sleep and went to get myself a drink and I found him in the kitchen. That's all. Okay?'

Claire said nothing.

'Anyway, as I said, he seemed pretty determined not to leave. To stay and win us back.'

'Maybe he changed his mind?' said Claire. Lizzie shook her head.

'Can we not just be happy that he's gone?' said George.

'Trust me, George,' Lizzie rubbed her tired eyes, 'I'd be thrilled if he was gone. But I can't believe he's taken off in the night. He's just gone for a walk in the woods, something like that. If we go look, we'll find him. And we need to do that. We need to hand him over to the Gardaí – or whatever – just get him gone.' Lizzie's voice was rising, she could feel a panic brewing in her belly.

The door behind her creaked and two sleepy heads appeared around it.

'What's happening?' asked Freya, tightening the belt of a blue silk embroidered dressing gown. Hudson, shirtless and wearing cotton lounge pants, stood behind her, his blond hair ruffled. He rubbed the heel of his palm against one eye and then the other.

'My father isn't downstairs,' said Lizzie.

'Has he left?' asked Hudson.

Lizzie shook her head.

'No. I've already explained to George and my mother that there's no way he'd go of his own accord. He was here to win us back and he wasn't going anywhere without us.'

Freya looked at her father and he shrugged.

'So where is he?' Freya asked, turning back to Lizzie.

'Outside?'

'Okay then,' Freya said. 'There's only one way to clear this up. We'll go out and look for him.'

'The estate is two hundred acres, darling...' said George.

'He's only one man,' she replied. 'If he's still here, he hasn't gone far. Right, maybe everyone should get dressed, put on your hiking boots. See you all downstairs in five minutes and we can go look.'

Five minutes later, everyone, including Liam whom Lizzie

had alerted to the situation, reassembled in the kitchen. The door to the back stairs opened, and the group were greeted by the bleary-eyed and confused face of Mia, the cook. She pulled her dressing gown around her.

'Do you need breakfast?' she asked, dubious, glancing up at the clock, noting the 5.50 a.m. time.

'We're sorry to disturb you,' Claire began. 'We're just...' Then she turned to George, whispering. 'Did you check up there? Could he have headed for a bedroom rather than the sofa?'

'I did. He's not.'

'Oh.'

'What's going on?' Mia asked, looking more awake but also more confused.

'Our extra guest has gone a bit AWOL,' explained Freya.

'Oh,' she replied. 'I see.'

'Did you hear or see anything?' asked Lizzie.

Mia shook her head.

'No, I'm sorry. I've only just woken up now, hearing you all down here.'

'Again, sorry for disturbing you,' said Claire. 'Please head back up, don't worry about us.'

'It's no problem. I hope you find him.' With a yawn, the cook turned and went back up the narrow wooden stairs.

'Come on,' said George, heading for the back door. 'Let's get this over with.'

Outside, they fell into pairs. Freya and Hudson, George and Claire, and Lizzie and Liam.

'We can go west,' said George, pointing towards a trail that took them into the woods and towards some tumbledown stone outhouses Lizzie could just about make out among the trees. 'Freya and Hudson, why don't you head straight – go by the graveyard and the walled garden, see if he's taken a stroll down there? Lizzie and Liam, you two go around to the front of the house and trek back along the trail we came in yesterday. Less chance of you getting lost if some of the woods are at least a little familiar.

'If anyone finds him, holler. And if he causes trouble, just scream. We'll come running.'

Everyone nodded and headed off.

Liam and Lizzie retraced the route from yesterday afternoon. They were silent, both lost in their own thoughts. Lizzie was sure her father was close by. Though she hoped she wasn't the one to find him. With luck George would be the one to stumble upon him, and then he'd grab him and take him to the quad bike without Lizzie ever having to see him again.

It was cool this early in the morning, even if the promise of yet another very warm day hung in the air. Lizzie pulled her pink hoodie closer to her. Zipped it up and pulled the drawstrings of the hood to close over the neck. The dawn chorus sang for them, filling the quiet that had settled between the siblings. They were soon in the thick of the trees, feeling the temperature drop. They heard scurrying scrabbles in the undergrowth, saw leaves and forest floor plants disturbed. Lizzie's thoughts strayed from her father and his whereabouts and settled on what she'd seen last night, Liam disappearing into the trees.

'Do you think he came this way?' asked Liam, the silence finally broken.

'No idea,' said Lizzie studying her brother's face. Struck once more by how like Declan he had become. So like him physically. Her fears that he might have gotten more like Declan had been unfounded, even if he'd added an understandable spiky edge when it came to interacting with her. She hoped it would eventually soften. And they'd get back to how they'd once been...

'What were you at last night, Liam?' Lizzie wound one side of the hoodie drawstring around her finger. Focused on the redness of the tip of her finger rather than looking at her brother.

'Why are you so interested? I remember telling you to drop it.'

Lizzie shrugged. Why *was* she so interested?

'It was strange. I was worried about you.'

Liam's eyes clouded over at Lizzie's words. His fingers found the scar on his jaw, traced the length of its raised white line. He looked down at his feet as he opened his mouth to speak. Kicked at some ivy.

'It would have been... nice, if you'd always been as worried about me.'

Lizzie pulled the drawstring tighter around her finger. It bulged slightly and went a dark shade of puce.

'True. I deserve that.' She released the cord from her finger, rubbed it. Looked over at Liam. 'I know you won't believe me but I always worried about you. I never stopped loving or caring about you. My problems just made me care more about me.' Lizzie shrugged. 'Selfish and shitty, I know. But I've changed. I'm me again. I promise.'

'Mam says—'

'What does Mam say?' Lizzie replied brusquely, cutting him off. Despite her attempts to build bridges, she felt the flicker of a flame to burn them too... *Mam says don't trust Lizzie*, was that it? Or *Mam says don't forget what she did*?

'Nothing.' He walked on, shuffling through the undergrowth.

Dammit. Lizzie sighed and followed him. Maybe he was about to say *Mam says let's try and get past this*.

'Liam, I'm sorry,' she said to his back. 'I didn't— Ouch!' She stopped and dropped down, grabbing her lower leg. A hidden bramble had nicked just above her boot, leaving a long jagged scratch. She should have put her jeans on rather than the shorts she'd grabbed in a hurry. Beads of blood swelled, then trickled down, leaving a crimson streak in their wake. She could see the drops inside her boot soak into her white socks, leaving a dark, deep red stain.

Liam, turned and looked back at her.

'You okay?'

Lizzie nodded.

'Uh-huh,' she mumbled, licking her finger and then rubbing the sore spot. She stood up again. Looked into the thick of the forest ahead of them. Ignoring the stinging cut, she caught up with him. She trained her eye on the forest floor, keeping a closer eye on where she put her feet. 'Look, I'm sorry, it's a journey and I do still have a way to go—'

'SHUSH!' said Liam. He grabbed her sleeve and stopped her. He cocked his head, held a finger to his lips.

'What...?' asked Lizzie, puzzled. Liam shushed her again. She went quiet.

Then she heard it too.

Far off, but clear enough that in the silent clear morning the sound carried all the way to them.

A scream.

A scream that didn't stop.

13

She looked at Liam and without needing to say anything they both turned and began to run.

It was a woman's voice. That Lizzie could tell. And it was coming from beyond the back of the house. Liam streaked ahead of her, stopping and pausing as they reached the clearing in front of the house.

'C'mon, Lizzie! What if it's Mam? C'mon, move!'

'I'm doing my best,' panted Lizzie.

They tore around to the back of the house. The screaming had stopped, but that only heightened her panic. Careering past the low pillared wall that bounded the side of the terrace, they spotted George and Claire emerging at speed from the path opposite. Mirrored looks of fear on their faces. Lizzie felt a surge of relief seeing her mother was okay.

'That's Freya!' yelled George, his eyes wide with panic. A terror Lizzie could see in them even from this distance. Without stopping he pointed to where Freya and Hudson had gone. He and Claire swerved in that direction, re-entering the woods, never slowing down. Lizzie and Liam followed, George leading the line, dodging and weaving through the trees as fast as he could.

'We're coming, Freya!' George cried, the anguish in his voice a siren.

Lizzie batted back low branches like a swimmer as she ran but still felt the whip and sting of the ones she missed. The bramble cut on her ankle was joined by a multitude of other small, shallow nicks. None of which she felt.

George veered right. They all followed. Lizzie felt a path emerge, compacted earth beneath her feet. It took them past a high, ivy- and moss-covered stone wall. As Lizzie ran by its perimeter she caught a streak of blue sky among the forest gloom.

The forest floor started to slope downwards and Lizzie heard water. The babble and rushing of a flowing stream. A rickety metal bridge provided passage across. George didn't slow down, just barrelled over, the metal clanking sound mixed with Lizzie's gasp; she fully expected him to plummet. But it held.

On the far side, among the dense trees, was a stone building. The size of a small cottage. A very odd little dwelling. Its patchy roof and walls were near entirely engulfed in ivy. Slim windows curved to a point, like a church. Metal bars instead of glass. And what wall could be seen was weirdly pockmarked. George disappeared around it, following the sound of sobbing, clear above the noise of the water.

Hudson appeared.

'We're okay,' he said. But even in the low light of the woods, Lizzie could see he was deathly pale.

'Are you sure? Where's Freya? What's happening?' Claire called across as they started over the bridge, showing more caution than George had.

'Look, you might not want to go round there.' Hudson stood his ground, as they assembled on the far bank.

'Is she okay?' asked Lizzie.

'She's fine. She's fine. It's just...'

'Is it...' Claire began, but didn't finish. She pushed Hudson out of the way and ran around the corner of this strange little building.

'Don't—' started Hudson. Liam and Lizzie followed their mother, rushing past him.

They came to a rapid stop. George was standing there, a shaking and weeping Freya in his arms. Her face buried in her hands. Claire stood just outside his reach, staring into the building's arched entrance, motionless.

'Claire. Darling, please,' entreated George, reaching out a hand to her. 'Guys, stay there,' he added, spotting the two of them. 'Really, don't come any closer.'

Liam stalled. Lizzie looked at him and then to Claire. George shook his head. Lizzie took a few steps forward. Towards her mother. She kept her eyes straight ahead, focused on Claire, not looking into the building.

She took her mother's hand. Felt the goosebumps on her arms prickle and her spine freeze like a river of ice.

Slowly, she turned.

It was one large open space. As strange on the inside as the outside. To the left a small rectangular pool, two steps down into it, was filled with stagnant water. Watched over by busy clouds of midges, traversed by spread-eagle water strider insects. Dark shadows reflected on the surface from the ceiling above it, the only part of the roof still fully intact. There was an ornate fireplace on the back wall directly in their eyeline. Small puddles of water pooled around the floor, rainwater from the holes in the roof.

But these details just framed the centrepiece of a grim tableau.

All Lizzie saw was the body.

Spread across the centre of the floor. The back of his head

caved in. A pool of dark, congealed blood, like a speech bubble next to it. The decanter, bloodied and chipped, was lying not far from the prone form.

'Oh. Oh no. No, no,' she whimpered. Lizzie dropped her mother's hand as she threw hers to her face.

Lizzie heard her mother take a deep breath.

'Well,' Claire sighed. 'I think we can say he's really dead this time.'

14

Lizzie took a step forward. Claire grabbed her sleeve.

'Don't. Don't touch him.' Lizzie stopped.

'Is it... is it... him?' A weak voice came from Lizzie and Claire's left. Liam's ashen face stared at them. His blue eyes replaced with dark holes, devoid of a spark.

Lizzie nodded. Claire broke away from her side and went to her son. She wrapped him in her arms, and Liam collapsed into her, sobbing.

Lizzie turned to George.

'The Guards. We... we need to inform them. Where is this quad bike, someone needs to go. I can go.'

Freya peeled away from her father, red-eyed and subdued. She nodded.

'Yes, Lizzie,' said George. 'I agree. Let's go back to the house and have a moment to calm down and then I'll go for the authorities.'

George led a shell-shocked train back to the house. Their limbs moving as if through treacle, like they'd used up all their speed on the way here. Lizzie forced one foot in front of another. She felt like she was on another planet, where the gravity worked differently. Retracing their steps, they came to the wall they'd run by. She stopped. Through an opening she saw it was an abandoned walled garden, strangled by overgrown bushes and plants. But for once no trees, the walls a defensive line that held off the invader here. This was where she'd seen a flash of blue. She stared in at the tangled mess of neglect and then looked up. There wasn't a cloud in the sky. The words of an Oscar Wilde poem came into her shocked brain.

> *I never saw sad men who looked*
> *With such a wistful eye*
> *Upon that little tent of blue*
> *We prisoners called the sky*

She looked at the others, ahead of her. Like a chain gang. Fellow inmates in this sudden prison of horror. She walked on. Leaving the sky behind. Plunging back into the murky darkness of the tree cover. Shaking her head, trying to dislodge the images of her father that flashed before her eyes. The bloodied decanter. The devastating mess of his head. The pool of blood on the ground beside him.

Back at the house, George paused outside the kitchen door and turned to the rest of them. He put his fingers to his lips, and then pointed it upstairs to Mia's window. Everyone nodded. They trooped in quietly.

'I think we could all benefit from a hot drink, I can make tea,' whispered Claire to George.

'Okay, but let's just keep it as quiet as possible.'

'Of course.'

Claire put on the kettle. Freya gathered cups and a teapot and put them on a tray.

'Will we drink it inside? In the drawing room?' said Claire, snatching a quick glance up at the ceiling. A chain gang again, they all followed Claire out of the room.

At the drawing room door, Claire stopped.

'Oh,' she said. Lizzie came around and looked for what had stopped her. She peered into the room. The blanket her father had been sleeping under still lay across the sofa. The pillow still rumpled at one end. Freya came behind them, taking in the scene.

'C'mon,' George said, and led them instead into the adjoining room. 'We can have our tea in here.' A grand rosewood table, fit to seat twenty or more, stretched the length of the room. They each pulled out a chair and sat. There was a baby grand piano in the window and portraits on the walls, ancestors staring down at them. Lizzie felt the weight of their gaze. She turned in her chair, trying to avoid their accusatory faces. She stared instead into the empty grate of the large marble fireplace. Sipped her tea without a word.

Each remained in their own cell of silence until George spoke.

'How is everyone?' he asked, leaning forward, his chair creaking beneath him.

'Shaky,' said Freya.

Lizzie looked across the table at him.

'Can we go get the Guards now? Please? I'm happy to go if you don't feel up to it.'

George shuffled in his seat. Further strained noises emanated from it. George cleared his throat.

'Someone else?' Lizzie asked.

He cleared his throat again.

'Lizzie,' he said, taking a deep breath. 'I've had a few thoughts... when the head cleared a bit, on the way back.'

'Thoughts about who was going to go for the Guards?' said Lizzie, staring him straight in his eyes. He dropped his gaze.

'Em, no,' he paused. And when he spoke again, his voice had an edge. 'I actually think we shouldn't go for the Gardaí.'

'Sorry, what?' said Claire, eyes screwed up.

'Yes, what?' repeated Lizzie. She placed her mug down on the table. 'What did you say?'

He sat forward, directing his words at Lizzie.

'I said, I don't think we should tell the Gardaí.'

'Oh, I heard you,' said Lizzie, 'I just don't understand why we wouldn't inform the police. Why on earth would we not tell them?'

'Yeah, why not? Someone killed my dad.' Liam's voice, still weak with shock, was barely audible. George sighed and then leant back in his chair. He ran his hands through his hair, pulling it back, laced through his fingers.

'What do we think happened to Declan?' he said.

'Huh?' said Lizzie. 'Someone attacked him!'

'Yes, obviously,' said George. 'And who attacked him? If you were the Gardaí, what would you think happened? Because it was one of two things. Either some random person got a car out here, managed to stop at the exact right place in the middle of nowhere to get onto my land. They then trekked an hour through the woods, probably in the dark – didn't get lost – and got to the house. Here they were lucky enough to spot your father inside and somehow lure him out. Even though we're in the middle of nowhere I lock the doors, so they didn't walk in. This house was burnt down once and there are a lot of valuable items in here. I keep it secure. So, he voluntarily left a locked house and was killed by a very lucky homicidal stranger?'

'My father hurt and swindled a lot of people, George. He made enemies.'

'That makes it even more unlikely that he'd willingly leave the security of a locked house to go have a chat with someone he knew to be murderous towards him.'

'Maybe he was outside already, getting some air.'

'True, but, add it all up. That'd be remarkably unfortunate,' said George. 'Plus, you're forgetting something.'

'What?'

'All of those he wronged think he's dead. They aren't looking for him.'

Lizzie didn't have an answer to that. She looked at her mother. Claire shook her head and looked at George.

'But you're not completely wrong, Lizzie. There are some people he wronged who knew he was alive.'

'Us,' Lizzie whispered.

'Yes. Option two for the Gardaí to consider.' George looked around the room. 'We were people who were definitely angry with him. Quite apart from how furious you three would be that he did this to you in the first place, he was also a grenade into all our new lives. Look at the potential destruction he was able to visit on us all in one short evening. Look at what he threatened... My darling Claire, you'd finally found happiness again. Lizzie, you've just conquered your demons. Liam, your family together and happy again. Freya, my sweetheart, you get to finally see me not lonely after so long. Which is obviously my feeling too. I've been alone and sad for so long. These past six months have been some of the happiest of my life. So, some random stranger in the woods? Or a house full of people whose lives you've obliterated? It isn't just the Gardaí who will think it was one of us. *I* think it was one of us.'

15

'What? No!' Lizzie cried, incredulous. 'How can you think that?'

'Jesus, this is insane,' said Hudson, shaking his head. Freya grabbed his hand.

'Daddy, surely not.'

Lizzie jumped up, sending her chair falling backwards. She knocked against her mug and it tipped over, tea spilling across the polished wood table.

'Calm down, child,' said George, standing. He produced a handkerchief from his pocket and mopped up the pools of liquid.

'That's all completely ridiculous,' said Lizzie. She looked to her mother for an ally, a fellow indignant voice. Claire didn't meet her eye.

But, as the last syllable of the word 'ridiculous' left her lips, Lizzie faltered. She was wrong. It wasn't ridiculous. Not entirely. At the very least George was right that suspicion would fall on them. And sometimes that was all it took to seal your fate.

Lizzie, feeling like someone had slowed time around her,

turned and righted her chair. A little dizzy, she sat. Looking around the table she saw an array of shocked and traumatised faces. Hudson dazed and unsettled, Freya pale and red-eyed. Claire and Liam seemed hardly here at all.

'We're just ordinary people,' she pleaded. 'It has to make more sense that it was some randomer hiding in the woods. That my father went for a walk and stumbled upon them. I know we were all angry... but to kill him? To do that to him?' Lizzie shook her head.

'I should clarify, I don't think anyone meant to hurt him,' said George, his voice soft, kind, looking at everyone. 'I can't believe anyone at this table did it intentionally. Someone went downstairs last night to talk to him... Went for a walk with him, to ask him to reconsider and to leave without a fuss. Something like that. An argument broke out. There was a struggle, a fight. He ends up as we found him. Can't you see it?'

Lizzie said nothing. Because she *could* see it. It was a classic example of Occam's razor – the simplest explanation is usually the correct one. And with a chill, she remembered the door she'd heard open as she drifted off to sleep last night. The footsteps on the stairs. Lizzie bowed her head. Rested it in her hands, elbows bent, on the table. If you'd told her only yesterday morning that her father would reappear, she'd have said you were being ridiculous. If you'd told her he was capable of faking his death and disappearing for five years, she'd have said you were being ridiculous. Things she didn't think could happen, did. And the quiet from around the table told her everyone else was coming to the same conclusion. Understanding it was not only a possibility, but a probability: that it was one of them.

'What are we going to do?' asked Freya, her voice unsteady. Hudson put his arm around her and pulled her close.

'Don't worry, sweetheart, don't fret,' he murmured. His turn to reassure her.

George got up. He circumnavigated the table. He rested his hand lightly on Freya's shoulder as he went.

'I have an idea,' he said. He stopped at the grand piano at the windows, sat down on the stool and opened the lid. His fingers rested on the white ivory keys, his thumb finding middle C. He pressed the note and the clear sound reverberated in the silence. He looked up at everyone.

'The fact of the matter is Declan O'Shea is dead. Officially. Legally. No one but us knows that wasn't the case. And if we all don't freak out, just stay here, keep with our plans, not rock the boat, then when this weekend is over – we can all just go on with our lives, put this behind us.'

'What? Just walk away?' said Claire. 'Leave him and not breathe a word?'

'We could lay him to rest in the graveyard. There are free plots. It could be quite dignified.'

'He doesn't deserve to go there,' said Freya.

'Honey, don't,' said George.

'You want us to act as if he never came back?' asked Liam.

'Yes,' said George. 'That's the idea.'

Lizzie turned to her mother and brother.

'How could we do that? Knowing one of us killed him? Seriously?' she said.

'Lizzie,' said George. 'I know this is all so shocking. And my suggestion is out there. But think about it. Your father wasn't a good man. By your own admission he destroyed all your lives. Are you going to let him do it again? Are you going to let his death destroy you a second time? No one here is a danger to anyone else. Your father brought an untenable level of provocation to the table.

'I say we let Declan O'Shea have his wish – and lay him to rest. Permanently, this time.'

16

'I don't want to railroad anyone into this... so maybe we could vote on it? How does that sound?'

Everyone looked around the table. Looking to see if anyone would object.

'Right, then,' said George. 'Raise your hand if you think we should just let this lie. Let Declan rest in the graveyard and not destroy anyone else's life.'

One by one the hands went up. Lizzie watched as they were raised and no one met her eye. She kept her hand firmly down. She couldn't believe she was the only one who didn't think this was crazy. Especially her mother. Liam seemed in shock – they all were, but he seemed worse. He probably wasn't thinking straight, if he was able to think at all. The Butlers she didn't know well enough to know where their moral compass pointed. But Claire, her upright, principled mother? How was she okay with this?

'Mam, really?' she said.

Claire nodded. 'I think it's the only way.'

'Well, you've all forgotten something,' said Lizzie.

'What?' asked George.

'The cook. She knew he was here. Won't she be suspicious about what's going on? Freya told her he'd gone AWOL, but that doesn't explain any of the rest of it. When she's more awake won't she realise how weird it was, all of us in the kitchen at 6 a.m.? All of us worried-looking and barrelling out the door. And what if she heard Freya screaming in the woods? How will you explain that?'

'I better talk to her then,' said Claire. 'Tell her something more.'

'Perhaps,' said George, looking at Claire, 'you could say that you and Declan had a row that woke up everyone upstairs. That's when he stormed out of the house. We decided to go after him – hence our appearance in the kitchen at 6 a.m. And if she heard the scream, then, well, that was you, frightened when we found him wandering in the woods. Tell her I insisted he leave. How about that?'

'Yes, I think that sounds plausible enough,' said Claire.

'And if we're acting a bit upset,' said George, 'his appearance in the first place is enough to explain that away. Let's keep her as much at arm's length though, just to be safe? Keep your distance from her. I'd be reluctant to suddenly dismiss her as that could look suspicious, but let's not let in any own-goals, alright?'

There was a flurry of nods around the table.

'Wait.' Liam's quiet voice piped up. 'What if it was her who did it? If it wasn't one of us then we could go to the police after all...'

Everyone stared at him, this new possibility hanging in the air.

Claire shook her head and spoke.

'No, I don't think so. Wouldn't she have taken off in the night as we all slept if she did it? Why hang around for us to find his body? It doesn't make sense. And, besides, what motive could she possibly have?'

'Maybe we ask her a few questions?' said Hudson. 'Just to be sure?'

'Yeah, and maybe we should ask each other a few questions while we're at it?' said Lizzie.

'No!' barked George. All eyes turned to him. 'No, no, no... no questions. For anyone. I agree with Claire. Surely she'd have fled if she was responsible. And if we start getting all nosey and asking her things other than what's for dinner, she could get suspicious. Which is the opposite of what we want to happen. It's too risky. And, as for asking each other questions? That'll foster suspicion and blame. That would only make it harder to walk away from all this. We need to just accept that it is what it is. And continue with our lives.'

'Christ,' Lizzie hissed through gritted teeth. Claire shot her a look.

'Is there anything else that might be a problem?' George asked the table. No one said anything.

'Okay then, with one respectful decline, it looks like everyone else is in agreement with the plan to let sleeping dogs lie.'

'Daddy,' said Freya. 'Until we're able to sort something out in the family plot, we can't just leave him in the bathhouse. The wildlife... we're lucky they hadn't been... at him already.'

'Ah, that's a good point.' George pursed his lips as he pondered the problem. 'Right... what do you think if we moved the remains temporarily to the icehouse? He'll be safe there.'

'Move him where?' asked Hudson.

'The icehouse,' said Freya. 'It's like, an old-fashioned outdoor freezer? All the old stately homes had them. They're usually a deep pit, with a roof and a door in the deepest, coldest part of the woods. Daddy's been experimenting with Butler Hall's one for years.'

'There's plenty of ice in there now too. It's perfect. He won't be left to the elements.'

'Has everyone lost their minds?' said Lizzie, and all eyes turned to her. 'It can't be this simple? Icehouses? Family plots? Surely we can't just walk away and pretend it never happened?'

'I think we might be able to,' said George. 'And I think we should.'

Lizzie stood up and stepped away from the table.

'It's clear that I'm on my own here. But I can't do this.' She stalked out of the room, and stopped in the hall. Looked to the drawing room door. Thought about her father's last night asleep there. Before he was killed. Before someone in this house smashed his head in. A maelstrom of feelings churned in her gut. She'd have admitted to hating her father last night. The love that she'd denied having these past five years, but had lingered hidden in the secret recesses of her heart, had been entirely annihilated. But still. That didn't mean she didn't care that he was dead. That this was what had happened to him.

'Lizzie.'

She turned. Claire was shutting the door behind her.

'Let's talk about this.'

'What's there to talk about? You all seem to have made up your crazy minds.'

Claire took Lizzie's hand, like a teacher taking a naughty child to the head's office, and led her across the hall to the half-plastered room. Claire closed the door behind them. Lizzie shook off her grip.

'How on earth are you okay with this, Mam?' Lizzie pre-empted whatever her mother had to say. Her words echoed around the cavernous space. 'I know Dad did awful things, I know he was about to do worse... but... but...' Lizzie felt inconvenient tears force themselves to the surface. She turned away from Claire and rubbed furiously at her eyes, trying to head them off.

'I'm not okay with it... not one little bit.' Claire talked to Lizzie's back. 'The sight of your dad... that will stay with me forever. He didn't deserve that. Despite everything. But... your brother, he's only eighteen. His life is about to begin. You've finally stopped trying to destroy yours. So, going to the Gardaí?' Claire took a deep breath. 'All I can see is disaster. For all of us. I think George is right, they'd only look at us. What if they think you're a good fit for the crime? You've got a conviction because of the drink driving last year and you threw a bowl at your dad's head last night. And what about me? I slapped him. In front of five witnesses.'

Lizzie turned back to her mother, pale.

'Do you think I did it? Do you think I killed my father?'

'Oh my God, Lizzie, that's not what I am saying. I'm saying that's what it could look like. To the Gardaí!'

A terrible thought bubbled to the turbulent surface of Lizzie's mind.

That whiskey decanter in the bathhouse. With blood on it. The weapon that killed her father. It had to be the same one from last night, the one Liam had emptied down the sink. It was identical. And when she pictured them all in the kitchen this morning, she remembered the stopper still on the island but the decanter missing from the draining board where Liam had left it.

His fingerprints would be all over it.

They'd gotten there when he'd been helping her, saving her from temptation. But that would sound awfully convenient to an interviewing detective, wouldn't it? Actual evidence to link him to their father's death. Not just circumstantial accounts of thrown crockery and slaps.

Lizzie slumped to the ground, all her strength gone. She sat on the dusty floor, her legs crossed in a mocking imitation of the yoga pose they'd learnt at St Brigid's. She felt anything but inner peace. Claire squatted down in front of her, her arms resting on her thighs, hands clasped in front of her.

'I need you to go along with this.'

Lizzie stared her mother in the eye.

'Do you think you can just enjoy your new life with your new husband and pretend this never happened? Do you think that will work?'

'Lizzie, don't spin it like that. I'm not asking you to agree to this for my sake, it's for yours. Yours and Liam's.'

'How noble of you.'

Claire stood up and loomed over her.

'You think I don't care enough about you to want to do this for you? That I'm being selfish? Can you actually hear yourself, Lizzie? Who never threw you out of the house when you stole from us? Multiple times. Me. Who collected you from the Garda station when you'd been arrested? *Multiple times.* Me. Who hung in there when you lied and manipulated and stole and raged? Who still didn't turn their back on you when you drove drunk and nearly killed your brother? Me!' Claire's voice rose to a shout. The sounds rocketing to the rafters above them. 'You're correct, it was all me, me, me. Your selfish mother.'

Lizzie placed her palms down on the dusty floor and pushed herself up. She kept her eyes to the ground, the weight of shame hanging her head.

'I shouldn't have suggested you were doing this for selfish reasons. I'm sorry. That was petulant of me. I lashed out because I'm upset and confused.' The lessons at St Brigid in understanding yourself, to give words to your actions and feelings, flowed from Lizzie. She wished the pain and guilt would leave with them. 'I was confused that you would agree to this precisely because you've always done the right thing.'

'I think this is also the right thing. Well, the best of two poor options anyway.'

'Maybe you don't understand, but I do. About trying to suppress stuff.' She sniffled as her tears reappeared. 'I know about that, only too well. It does bad things to you. And I understand the weight of guilt better than most too. It'll catch up with you.'

'That's a chance I'll have to take. And if you want to assuage some of that guilt, you'll do this for me.'

'Will nothing convince you?'

Claire shook her head.

'Fine.' Lizzie turned to go. 'I'll do it. For you. To show you I'm serious about making amends. That I've changed. But...' She walked slowly, unsteady on her feet, to the door and then stopped. She looked back at Claire. 'You need to really think about this. You've got to understand what you're doing. It could destroy us. Just as thoroughly as involving the Gardaí.'

17

Lizzie went upstairs. Claire could go back to the others and tell them she'd capitulated. She was going to take a shower instead. The wafer-thin symbolism wasn't lost on her. Washing herself clean, washing off the guilt of collusion.

Hanging her towel on the brass hook on the back of the door she turned on the shower. It warmed up and Lizzie stepped under the large chrome attachment which hung over one end of the bathtub. As steam filled the room, she let the hot water flow over her. Let it provide some warmth and comfort which she desperately needed. She kept it running for twenty minutes, knowing she was using up the hot water. But she didn't care. This mini-rebellion made her feel better, briefly...

As she rubbed her fingers through her wet soapy hair, Lizzie let her mind wander back to one insistent worry among the many. The fingerprints on the whiskey decanter. Liam's fingerprints. What to do about them? If there were no repercussions from this plan, to just walk away, then it wasn't a problem. But that was an "if" Lizzie wasn't sure she could live with. And that then meant she had to do something about it. Just in case. But what? Wipe it clean? Destroy it? She was no expert, but Lizzie knew enough to know that she was no match for forensic science. She'd probably leave some other trail on the decanter if she tried anything. And then she'd have tampering with evidence to add to the making-them-look-guilty pot. She felt cornered. But at least she had the weekend to think of something.

The water began to run cold. Lizzie shut it off. Wrapping the towel around her, she listened at the door for the others. She didn't want to see any of them. Silence told her the coast was clear, so she scampered back to her room.

Lizzie pulled on a pair of denim shorts and a red T-shirt. Left her wet hair loose. She lay down on the bed, its softness once more welcoming her, embracing her. She didn't care that the pillow would get soaked by her hair. The day would be another warm one, everything would dry. She lay there, staring up at the ceiling. Following the cracks as if they were some sort of map that would show her a way out of this mess. She heard quiet voices outside, on the terrace. George and Hudson. The word 'icehouse' floated up to her. She turned her back to the window, rolling onto her side. Trying not to think about the job they were off to do. Despite her overwhelming tiredness, Lizzie was reluctant to close her eyes. She knew she'd see him again. Lying spread out on the bathhouse floor. The dark, crimson pool of blood by his head. She'd spent the last five years running away from imagined images of her father being dragged under waves. His lungs filling up with water. This new horror movie was even worse. She didn't have to invent these images.

But despite her reluctance, sleep came anyway. Her eyelids grew heavy and as a gentle breeze got lost in her room, she drifted off to sleep.

Lizzie woke with a gasp. Sat up, heart pounding. Half-remembered dreams of dappled shadows and rippling water were wrenched from her as she came to consciousness.

Tendrils of panic snaked through her. Searching for her lungs, encircling them, squeezing. She felt her heart, barely slowing from her dreams, speed up again, as if desperate to outrun the invading enemy. Beads of sweat that had nothing to do with the day's heat formed on Lizzie's forehead.

She sprang up from the bed. Pupils wide. Sucking in shallow, juddering breaths. Her therapist from St Brigid's whispered to her. *Slow down. Ground yourself.* She searched for her senses, pressing the soles of her feet onto the warm wooden floor. Forced herself to inhale and examine the earthy scents from the forest air wafting through her room. *Slow everything down*, Lizzie whispered to herself, *breathe...*

She closed her eyes. She listened to the birds outside for some time. The panic receded. Eventually opening her eyes again.

She should get out of this room. Do something to keep busy. This estate might not be a farm like St Brigid's, somewhere that made work for idle hands, but surely there were things she could do around here. Things to occupy her while she sorted out how the hell she was going to cope with this madness. Her mother didn't understand what she was asking of Lizzie. Or of herself.

Lizzie looked at the clock on her bedside table. It was twelve noon. She'd slept for four hours. She'd go explore the house. Something. Anything.

Lizzie found her flat red sandals and slipped them on. Tied her hair back. She didn't bother combing it first. She passed the dresser mirror without looking at herself.

Opening her door, she looked across the landing. Liam's room was directly opposite. She walked slowly over. She'd check on him. Raising her hand, her knuckles tapped the door.

'Liam?' she called out, quietly.

Nothing.

'Liam, hon?' she tried again.

'Go away,' his gruff voice came back to her.

'Are you okay?'

'Go the hell away!' he yelled, louder this time.

She backed off. She'd try again later.

Downstairs, Lizzie paused in the hall, deciding what to do. She should go outside, it was a beautiful day and nature would help. But she wasn't ready for the bright, cheerful sun. It would feel like it was mocking her. She wanted to hide away.

She looked at the options around her. The first door was to the drawing room. She certainly wasn't going in there. The second was the dining room. Another room she'd take her time going back to. She headed for the last door in the row.

She stepped into a dark room. Beautiful oak built-in shelves covered every wall. Filled with books. It was the library. A pedestal desk with a green leather inlay took pride of place in front of wooden French doors. Lizzie could see the garden beyond. This was where the music had been playing last night. She felt calmer in the dim light, surrounded by quiet and books.

Two large, rust-coloured leather wingback chairs sat by a fireplace. It was the kind of room that felt like it should always have a fire roaring in the grate. A small, ornate round table laden with – empty – crystal decanters occupied a corner close to the chairs. Lizzie had an urge to go over and lift the stoppers, smell the crystal containers.

She shook herself and looked back at the shelves. She'd find a book.

She took a step towards them.

'Hi there,' came a voice from behind her.

'Jesus!' yelped Lizzie, jumping out of her skin. She spun around.

18

Freya, her blonde head now visible, looked at her from around the side of the nearest armchair. The petite woman had been concealed behind its high back.

'Sorry, Lizzie. I didn't mean to startle you.'

'I just... just didn't see you there,' said Lizzie.

'That's these chairs for you. You can sit here, in this one, and no one can see you're here. Great for Hide and Seek when I was little.'

'I'm sure. But look, sorry, I'll leave you in peace.' Lizzie started to back out of the room.

'Oh, no, stay,' said Freya. 'I wanted to talk to you actually.'

'Okay...' Lizzie's heart sank.

Freya shifted forward in the chair and perched on the edge so that Lizzie could see more of her. She stared straight ahead, into the opposite chair, gathering her thoughts. She tucked her hair behind her ears and looked up.

'Do you want to sit?' Freya pointed to the chair opposite.

'Do you want me to?'

Freya chuckled.

'Whatever makes you more comfortable, I don't mind.'

'I'm okay here.'

'Sure,' said Freya. 'So, like… I just wanted you to know that I didn't vote in favour of… *the plan*… lightly. I thought about it and just felt that Daddy was right.'

'Okay,' said Lizzie. She looked into Freya's pleading eyes.

'Buddha says that there is no path to happiness, that happiness *is* the path. You know? Like, I think we need to stay on the right path, if we diverge, let what your father did take us a different way,' she shook her head, 'I just think unhappiness would be underfoot, it's the wrong way.'

Lizzie nodded. Wondered what Freya wanted her to say in response. This little speech needed to be framed with a sunset, or a beach, and posted on social media.

'I understand,' she finally muttered. A response akin to those faux non-apologies: *'I'm sorry if what I said offended you.'* It was the best she could come up with. If Freya was looking for absolution, she didn't have it for her. She didn't have it for herself.

In the chair, Freya gathered up her long blonde hair. Twisted it into a messy bun and slipped a hair tie from her wrist over it. Lizzie was transfixed. Freya's biceps flexed and relaxed as she corralled her hair. She was small and petite, but clearly strong. A woman who looked after herself. Someone who did her strength training as well as cardio. Lizzie shivered. Was she strong enough to wield a hefty crystal decanter, smash her father's head in? Probably. Like the athletic Hudson. Like her brother. Like George too. He might be older, but he had the brawny strength of an outdoorsman. And what about Claire? Her mother? Could she have done it? Was she strong enough? She wasn't the gym bunny Freya obviously was, but adrenaline had been known to lift cars off trapped children. Would it also help someone swing a decanter, release a pent-up rage murderously? Probably. Lizzie felt the foot press down on the pedal of her pulse.

'Are you okay?' asked Freya.

A little dizzy, Lizzie slowly shook her head. She was beginning to understand what George had meant when he'd demanded they didn't interrogate each other. It was upsetting and overwhelming, just thinking about it all.

'No. But surely no one is okay right now?'

'Ah, true,' agreed Freya, slumping down into the chair.

Lizzie looked towards the door to the hall and then the French doors. She wanted to get out of here, get away from Freya. Her darting eyes were distracted by a photograph on the mantelpiece. In a large silver frame was a photo of a very beautiful fair-haired woman. She was smiling, her blue eyes sparkling, radiating a connection and love with whoever was behind the camera. Her chin was raised as if she'd been caught just before she threw her head back in laughter.

Freya followed Lizzie's gaze.

'That's my mum, Grace.' Freya stood up. She touched a finger to the frame, leaving a fingerprint where it rested. Leaving a little of her DNA on it. Like a connection, a communion between mother and daughter.

'She was beautiful,' said Lizzie.

Freya nodded her head. Lizzie couldn't see Freya's face, but it didn't take much to imagine her expression. It was clear in the slump of her shoulders, the wordless response. Lizzie wondered what it was like to feel that sort of grief, a pure and uncomplicated kind. To be able to just be sorry that person was gone.

'What happened to her?'

Freya sat back down in her chair.

'Cancer. Though I didn't understand that at the time, I was so small.'

Lizzie relented and sat down in the chair opposite. The shift in focus, this gear change, was a reality check. Other people had real problems too, had suffered.

'The memories I have are fuzzy. They're of her being different, not like my mum any more, if that makes sense. Dad filled in the gaps when I was older.'

'It still must have been hard.'

'Yeah, I mightn't have understood, but things were weird,' Freya sighed. 'I remember Daddy telling me we had to be quiet, because Mummy was upstairs in bed with her headaches. He was so good, he made a game of it. Who could be the quietest the longest. I'd get a packet of chocolate buttons when I "won" that game. And I always won.' Freya shook her head sadly at the memory. 'When she did come downstairs she'd have dizzy spells and we couldn't leave her on her own in case she fell. I'm not sure what I was meant to do; a five-year-old was hardly going to be able to catch her. Though, she'd lost so much weight I probably could have.'

Freya wound a strand of hair through her fingers.

'I'm happy I don't recall much more. Daddy told me years later that at the end it affected her heart and she lost her sight.' Freya shook her head. 'I'm particularly glad I don't remember that bit.'

'Freya,' said Lizzie, 'I'm so sorry. That sounds awful.'

'Ah, in truth it was far worse for Daddy. As I said, I was just a kid who barely remembers it all. He lived it. He might seem such a happy man, but he's kept this sadness deep inside. It didn't help that, apparently, they missed the cancer for a long time, it's why it got so bad. For some reason he blames himself for that.'

'Oh, that's terrible.'

'I know. I've told him he shouldn't, like, it's not as if he's a doctor or something.'

'I'm sorry for bringing this up. It was tactless of me.'

'No, don't apologise. Makes us even, hey?' She smiled. 'I was so young I never understood it all. When I talk about it now, I feel more like I'm retelling a story I once heard. If I'm honest I'm not sure now what is a real memory and what is some weird amalgam of anecdote and photograph and my imagination.'

Freya leant over to the small drinks table. There was a framed photograph of Grace there too, beside the empty decanters, which Lizzie hadn't noticed in the dim light. Freya picked this one up and examined it closely, then put it back.

'There's another one there,' she pointed to one of the bookshelves, 'and another.' She indicated one last image on another shelf. 'This room is a bit of a shrine. I hope your mother won't be upset by it.'

'My mum is a very practical person,' said Lizzie. 'She'll understand.'

A shadow passed by the window. Lizzie and Freya both looked up. Hudson and George were walking outside. George was leaning into Hudson, his hands gesticulating enthusiastically. Hudson was nodding but didn't appear to be talking.

'Oh God, Daddy is bending Hudson's ear. I bet it's something to do with the house, the timber he used or the exact replica eighteenth-century nails... something equally dull. I'd better go rescue my poor husband.'

'Of course,' said Lizzie, working to keep the relief out of her voice that Freya was going.

Freya stopped at the door out to the garden, her hand resting on the door handle. She looked back at Lizzie in the wingback chair.

'Sorry. I just heard that sentence there. Making Daddy and Hudson sound so... flippant. We're reeling, honestly. Shook. Hudson's very upset by everything that's happened, he's such a sensitive man,' she said, her voice quiet, woven with emotion. 'Like the rest of us. He really feels for you guys. This isn't quite how I imagined introducing him to Ireland and to my home here.'

'I can imagine,' said Lizzie.

Freya looked out the window as she spoke again. Watching her father and husband.

'And, if Daddy seems to just be himself, please don't think he's not shocked by all of this. That he doesn't care. It's just that there's a bit of the old stiff upper lip in the gene pool. It's how we cope.'

'I understand,' said Lizzie. Not that she really did. She'd tried ignoring her pain and it came out anyway, in the most destructive manner possible. If only it had been as simple as planting a smile on her face.

Freya slipped out, leaving the door ajar as she left. A lazy summer breeze wound its way into the room. Lizzie could hear George's booming 'Hello!' as he spotted her. Followed by Hudson's relieved 'Darling.'

Lizzie stood. She wasn't interested in eavesdropping. She walked over and shut it. But she stopped a moment and looked out at them. Under the overhang of a large sycamore tree, they chatted. She could see what Freya meant about Hudson. He looked tired and drawn. His smile, unlike his father-in-law's, was strained and tentative. George appeared relaxed. Happy even. Lizzie would have to take Freya's word for it that he was hiding his true feelings. But whatever Freya's assurances, they definitely, all three, had an ease of body language that the O'Sheas didn't. Because Declan wasn't one of theirs? Probably. But she couldn't help looking at the three of them, and again, sizing them up. One of them could have done it. There was a one in six chance they had. Were they play-acting now, carefree or careworn as a cover?

She watched them until George turned in her direction. She whipped her head around, didn't want him to catch her staring. Lizzie was going to drive herself mad if she kept doing this. Speculating. Unless she locked herself in her room for the weekend she was going to have to spend the next few days mixing with them. Doing what her mother wanted and agree to this, how would she cope? Distract herself? Adopt a Schrödinger's Cat approach? Everyone is both a killer and not a killer. Perform some kind of mental gymnastics that made her okay with all this madness.

She'd start with trying to distract herself anyway and turned to one of the bookshelves. She cocked her head sideways, reading their spines. Forcing out difficult thoughts with other, easier ones. She ran her finger along the old leather spines. Feeling their velvety warmth. Like stroking a sleek-coated dog. She paused at a copy of *Treasure Island*. A favourite as a child. A smile spread across her face for the first time in twenty-four hours. She pulled it off the shelf. As she did so, something came with it. Something that had been pressed in between *Treasure Island* and the book beside it. Whatever it was fluttered past her, landing with a quiet smack on the ground.

19

Lizzie put the book back on the shelf and dropped down, picking up the fallen item. She turned it over in her hands.

It was a letter. And it looked old. The edges of the browning envelope were brittle where a long-ago hand or letter opener had ripped it open. It looked like it should be in a museum, not here, carelessly jammed between two books. The looping handwriting on the front of the envelope was hard to read, but after a moment staring at it, tracing the letters with her finger, Lizzie made out the name of the recipient. Miss Mary Butler. She looked up and out the window. Her eyes, loose and unfocused, half watched Freya and George under the tree, as she pondered the name. It must be some previous inhabitant of Butler Hall. A past relative of George and Freya.

Lizzie was intrigued. What were the ethics of reading private letters when the sender and recipient were a long time dead? It would be okay, wouldn't it? It wasn't like she was opening George's private post. Lizzie retreated to the wingback chairs, this time taking the one Freya had been concealed in. She curled her legs up under her then slipped out the letter and carefully unfolded it. The creases of the paper were darkened and it was hard to read the words where they ran, but the rest of it was legible. Due to the same looping script from the envelope, though, it took time to decipher.

10th May, 1910

It was over a hundred years old. Lizzie began to read.

My dearest, darling Mary,

You didn't say no when I asked if I could write, so here I am, writing to you. I only hope that you do not fling this in the fire and instead take the time to read my words.

Seems like this Mary had at least taken the time to read the letter and hadn't burnt it as the writer feared.

Tell me there is still hope? Tell me that your rejection is not final. That I can dream that you will change your mind.

You should be aware that not every suitor will be as understanding as me. I do not care that you drive about in that horrid automobile, and head to Dublin for those appalling Women's Suffrage marches. Stay away from the Skeffington woman and her band of harridans at least, I beg you.

Not every prospective husband would be willing to let you have such freedoms. I do not even care that you have a dram of whiskey in the evening. You said when we last met that you did not love me and that without love you could not marry. And that you had little inclination to marry in the first place. Your father will not be pleased

with you. Would you not want to make your poor father
happy at least? Your words are still ringing in my ears...

A crease obscured whatever Mary Butler had said to her poor suitor, but Lizzie had a feeling it wasn't the most complimentary. She took up the rest below.

...And I do not like to remind you that, despite your
obvious charms, you will not have so many options for a
husband. That is the sorry state of affairs. Butler Hall is a
beautiful home, but we are no longer living in a time
where such houses are easily kept. The English gentry
are having similar troubles, that is why so many daugh-
ters of Yanks are Lady this and Duchess that these days.
They bring their vulgar American money with them. But
it seems my money is vulgar to you. I don't see how the
continued good fortune of your family could invoke such
a reaction from you, but so it does, it seems.

I will write again when...

Another crease obscured the next line, leaving Lizzie in the dark about when he would write again.

...I would have visited but I am unwell and confined to
my bed. It is like the love sickness in my heart has taken
up residence in my bones. But I will persist. I think I can
convince you that marrying me is the right choice. The
only choice.

All my undying love,

Robert

Lizzie looked up from the letter. Poor old Robert. It sounded like Mary Butler was pretty clear about how she felt about things. And she sounded like a bit of a handful too. But in a way that made Lizzie like her. Obstreperous daughters were Lizzie's lane. She looked over at the bookshelf. Were there any further letters? It felt like she was reading someone's diary, but she was curious.

Lizzie went back to the shelf where she'd found it. It was strange, it being stuffed between two books. But there was no way it had been sitting here since Mary Butler had been in residence. The house had burnt down and been rebuilt since. Lizzie scanned the books and took out *Treasure Island* again, placed it down on the desk, and moved about the other books on the shelf, looking. But there was nothing. She scanned the other shelves for a box, any kind of container where other letters might be kept. Again nothing.

Disappointed, Lizzie turned and picked up *Treasure Island*. She'd sit and read it. She held it in her hands a moment. Maybe the letter had actually fallen from its pages? Had been used as a bookmark or something? She opened it. To her surprise the book didn't flutter open fan-like with near translucent paper pages. Instead, like a movie prop, the centre of the book was hollowed out. And sitting within was a trove of letters. All with the same hard to decipher handwriting on the envelope. Poor, lovelorn Robert had persisted. Lizzie smiled, delighted. There was one odd note though. In this hollowed-out book, the sliced pages looked freshly cut. The edges weren't discoloured or brittle. These hadn't been hidden by Mary herself. Someone far more recently had done it. Lizzie couldn't fathom why.

Fake book in hand, Lizzie looked out the library window again. Claire had appeared from upstairs, her face still pale and strained. Lizzie watched as she stopped next to George, Freya and Hudson. She started chatting. Curious now to hear what was being said, Lizzie snuck out a hand and cracked one side of the French doors. She caught the end of a sentence from Claire. '...I'm going back to the walled garden.' That sounded about right. The garden had always been her mother's refuge. George's booming 'enjoy' followed Claire as she headed towards the path they'd all careered down this morning, running past the walled garden to the bathhouse. Barrelling at top speed to a new nightmare. Even with the promise of the walled garden's solace, Lizzie wouldn't have been keen to head back down that way. She might have to though, if she could come up with something to do about the whiskey decanter. That was if it was still in there. Hudson or George might have taken it. When they'd moved her father. Or had they similar qualms about disturbing it? It wasn't a question she was keen to ask.

As if summoned by her thoughts, Hudson also broke away from the group. 'I'll get them,' she heard him say. Then he was coming her way, directly towards the library. Lizzie shoved *Treasure Island* and its hidden contents back onto the shelf.

Hudson pushed open the door and spotted her. A cautious smile tentative across his face.

'Hi there, Lizzie. How are you feeling?' He stepped fully into the library.

'Oh well, you know,' she said, flustered, her back against the bookshelf as if she'd nearly been caught doing something she shouldn't.

'I'm just going to go get our yoga mats. Freya and I are going to do a bit of yoga among the trees. It's very soothing. And after everything that's happened... you know?'

'I do.'

Hudson loitered, shuffled his feet.

'He's... em, he's safe in the icehouse now.' He looked back up at her. 'I thought you might like to know that. He's not just... lying, like we found him. I said a few words too. Asked the universe to speed him gently on his journey.'

Lizzie felt her eyes being drawn to his hands. This time not considering their fatal potential, but instead imagining them lifting and carrying Declan. His dead weight. White-skinned. Lifeless. She shuddered. But she also felt a weird block to feeling more than this distaste. Her emotions were a Frankenstein's monster of sadness, horror, guilt, regret, all stitched together. But they were lying on the table, unmoving, no electricity sent through them yet. *Beware; for I am fearless, and therefore powerful*, Mary Shelley had written. Reanimated, would Lizzie's grief be too fearless, too powerful?

'Thanks, Hudson. Thanks for looking after him.'

'It's okay. It doesn't matter what he might have done, we all deserve respect in death. I'm sorry, also, that I got a little up in his face last night at the table. I just hate a bully. I can't bear it. Just seeing the effect he was having on you all, and it wasn't just the shock. But now... well.'

'Please, Hudson, don't worry about it. Last night...' Lizzie shook her head. 'Really, don't give it a second thought.'

Hudson nodded, his blue eyes tired and troubled.

'What are you doing now? Would you like to join us meditating?'

Lizzie couldn't think of something she'd like to do less than go into the forest with these two. To lie under the trees with them, thinking of what had happened, while trying to control her breathing. It would be anything but relaxing.

'Thanks, but no, it's okay. I'm just going to read.'

'Ah, that's a good idea too. Reading's great! An excellent de-stressor. Very mindful. But if you change your mind, we'll be going in about five minutes.'

Lizzie forced a smile.

Hudson kept going, heading for the door to the hall. Lizzie willed him on. But he paused a second time, at the door. Holding on to it, half turned back.

He looked at her, his face arranged into a sympathetic

shape. He then opened his mouth as if to say something. If he spouted any so-called eastern philosophy at her Lizzie would scream.

'Yes?' she said.

He shoved his hands into his pockets, forcing his elbows out at obtuse angles. He dithered, but spoke again after a moment.

'No, actually, it's nothing.' He turned back to the door. 'Sorry. Right, I better go get those yoga mats,' he said. 'Freya will be wondering what's taking me so long.'

Hudson tipped an imaginary hat, then slipped out of the room. Lizzie heard his feet on the stairs a few moments later.

Lizzie hadn't moved when he returned two minutes later, blue and pink yoga mats under each arm.

'Last chance to join us?' he said as he headed for the door.

'Thanks, but it's okay. Enjoy.' He smiled and was gone. She watched his progress across the terrace and down to the lawn, Freya joining him as they waved to George and headed off along one of the paths into the forest. Lizzie made a mental note to find Freya's Instagram account whenever they left this place – she suspected she'd see pictures of what she was missing.

Now, only George remained. Still under the shade of the massive sycamore tree. He stood there, serene, calmly surveying the quiet garden and woods. Lizzie was turning, ready to retrieve the Mary Butler letters. From the corner of her eye she saw him stiffen. His calm, contented demeanour replaced with a pin-sharp focus. He was staring at the back of the house. From her angle Lizzie couldn't see what had caught his attention. But it didn't take long for what it was to be revealed.

Or rather, *who.*

Mia.

She'd stepped out onto the terrace. She turned and began to scan the back of the house. Lizzie threw herself back, pressed against the wall beside the doors. She held her breath and waited, giving the cook time to complete her search. Carefully she peered around. Mia was now looking over at George. With a barely perceptible nod she headed off in the direction of the path to the stone outhouses. As the woods swallowed her, George looked all around him and then slowly, casually, he followed her.

20

Lizzie's heart was thumping. But this was not like the near panic attack of earlier. This sent energising adrenaline through her limbs, propelling, not paralysing her. She let George disappear into the trees then shoved the fake book back on the shelf, the letters instantly forgotten. Her pulse pounded in her ears as she slipped out the door.

She crossed the terrace, skipped down the steps onto the small lawn. The temperature and light dipped as she stepped through the leafy curtain. The skin on her arms goosebumped. And not just because of the coolness of the forest.

There was a dirt track here that stretched into the thickness of the trees. Scattered with fallen leaves and twigs, Lizzie danced over them, moving quickly, but quietly. She came upon the outhouses and listened for sounds. Was this where they were? She rested her hands on the cool mossy stone wall of the first building. She heard nothing. She kept going, spying through cracked glass, the quad bike inside. It looked old and unreliable. Lizzie wouldn't fancy having to ride on it anywhere.

She pushed on, following the path deeper and deeper into the wood, listening all the time for George and Mia. Where were they? Lizzie stopped and spun around. Had they gone off the path at some point into the woods? Doubts began to replace her initial frenzy.

Then she heard it.

Angry voices. Further down the path.

She sped up but was still careful to be quiet. Watching where she put her feet. Closer, as the voices got louder, she slowed and slipped from tree trunk to tree trunk, concealing herself.

The path had wound its way down to yet one more half-consumed relic in this insatiable forest. Round, with stone pillars supporting a domed roof, dressed in the ubiquitous and enthusiastic ivy, was a forgotten folly. The ornamental building with no purpose other than to appear pretty. Though this one now was a faded beauty, trading off past glories.

And within, were George and Mia.

Faces twisted and angry.

The normally genial George was jabbing his finger at Mia. She was giving as good as she got. Lizzie risked moving closer, to a nearer tree. Crouching and creeping, tiptoeing through the undergrowth, her heart hammering. She slipped down behind a fallen tree trunk that was perched at an angle on a second prone tree. Colonised by exuberant ferns, which fanned out in sprays of cover, Lizzie felt safe she couldn't be seen. She knelt, sinking into the soggy forest floor. Dampness ran the length of her bare legs. She suppressed a shudder at tickles on her bare calves, God knows what was scurrying over and around her.

She tried to make out the jumble and tumble of angry words that spat and sparked from the folly.

'What are you...' George's voice harsh and demanding.

'How dare you...'

'I'm not leaving!' That came from Mia. The clearest snippet yet.

As Lizzie watched, it became clear that, for all his height

and physical presence, it was Mia who had the upper hand. George was pleading. Flashes of anger flared and he pointed and gesticulated, but mostly he seemed cowed, desperate. His voice whiney, shoulders slumped. He backed off as Mia advanced on him, her voice shrill and insistent. Lizzie was getting frustrated. For all her observations, and the words she was catching, she was still too far to catch the sense of the argument. She looked around. Could she get closer?

Then she heard two words. Clear as day.

George, rallying, standing taller.

Extortion. Blackmail.

Mia threw her head back and her laugh echoed around the folly.

If you want to call it that. I call it justice.

Lizzie heard every word of that sentence. Forgetful amid her mirth, Mia let the volume of her voice rise.

Blackmail? Extortion? Mia, the cook, was blackmailing George? Thoughts exploded like a frenzy of fireworks trapped in a box, detonating and ricocheting off the walls of her mind. Was this to do with her dad? Was George responsible? And somehow Mia knew? But hadn't she spotted that moment between them when they'd arrived yesterday? That was hours before Declan had shown up.

Lizzie needed to get closer, to hear more.

She looked around. There was a very large tree closer to the folly, a horse chestnut. It could conceal her if she stood very still behind it. She'd have to get to it first. Lizzie looked at the ground. If she crawled on her belly she might make it.

Lizzie lay down, elbows at right angles like she'd seen them do in the movies. She felt her T-shirt soak up the wet from the damp forest floor. She stifled a retch at the rotting aromas that oozed along with the moisture. She started to inch forward.

She felt a painful poke to her belly.

Then a loud crack.

She was only inches from her hiding place and she'd crawled over a fallen branch hidden in the forest floor ivy.

The crack reverberated around the woods, bouncing from tree to tree. Lizzie froze. As did George and Mia. With a sinking horror, Lizzie saw them step out of the folly, looking all around them. She was still just about hidden by the ivy and ferns. But they'd see her pretty quickly if they kept coming. As they came closer, Lizzie realised that – for a split second only – the large horse-chestnut tree would block their view of her. Spinning, she rolled back under the fallen tree trunk she'd been hiding behind a moment ago.

There was just enough space for her to lie flat. The under-growth and gloom would keep her hidden. She lay there, not moving a muscle. The dark, confined space felt like a coffin. A dank, dark coffin. The tree above her – inches from her nose – its lid. Her hair began to soak up the even wetter forest floor here. Fungus, stinking mushrooms and toadstools grew all around her. There was a spider, as big as her fist – or at least this close up it felt like it – right above her head. Lizzie whimpered to herself.

She closed her eyes. It would be better to not see any of this. Pretend she was just back in her bed. Or at home. Dublin home, not this cursed house. Be like a baby and close her eyes – if she couldn't see the world then it couldn't see her. But she could hear them getting closer. She heard the crunch and snap of their slow, suspicious footsteps. Their whispers. She held her breath. Closer they came. Lizzie felt tears bulge at the corner of her squeezed shut eyes.

And then the footsteps stopped. She opened her eyes – how close were they? She saw their ankles and feet barely a metre away.

'Maybe it was nothing?' Lizzie heard the hope in George's voice.

'I don't know,' said Mia, 'it was pretty loud for an animal.'

'Maybe it was a fox.'

'They're nocturnal, George,' said Mia's irritated voice. 'You know that better than me.'

'Well, whatever it was, dear, it's gone now.'

Lizzie, despite the stress, noted the *dear*. Even sarcastic it was intimate, familiar. These two knew each other. Well. This sounded more personal than what had happened here in the last few hours.

'Okay.' Mia spoke again. 'I think you're right, it's gone. And I better go too. You and your new family need feeding, it's nearly lunchtime.' Her voice dripped with disdain.

'You haven't answered me that. How did you get here? How on earth did you trick Claire into hiring you?'

'Oh, it's easy to dupe someone if you know how. And I learnt from the best, darling. Didn't I?'

'Maggie, please.'

'Don't you "Maggie please" me.'

Who was Maggie? Was Mia Maggie? She was using a fake name?

'I have to get back,' Mia – Maggie? – continued. 'You've heard my terms. If you don't follow them I'm telling your wife everything. See how well that works out for you.'

'Maggie, please, I'm sorry...'

'I'll bet you are. You're only lucky that going to the Gardaí would interfere with my plan. Blackmail is still illegal. But don't put it past me. Especially with that body in the bathhouse. It's quite tempting to dump you in it. But I don't want them involved any more than you do. Not right now, anyway.'

'Perhaps *I* will call the Guards,' spat George. 'You'd have to prove everything.' But even Lizzie heard the lack of conviction in his voice.

Mia laughed.

'I don't think you will somehow. Now, I'm going back to the house. You might want to give it a few minutes before you set off. And hey, keep a close eye on that sweet, darling new wife of yours. She's so precious. I quite like her.'

'Stay away from her! Don't say a word to her! Do you hear me, Maggie? Stay the hell away!'

'Then you know what you have to do.'

Lizzie held her breath. One set of footsteps walked away. Lizzie could hear the heaving, frustrated breathing of George as he waited. 'Bitch,' he muttered under his breath. She heard the thump as he lashed out. A broken branch, launched by George's foot, landed close to her, rolling and coming to a stop inches from her hiding place. Lizzie struggled to keep still. Her muscles were starting to shake under the strain. Just as she thought she couldn't do it a moment longer, George started walking, heading back down the path. Lizzie gave way to her stalled tears. Somewhere between relief and fear. Crying, she rolled out from under the tree. She leant against the tree trunk and rubbed her eyes. Shaken and confused. She could see George disappearing in the distance.

What had he done?

21

Lizzie scrambled up. George was gone, but she was shaken. What was with this cursed place? First her father killed, and odds on by one of them. And now George was being black-mailed. Lizzie had one thought. Claire. She needed to tell her everything she'd overheard. Her mother had to know there was something not quite right about her new husband. And to be careful of this cook.

Lizzie wasn't certain but thought she could cut across the woods here and come out near the walled gardens. Where Claire was. Diving into the undergrowth, thick and uneven, her feet wobbling every few steps. Her sandals completely unsuit-able footwear. But she pressed on, moving deeper into the untamed wood. Birds above her sang, oblivious, their tune doing nothing to soothe Lizzie's frightened soul. She stumbled left, her foot dipping into an unexpected depression. She righted herself.

There was a flash of movement in the distance and Lizzie froze, terrified. Had George doubled back? Or Mia? Her heart tried to escape her chest in fright, but her brain caught up, made sense of what she was seeing. Deer. It was just a group of deer.

Like guardians of the forest, they stood and watched her. At the edge of the group was a doe and its fawn. Lizzie was sure it was the same pair from last night. With their large, sad eyes they stared back at her.

She turned away from the animals and picked up the pace, risking falling, but not caring. Dipping and dodging, diving around trees, jumping over brambles. Moving forward, quicker, quicker.

She was gaining confidence when she faltered. A hidden root snagged her foot. Lizzie fell, twisting and tumbling, landing with a thud. The wind knocked out of her. Flattened and disorientated, it took Lizzie a moment to realise she was staring upwards, towards the treetops. Her chest heaved from the effort and emotion. Pain radiated from her left wrist but it wasn't too bad. Nothing broken. She must have landed heavily on it. And thankfully otherwise she didn't seem to have done any serious damage to herself.

'Lizzie!' a voice cried out in the silence.

Lizzie arched her neck, viewing the source of the voice from an upside-down viewpoint.

Freya. And behind her Hudson. As if from nowhere. Summoned forest sprites.

They ran up to her. Hudson reached out a hand to help her stand.

'Are you okay?' he asked, pulling her up.

Lizzie eased her weight onto the ankle that had been caught and brought it down. Like her wrist, it was a little sore, but fine. There was no serious damage there. She nodded.

'I'm okay.'

'We were doing our meditation over there.' Hudson nodded over her shoulder and Lizzie turned, seeing the his-and-hers mats rolled out in the undergrowth. They were lucky it hadn't been them she'd tripped over.

'We've been doing deep relaxation for the last twenty

minutes, but the sound of you falling brought me out of it,' said Freya. 'It was quite a thump. Are you sure you're okay?' She looked her up and down.

'I am, thanks.'

'I thought you were going to stay in the library and read a book?' said Hudson.

'I changed my mind,' Lizzie improvised. 'Maybe it was you mentioning the meditation. I decided to run. Run off my feelings, you know.'

'In sandals?' said Freya, looking at her feet, eyebrow raised.

Lizzie shrugged. Tried to fix her face into a 'silly me' expression.

'Yeah, not my smartest hour.'

Lizzie took a tentative step forward. She didn't want to hang about. Freya stopped her. Put a hand on her arm.

'I know that sounds rude, but you look a mess,' she said. 'Are you okay? Like, relatively speaking.'

Looking down at herself, Lizzie could see how wet and dirty she was. She looked like she'd been living outdoors for a month. She was reminded of her lowest points. When things had gotten really, *really* bad. When she hadn't gone home for months on end, stayed with her so-called friends in squats and moved around, one step from the streets. Memories that weren't helpful right now.

'I also tripped back there too, it was wet,' said Lizzie, thinking fast. 'I'm sure I look a state.'

'Let us help get you home and cleaned up. And if, like, you want to talk about anything, Hudson and I are good listeners.'

'You're very thoughtful, but I'm going to go to the walled garden. That's where Mam is.'

'We can go there with you then.'

'Seriously, no. Don't interrupt your session just for me. I'm fine, honestly.' Lizzie didn't want a chaperone. She wanted to get to Claire, on her own.

'It's no trouble,' said Freya, a sweet smile on her face. 'Grab the mats, Hud, yeah?'

Hudson trotted over to the mats and began to roll them.

'Really, I'll be fine,' said Lizzie frostily and started walking, hiding the slight limp from her wrenched ankle.

'The walled garden is that way,' said Freya. Lizzie looked back and saw Freya indicating a direction some way off where she was heading.

'Oh,' she replied.

'Hudson,' commanded Freya, 'c'mon.'

Lizzie sighed, but stopped.

Their mats gathered up, Freya led the way, guiding them through the undergrowth until they joined a new earth track. Hudson dropped back beside Lizzie.

'You doing okay? Today has been a pretty surreal day.'

Lizzie nodded but said nothing. It had just got more surreal, but she wouldn't be sharing that with him. Or anyone other than her mother.

'Look,' he said, keeping step with her. 'Earlier, in the library, I was going to say something to you, but I didn't.'

'Uh-huh?' Lizzie had noticed that.

'It was about this morning, when George asked us all to vote. I felt bad, no one supporting you. And I said nothing.'

Lizzie shrugged. 'It is what it is.'

'You probably thought I was an awful person. You probably *think* I'm an awful person.'

'Don't worry about it. You don't owe me any explanations.'

Hudson shook his head.

'I feel like I do. And there is one... You see, I had this cousin...'

'Okay,' said Lizzie. Despite herself, intrigued.

'He was an idiot. Well, we all were. Our family, we're wealthy. Old money, they call it in the States, but that makes me laugh when you come to a place like this. Anyway, we were spoiled. Ran wild. He ended up killing someone. An old lady, knocked her down in his car. He'd been drinking. My aunt and uncle did the right thing, marched him right down to the cops. We're good people, you know? They didn't try to make the problem go away. They wanted him to take responsibility for what he'd done. They hired him the best lawyers, sure, but there was no running away from it. But those lawyers couldn't change the facts. He went to prison. He got less time than he should have because money will get you that much. But ten years or thirty,' Hudson shook his head, 'it was the end of him. He was introduced to hard drugs inside, made bad, bad friends. He came out and was never the same. Eventually he was found under a bridge, cold, with a needle in his arm. He wasn't even thirty. My aunt and uncle were never the same either. And that old lady is still dead. I know that's a bit reductive. Justice is important. But... I guess I've seen that sometimes doing the so-called right thing doesn't make anything better.'

Lizzie let his words sink in.

'I just wanted to explain.'

'Thanks, Hudson,' she said.

'I didn't want you to think I didn't care, that it should just be brushed under the carpet.'

'That does help,' Lizzie said, and she wasn't lying. 'I felt very alone this morning.'

'I know,' he replied. 'That wasn't right.' He reached out and squeezed her arm. Lizzie nodded but said nothing more, emotion muting her.

The walled garden came into view. Freya slowed down and Lizzie and Hudson caught up with her.

'I've got it from here,' said Lizzie. 'Thanks for showing me the way.'

'We'll just make sure your mum is actually here,' said Freya.

'I'm not five...' replied Lizzie, but Freya was already stepping through the archway into the walled garden.

Lizzie followed. Hudson after her.

And as if a switch was flicked they were enveloped, squinting, by the sweltering summer sun. It was like a mother's embrace.

'Claire?' called out Freya. They spread out, Hudson turning to the right path, Freya taking the centre and Lizzie going to the left. Each of them peering around the wild, overgrown shrubs and plants. The once symmetrical, organised garden hadn't escaped the rewilding of the Butler estate. But without the encroachment of the forest, there was still some semblance of what it had once been.

'Mam?' Lizzie cried. She stole a glance over at Freya and then Hudson. She wished they'd just go away. 'Mam?'

From behind the tall tumble of a yellow flowering plant, Claire appeared.

'Oh, hi there, guys,' she smiled. The smile faded when she spotted the dirty dishevelled state of Lizzie. She strode over to her. 'Lizzie. Are you okay? What's happened?'

'It's nothing. I'll explain in a moment. Listen to me—'

Lizzie stopped. A familiar wariness was asserting itself in Claire's eyes. Her guard had dropped briefly in alarm at Lizzie's state. Now Lizzie saw her eyes dart over to Hudson and Freya.

Claire opened her mouth to say something, but stopped.

'What?' asked Lizzie.

Claire pursed her lips, kept her thoughts to herself. But Lizzie had a suspicion about what she was thinking.

'I haven't been drinking, if that's what you wanted to ask. I look like this because I fell over like a normal, sober person.'

'I didn't say anything...'

'You didn't have to. You've got to change the record.'

'Lizzie, five minutes with you sober doesn't erase the five years you were a mess. If I see you dirty and dishevelled... well... that only ever meant one thing...'

Lizzie fought the urge to respond. To argue. But she was

getting sidetracked. She had to prioritise. She had to share what she'd discovered. With another quick glance at Freya and Hudson, she dropped the level of her voice and stepped closer to her mother. The words tumbled out. 'Okay, fine. But, I need to talk to you about something. It's serious...'

'Speak up, what are you saying?'

Lizzie looked back again; Freya and Hudson were approaching.

'I need to talk to you in private, about George...'

'Oh, Lizzie, please, you agreed this morning to go along with—'

Lizzie cut her off. 'No, it's not that. Mam, listen to me—'

'Hey there, gang!' rang out behind her. Claire looked over Lizzie's shoulder. Lizzie turned. Carrying a large bunch of wildflowers, George strode through the walled garden door. 'I thought I was just going to find my darling wife here. Look at you all, what a lovely surprise.'

Lizzie froze.

Claire turned back to her daughter, but her eyes stayed half focused on her approaching husband.

'Sorry, Lizzie, what were you trying to tell me?'

'Nothing,' said Lizzie. She forced a smile. 'It was nothing.'

22

George divided the flowers between Claire, Lizzie and Freya.

'For the three lovely ladies,' he said.

Lizzie suppressed a shudder when their fingers touched as she took her offering. George straightened up and smiled. The smile faded as he took in the state of her.

'Goodness, child, what happened to you?' He looked from Lizzie to Claire.

'Don't know.' Claire shrugged. 'I was just about to hear all about it.'

'Oh, there's nothing to know. I fell, that's all,' said Lizzie, squirming under the attention.

'She was running. In sandals,' said Freya, disloyally. Lizzie shot her an irked side-eye.

'Freya,' admonished Hudson.

'Well, she was.'

'It was nothing serious,' said Lizzie. 'I look far worse than I am.'

'I can't lie, you look pretty bad,' said Claire.

'Are you holding your ankle there? Is it sore?' George asked.

Everyone looked at Lizzie's foot, including herself. She placed it flat on the ground, wriggled her toes.

'No, it's fine. Honestly.'

'If you can move your toes,' said Claire, 'and you're not screaming in pain, you're probably right and you're fine.'

'Well, that is good news,' said George. 'Take it easy in future, this place isn't quite up to code on its Health and Safety.'

He exhaled and happy-sighed. Tilting his face to the sun's warming rays, his eyes closed and a calm, beatific smile played across his lips.

'We should all hang out in the walled garden more often,' he said. 'You get a lovely bit of sun in here.'

'It is lovely,' agreed Claire.

Lizzie was transfixed by this performance from George. Not twenty minutes ago he had been at his wits' end, arguing with Mia at the folly. Threatened, under siege. He looked now like he hadn't a care in the world. She watched him turn to Freya.

'How was the meditation? It help?'

'Yes, it was lovely, we're feeling calmer now, aren't we, Hud?'

'For sure,' said Hudson.

'Good, good.'

Lizzie examined George's face for any hint of strain. He was very convincing. She looked away, she didn't need him to spot her scrutiny. As she turned, Lizzie noticed she wasn't the only one watching him closely. It had been fleeting, but for a moment Freya had stared at her father, looking at him as if she too was trying to work something out. The expression had gone as quickly as it appeared, but Lizzie was sure she'd seen it.

'So, Claire darling, what do you make of my walled garden? Will this be your personal project?'

Despite the dark circles under them, Claire's eyes lit up.

'This place is a dream. Oh, and I found something really

interesting. Down in the back corner. If you'd actually been hurt, Lizzie, I could have helped. I think I've found the remains of an apothecary's garden down there.' Claire turned and pointed.

'Really?' said George. 'Have you actually found a poison garden, here?'

'Oh, don't call it a poison garden. That's just a trendy made-up name a marketeer came up with.'

'What are you two talking about?' asked Lizzie.

'There's an apothecary's garden – or a poison garden if you want to attract the tourists – down there. It's a garden for growing medicinal plants that an apothecary would have used. Long ago.'

'That sounds dangerous,' said Hudson.

'Well, it is, particularly if you don't know what you're doing.'

'This is exciting!' said George. 'I never realised. A poison garden at Butler Hall... show us!'

'Only if you stop calling it that... and anyway I think that's what I've found, I'm no expert.'

'What plants are there?' said George, pulling on Claire's hand. 'Any of the big boys? Any belladonna? Hemlock?'

'I think I spotted some pennyroyal. And there is what might be an ephedra shrub, though I haven't had a proper *proper* look yet.'

'I've not heard of those,' said George, looking disappointed.

The group followed Claire to the back corner of the garden, pushing back overgrown bushes and shrubs that caused obstructions to the once neat paths. She stopped in front of an innocent-looking flowerbed full of innocuous-looking plants. Large and small, flowering shrubs of all different hues. It didn't look special, or dangerous, and was as wild and out of control as everywhere else within these walls. Claire handed her bouquet of wildflowers to Lizzie, and then crouched down to examine some leaves and flowers. She looked up at her audience.

'You all look a bit underwhelmed.'

'I don't know about everyone else, but I was expecting...' mused Hudson, 'I dunno, something with teeth perhaps.'

Claire laughed.

'Nope. They look pretty much like any kind of plant. Sorry to disappoint.'

George poked at the plants with a branch he'd picked up.

'I'll be going through them with my gardening app,' Claire waved her phone about, 'which will identify any I don't recognise. I'll let you know if I find anything notorious. I promise.'

'Super,' said George.

'Daddy,' said Freya, looking down at her watch.

'Yes, darling?'

'Have you seen the cook lately? What time is lunch? I'm beginning to feel peckish.'

'Oh right, no... no, haven't seen her. But what time is it?' George made a big deal of checking his watch. 'Ah well, would you look at that. It's nearly one thirty. Right, troops, perhaps it's time to go back for rations.'

As they trekked back to the house, Lizzie walking by herself at the back of the group, it started to dawn on her that telling Claire might be more complicated than just waiting until they were out of earshot of George. She watched Claire and George walk together. Holding hands like teenagers. In her free hand her mother held the bunch of flowers George had picked for her. They were a picture of pure happiness, despite everything, despite the whole horror show. What would happen when Lizzie told her mother about what she'd witnessed? Her destroyed mother who had finally met someone, finally had her shattered heart mended. It was hard to imagine Claire thanking her for it. It would be like the dead, mangled bird a cat dropped at its owner's feet. A repulsive, entirely unwanted, present.

But even that, Lizzie realised, rested on Claire actually believing her. She was still conditioned to be suspicious of Lizzie. Lizzie's years of lies and manipulation had taken their toll. And those six months in St Brigid's, while it had seemed a good idea to take a break from each other as she got better, it meant that Claire and Liam hadn't seen her shake off the sheep's clothing of her addictions. How could she convince them that she wasn't still the girl who cried wolf?

23

'What's that?' asked Hudson. George had taken them the long way back to the house. Taking the opportunity to show off some of the grounds.

A low stone wall appeared among the trees. Lizzie thought she could see a cross, or two.

'The family plot,' replied George. 'Last resting place of all the Butlers since the eighteenth century.'

As they got closer, Lizzie looked over the low stone wall that enclosed a square of graveyard. Inside were the crumbling crosses of long ago, mixed with headstones of relatively newer vintage. It hadn't escaped the rampant trees. These walls, unlike the walled garden, were not quite as effective at resisting the invader. Through breaches in its perimeter they'd made their way in, pushing aside resistance, planting themselves in spaces between graves and paths. But there was something beautiful about this graveyard. The canopy overhead thinner too. Some sun made its way in, falling kindly around the place. There was a serene atmosphere. This was where George said they would put her father. Lizzie looked around the plot. A part of her she didn't understand felt some comfort at that thought. Was it the finality of it? Something they'd been robbed of when they'd thought his body had been washed away to the ocean deep.

Freya stopped midway along the wall. She stared intently at one of the graves. George stopped beside her and put his arm around her. She leant her head on his chest. Its headstone not quite so decrepit as all the others.

George looked around at them all.

'This is where my darling Grace rests. It's been about eighteen years, but we still miss her.'

'What was she like?' asked Claire. A wistful smile played on George's lips.

'The best. She was quite serious, but when you managed to make her laugh, she really laughed, from her toes. It made you feel good, like you'd really achieved something. Like you, Claire, my darling, she was thoughtful, smart.' He turned to Freya, touched her cheek with his crooked index finger. 'And she loved this one so much.' Freya's downcast eyes looked on the verge of tears.

'It feels like she slips away from me more every year,' said Freya quietly. 'I was so young, my memories are so fragile...'

'Poor darling,' said George, squeezing her harder. 'She's in your heart, she's part of you. Don't forget that. You can never lose that.'

'Thank you, Daddy.' She smiled sadly. 'And thank you too, Claire. For putting a smile back on my father's face.'

'He's put a smile on my face just as much.'

George released Freya to Hudson's embrace. Took up Claire's hand again.

They followed the graveyard wall, looking at the headstones, less emotive ancestral ones, as they went. Hudson with his arm around Freya, Claire and George following, and Lizzie at the back pondering the strangeness that both George and her mother's former partners would end up here. They passed a particular gravestone and a name jumped out at Lizzie. *Mary Butler.* Was she the Butler from the letter? Lizzie leant over the wall and looked closer. The dates on the headstone, 1890–1945, sounded right. She'd have been about twenty when the letters were written in 1910. It had to be her.

'Who's caught your eye there?' asked George, spotting her interest.

'Oh, I'm not sure. Can't quite see the name?' said Lizzie, feigning ignorance, pointing to the grave.

George scoffed.

'Ah, that's the infamous Mary Butler.'

'Infamous?'

'Oh, Daddy, don't start, please,' said Freya.

'What?' said Lizzie.

'You've stumbled across one of his pet peeves, Lizzie. Brace yourself for the patriarchal spin!'

'It is *not* patriarchal spin,' refuted George. He turned to Lizzie and fixed her with an intense look. 'Mary Butler was the daughter of Charles Butler, the last Butler to live here before it burnt down. He's there, next to her. He was my great-*great*-grandfather.'

'So what was so infamous about her?' said Lizzie.

'She was a handful. And I'm sorry to say it, but she's the reason for the family's ruined fortunes.'

'No she wasn't, Daddy,' Freya sighed. 'That was all Charles's fault.'

'What did she do?' Lizzie thought about the letter she'd read. The references to the family's financial difficulties.

'It is more what she *didn't* do. The family was in financial trouble, things were going badly, they were going to lose the house, total disaster. Charles managed to find her a rich husband – a man who didn't mind that she brought nothing but her beauty to the match – and what did she do? She turned him down. Refused to marry him, said she didn't love him and that was that. Despite the fact that it would have saved them all. She let the family be ruined.'

'Again, where's the blame for Great-Grandaddy Charles who let the situation get that bad?' asked Freya.

'Don't blame him, it wasn't his fault, his gambler father started the rot. By the time he was in charge, things were spiralling.'

'You have to sort of respect that she wouldn't marry a man she didn't love,' said Hudson.

'You do,' agreed Lizzie.

'Yeah, well,' said George, 'it's all very noble having principles, but they don't put food on the table, do they? They don't keep a grand house running. She should have done it for the family, for the Butlers. Our lives, Freya, could well be very different now, if she had.'

'But she didn't and our lives are just fine, Daddy. Not perfect, but whose are?'

George harrumphed and they all continued on along the wall of the graveyard, past its worn ornate metal gate that was hanging off its hinges.

'The ironic thing is...' restarted George. Freya rolled her eyes. 'This suitor, the man she rejected, he died quite young. I can't remember how long he lasted after she turned him down but it wasn't long. If she'd just married him she'd have been a very rich widow and made her father very happy.'

'Daddy, please,' said Freya. She looked at Lizzie. 'Look what you started! I've been hearing this rant since I was a child. I feel for Mary Butler if she had a daddy as bad!'

'Ha!' barked George. 'I'm just saying, darling, wouldn't you have loved to have me all to yourself all these years, not shared me with rebuilding this house? That's what you could have had if she'd done the right thing a hundred years ago.'

'You can't say that, Daddy. Who knows what might have

happened? And don't lie, you love renovating this place. You'd be lost without it.'

'Hmmm,' muttered George. 'Maybe, maybe...'

The group walked on. Parallel to them now was a second path which curved and joined them from deeper in the woods. Something was moving further back, down this path. Everyone stopped. Despite the veneer of getting on with things, they were all still a hair-trigger away from fear. A person emerged. Lizzie relaxed and noisily exhaled when she spotted it was Liam.

'Heya!' she called out. 'Liam!'

She waved her hand. His head shot up; he hadn't seen them until she cried out. His face was pale, there were dark circles under his eyes. They'd all thought he was still in bed, not out wandering the forest. And he looked like he should still be there. Grey and wan, he half-heartedly returned Lizzie's wave and crossed the undergrowth to join them all.

'Hey,' he said. Eyes meeting no one. Lizzie noticed Hudson, Freya and George recoil, step back. She felt a fire ignite in her belly. How dare they react to her brother that way. Claire broke away from George and linked her arm in Liam's. They walked ahead, Claire talking quietly in his ear.

'Can you all please not react to Liam like that,' Lizzie hissed, out of earshot of her mother and brother. She'd thought about who might be responsible for Declan's death, and so must have they. But instead of deciding, like she had, that they couldn't say who was responsible, had George, Freya and Hudson instead deemed Liam most likely? Was that part of the reason they, compared to the O'Sheas, were relatively speaking so relaxed? Not their victim. And not their killer. 'He didn't do it.'

George and Freya fell over themselves with stuttered denials and awkward eye contact.

'Oh, no, we don't think that,' coughed George.

'Sure,' Lizzie fumed. She'd seen how well George could pretend in the walled garden. He could try harder here, no?

'He didn't do it,' she repeated. This was a narrative that needed to be stamped out right now.

Lizzie hung back. She let them walk on together. On ahead.

Hudson looked over his shoulder at her. Caught her eye. Lizzie looked away.

He dropped back.

'You okay?' he asked.

'Peachy.'

Hudson sighed.

'No one knows who did it,' he said, haltingly. 'But, yeah, I think George and Freya are wary of your brother. He is very upset.'

'We're all very upset! Our father was killed.'

'I know. I know... but...'

'But what?'

'It's not just that.'

'What is it then?'

Hudson said nothing for a moment. Opened his mouth then closed it again.

'Spit it out,' said Lizzie. Wishing he'd just leave her alone.

'That path...' started Hudson, bobbing his head in the direction Liam had emerged.

'What about it?'

'I don't know this place, I'm only here like you. But, I've already taken that path. Earlier. And I know from George that it only leads to one place.'

'Where?'

'The icehouse.'

24

'The icehouse?' Lizzie repeated. Hudson nodded.

Lizzie didn't say it out loud, but that was unsettling. Ghoulish even. What was Liam thinking?

'He didn't see the body at the bathhouse,' she said. 'Maybe he needed to see Dad, for closure, or something.'

'Sure,' said Hudson. 'It's a bit extreme though, don't you think?'

'This whole situation is a bit extreme. You can't judge anyone on their behaviour right now. I could say you lot are all a bit too relaxed. I could make some judgements on that. How would that make you feel?'

Hudson held his hands up.

'I just wanted to tell you where he was coming from. Okay?'

Lizzie went quiet and Hudson slipped back to Freya, who shot Lizzie a quick glance. But Lizzie didn't care this time. Her thoughts were lost in thinking about her brother. He was struggling, that was clear.

They all emerged from the woods onto the lawn. As before, it felt like someone had ramped up the thermostat when stepping out from under the tree cover. On the table on the terrace

Lizzie could see lunch was being laid out. Liam pulled ahead, took the steps and crossed the terrace. He didn't stop at the table, but kept going, into the house, without a backwards glance.

'Liam!' Claire called after him, frowning.

'Let him go,' said George. 'Give him space. He'll be okay.'

'I'm worried about him,' she said quietly. 'He's so young, and to have his father reappear and then... you know...' She shook her head.

'You just need to give him time. He'll be okay, I'm sure,' said George as he, Freya and Hudson sat down at the table. He grabbed a bread roll, took a giant bite out of it and chewed. Claire sat down next to him, her face a tapestry of worry. George swallowed and looked at her. He reached out and patted her hand. 'Look, I'll do something with him, hey? How does that sound? Take some time and talk to him?'

He looked over at Hudson. Avoided catching Lizzie's eye.

'Tomorrow, I could take you two out and about around the estate for the day. We could even attempt to bag a pheasant or two for dinner. What do you think, would you be up for that?'

'Hunting?' said Lizzie, horrified.

'Em, yes, but just a bit, it would mainly be a glorified nature walk. Good for the soul, you know?' said George.

Lizzie struggled to find the words. This helpful, fatherly version of George, obviously a pretence for her mother – she'd seen him only minutes ago look at her brother as if he was infectious – could he be *that* tone-deaf to think a day of violence would fix what ailed Liam?

'After what has happened here? To my father. You're suggesting that going killing will make Liam feel better? Seriously?'

Flustered, George huffed and puffed.

'Well, I don't think—'

'Lizzie...' cautioned Claire. Lizzie shook her head at her mother. Looked back at George.

'I hear you, Lizzie,' George said, regrouping. He intertwined his fingers, steepled over his lunch plate. 'That's a valid point. As I said, it would be more of a glorified nature walk, spending the day hiking the entire estate. I've given the wrong impression, I just want to get him out, distract him. Some country air, a day out and about. I guess I thought a chance to bag a pheasant or rabbit for dinner might make him feel good, that he'd achieved something.' George shrugged. 'I'm afraid I come from stiff-upper-lip stock. Walk it off, certainly don't talk about it. This is all I know how to do.'

He looked at her, the corners of his mouth downturned, his head tilted to the side.

'I just want to help,' he finished.

'We can always ask him?' said Claire.

'Maybe.' Lizzie wasn't convinced.

Mia appeared from the house carrying plates of cold meats and salads, to add to the freshly-baked bread. The cook kept her focus on her work, politely ignoring them. Ignoring George.

All talk of Liam stopped.

In front of Mia, everyone was smiling, body language was loosened and relaxed. But Mia was playing her part too. Not a hint of anything from her but helpful staff. Eyes down, unobtrusive as possible. Everyone playing their role.

'I'll go talk to him, Mam,' said Lizzie. 'I have to get cleaned up before I sit down anyway, I'm a mess.'

Lizzie headed for the kitchen door, Claire got up and followed her. Inside, Lizzie stopped and looked at her mother questioningly. Claire eyed Mia as she came and went. Waited and then dropped her voice.

'Let me know how you find him? I'm worried about him.'

'Sure, of course, Mam.'

Mia came back into the kitchen and Claire looked up and smiled at her.

'Everything looks delicious, again. Thank you, Mia.'

The cook looked at her. Lizzie studied her reaction.

'You're welcome, Mrs Butler,' she replied, with a smile, no trace of the angry woman Lizzie had seen threatening George in the woods. She left the kitchen again with more of their lunch for the table outside.

'"Mrs Butler",' repeated Claire. She turned to Lizzie. 'Ha, did you hear that?'

Lizzie couldn't bring herself to say anything in reply. She shrugged and started moving again, heading out of the kitchen. Claire followed her to the hall, and shut the kitchen door behind her.

Claire's eyes narrowed. 'What? I thought you were liking George well enough? I know it's early days, and so much has happened.' She checked the door behind her. 'You can't blame him that we all... that we all agreed with and voted with him.'

'It's not that.'

'So, there is something? Honestly, Lizzie, he's been nothing but nice to you. Plus, you need to give him more time. You've only known him twenty-four hours.'

'Nearly as long as you've known him then.'

'You, of all people,' snapped Claire, 'you don't get to judge my choices.'

Lizzie sighed. Her stupid big mouth, couldn't she manage to not snipe at her mother? She was meant to be making things better, not worse.

'Sorry. I shouldn't have said that. I'm not judging you, Mam... I just worry about how well you know him.'

'I know him well enough.'

Lizzie knew she shouldn't but she kept pressing.

'You got married so quickly. And was it not a bit sketchy meeting him on Facebook? What do you know about his past?'

'People meet online all the time these days. Surely I don't have to tell you that? It's not "sketchy" in the slightest,' said Claire, air-quoting the word. 'He's told me enough about his past too, you don't have to worry about that.'

I've a feeling I do, thought Lizzie, but managed to keep her opinion to herself this time. As she'd predicted on the way back from the walled garden, Lizzie could hear the defensiveness as well as anger growing in Claire's voice. Time to stop. For real this time.

'Mam, I'm just tired, like Liam. We're all on edge.'

'Okay,' said Claire, eyeing up Lizzie warily.

'Speaking of whom...' Lizzie took a few steps further into the hall. She stopped and looked back at her mother. She wanted to tell her that she'd really changed. That it was her, not George who she could trust. But she knew it wouldn't work. She'd scoffed, like the rest of them, when Declan had said he'd returned because he wanted to win them back. That he was sorry. Words were poor medicine for the sickness she and her father had inflicted, in their different ways, on Claire and Liam.

With a shake of her head, Lizzie continued towards the stairs. She took them two at a time, and turned left at the top, heading to Liam's room. She knocked on his door.

'Liam,' she called out.

Nothing.

'Liam,' she called again. And once again, no response. She put her hand on the handle and turned. 'I'm coming in now, don't get a surprise...'

She opened the door.

The room was empty. She stopped and listened. Took a step back onto the landing. It sounded like he might be in the bathroom. She looked back into the room. His stuff was scattered about the place in his usual messy fashion. How could they be here such a short time and already he had the place trashed? Lizzie shook her head. She began to close the door again. And

then she stopped. Dithered. Lizzie had an urge – which immediately made her feel guilty – to go in. To have a look around.

With a glance in the direction of the bathroom, she made a
snap decision. She went in and walked around the room,
treading softly. His bed was unmade. Chargers and headphones
lay tangled on his bedside table. On the desk by the window
were an empty water bottle and a crumpled packet of gum.
He'd left a pile of clothes on a chair by the window. Lizzie
recognised the T-shirt he'd been wearing last night, when he'd
come in from whatever it was he'd been doing out in the woods.
She lifted it up. Saw the dirty stain from where he'd wiped his
hand. She went to put it down again, but stopped. It had been
lying on top of something. Two small, cheap-looking mobile
phones.

25

Lizzie picked up the two phones, turned them over in her hands, frowning. Neither were Liam's smartphone with its overly large screen and purple anime case. She pressed the home button on one of them. Nothing. It was off or out of charge. She pressed all the buttons, still nothing. She put it back and tried the second. Pressed the home button again. This phone lit up.

No SIM card installed came up on the screen.

Belatedly, Lizzie heard the bathroom door opening. She dropped the phones back, and dumped the T-shirt on top. She scampered towards the door.

Meeting Liam at the threshold.

'What are you doing in my room?' he asked, his tired eyes narrowed.

'I was looking for you.'

Liam stepped around her. She saw his eyes dart towards the clothes on the chair.

'Pretty obvious that I wasn't here? No?'

'Yeah,' replied Lizzie, leaning against the doorframe. 'I stayed to check out your view.'

He looked at her.

'Trees, Lizzie. Just more fucking trees.'

'I noticed.'

'Were you looking to rob something? Is that it? I've nothing you can sell.'

'That's not true, I'd get a few bob for your iPhone,' said Lizzie, forcing a smile onto her face. Liam's eyes darted to his bedside locker and then with a relieved sigh, patted his back pocket for his mobile.

'Jesus, Liam, I wasn't here to rob anything,' said Lizzie, her attempts at light-heartedness crushed by her brother's reaction.

Liam crossed to the bed and sat. He looked up at his sister.

'You know I used to hide my stuff every morning? Before school, to make sure it was there when I got back?'

'I didn't know that,' said Lizzie in a small voice.

'Yeah, every morning before I went to school I'd unplug the games console, grab my tablet and hide them. I'd pick a different place every day, just in case. Keep you guessing. So joke all you want but it's been a nice six months not having to worry about that.'

'I know sorry doesn't cover it...'

'You're right, it doesn't.'

He started undoing the laces of his boots. Then he stopped, staring down at the half-loosened boots, the laces slack in his fingers. He looked up at her.

'Do you know what still gets to me? After everything, after everything you put us through?'

Lizzie shook her head. Forced herself not to look away from him.

'I got in the car. That night with you. I could tell pretty quickly that you'd been drinking. I should have gotten out, but some stupid part of my brain refused to believe you'd put me at risk like that. I was an idiot.' Liam shook his head at the memory, his face screwed up with anger. He gulped back a shaky breath. 'Dad messed us all up, you didn't have any special claim on that.'

'Oh, Liam.' Lizzie felt sick with guilt. They'd never talked about it. There hadn't been the chance, Claire had whisked her away to St Brigid's before they could. She'd known he must have felt awful. But hearing it straight from him. It was devastating.

And he was right, she didn't have some monopoly on pain. Even if she'd thought at the time that her pain was worse than theirs. That it plumbed deeper depths. The arrogance of her. Just looking at her brother here, now, as new traumas dragged him down. It cut deep. It was time she started earning the trust again that he'd once put in her.

'Liam,' she said softly, exhaling an anxious breath. He looked up at her, weary. 'Are you okay?'

He snorted.

'Yeah, I know, stupid question,' she said.

He shrugged. Pulled off his boots.

'Why'd you go to the icehouse?'

He stared at the floor. Didn't reply.

'That was... Liam, I know everything is messed up, but...'

Liam reached under the bed and pulled out a pair of trainers. He pulled them on and stood.

'I'm going down for some food,' he said.

'You not going to say anything about the icehouse?'

'No.' He headed for the door.

'Well, are you going to at least tell me then what the two random phones are about?'

This stopped him. He froze, back to Lizzie.

'Yeah, I found them. Over there, under that T-shirt you were wearing last night. When you disappeared into the woods. Whatever that was about. What's going on with you, Liam? Only criminals and love cheats need burner phones.'

He turned to face her, eyes blazing.

'How dare you go through my things.'

'I wasn't going through anything. Not really. I found them by accident. I'm just worried about you. And more so now since I found the phones. What are they for, Liam?'

'None of your business.'

'I want it to be my business. I want to help you. The Butlers already think you killed Dad.'

'They do not!'

'They do too! You should have seen them earlier when you emerged from the icehouse path... they couldn't back off quick enough!'

'But... but why me?' Liam's bravado evaporated. 'What have I done that they think it was me?'

'I don't know, but visiting the icehouse certainly did nothing to help. And if they were here now and knew about these weird phones? They'd be having a field day. So, again, what's with them, Liam, seriously?'

Once more, he clammed up. Lizzie threw her hands up.

'Christ, Liam! It's all well and good everyone voting for all this – but if the plan to just pretend Dad's death didn't happen goes south and the Gardaí end up getting involved, you can be sure as hell the Butlers will throw us under the bus. And there'll be burner phones to throw with you!' *And a whiskey decanter with your fingerprints on it*, she wanted to add but Liam was looking worried enough. 'The police will think you did it.'

'But I didn't!'

'You might have to prove that, Liam, and if you won't even talk to me—'

'Why would I talk to you, Lizzie, of all people? You're clean for five minutes and suddenly you're who I'd be talking to if I'm in trouble?'

'*Are* you in trouble?'

'Oh, stop reading into things,' Liam snapped. 'I'm going for my lunch.' Lizzie wanted to grab him by the shoulders and shake him. She followed him out of the room. Watched as he started down the stairs.

'Liam—'

He stopped and looked back up at her, scowling. 'What?'

There were so many things she wanted to say. *Talk to me. You can trust me now. George is hiding something.* But she could clearly see the anger in Liam's eyes. Like Claire, would he hear her? She settled on something he might.

'Just so you know, George is going to suggest taking you and Hudson for a day out around the estate tomorrow. He actually suggested a little bit of hunting.'

'Sounds good.'

'Sounds good? Seriously? Even with everything that's going on around here? And knowing they're totally suspicious of you?'

'It's fine.' He turned and stomped heavily down the stairs.

'Christ, Liam. What's going on with you?'

26

Lizzie stood at the top of the stairs, the sound of Liam becoming more distant. She looked back towards his bedroom door. Thinking of the phones within. What were they for? She couldn't think what he was at. The fear that had gripped her last night, that maybe he was involved with drugs, reared its ugly head again. But that didn't really explain it either. Lizzie's tummy rumbled. She needed to eat. She looked down at herself. She was still a mess. She'd have to get cleaned up before she did anything. Grabbing a fresh towel from her room, she was a little sorry now that she'd spitefully used up the hot water earlier.

In and out of the lukewarm shower in double-quick time, Lizzie dug out a fresh set of clothes from her bag. Sitting on the bed she combed her long hair, freshly washed for a second time. With the meditative strokes of the comb, Lizzie's mind wandered back to the phones and the decanter in the bathhouse. What was up with the phones? It was weird. Lizzie couldn't see that they made Liam more likely to have been the one to hurt Declan... but a ready explanation for their existence wasn't coming to her either. Regardless of their origin, it did make neutralising the bathhouse decanter even more important.

She didn't need there to be a stack of evidence making her brother look suspicious. She still hadn't come up with any idea what to do with it, but perhaps the first step was to just confirm it was still there? And maybe now was the time to do it, while the rest of them were eating lunch. Lizzie got up and looked out her window, checking they were all seated down below.

Pulling on her boots, she also grabbed her hoodie and tied it around her waist. She knew it had been early morning when she'd been in the bathhouse, and she'd been in shock too, but all she remembered was how cold it had been.

Downstairs, everyone, bar Liam, turned to look at her.

'Ah, there you are, Lizzie,' said George. He leant over and pulled out a free chair. 'Sit, come enjoy some lovely lunch.'

'Thanks, George.' Lizzie strolled across the terrace, in the direction of the steps. 'But I've a headache, I think I'm just going to go for a walk, clear the head.'

'You have to eat, Lizzie,' said Claire, with knitted brows. 'You missed breakfast too. That's why your head hurts. Come on now and eat something.'

Lizzie shook her head. Grimaced a little as if it aggravated her phantom headache. She felt her tummy rumble at the sight of the table laden with food. She hoped they couldn't hear it. Lizzie looked over her shoulder as she went.

'Don't worry. Save me something, I'm sure I won't be long.'

Down the incline, deep into the heart of the woods, she approached the bridge over the stream. She slowed and stopped. It felt darker here than the rest of the woods. She shivered. It was noticeably cooler too. She untied her hoodie, glad she'd brought it, and draped it over her shoulders. The building across the bridge was even murkier and shadowier than it had seemed when they found her father. More sinister.

One foot in front of the other, Lizzie crossed the rickety

bridge. On the other side she had to remind herself to breathe. She rounded the building, trembling. Flashing back to hearing Freya's scream echo about the woods. To seeing Declan lying there, the back of his head bashed in. She stepped in front of the arched door opening. Looked inside the dark, damp building. She could see the dried dull stain of her father's blood, beside where he'd lain. Lizzie looked left and right, but didn't see the decanter. With a racing heart she stepped into the building. The temperature dropped further inside here. She looked around.

There it was. Just inside the door, against the wall. It must have been moved when Hudson and George had taken Declan's body away. One of them shifting it with a foot as they left. Something like that.

Lizzie crouched down. Stared at it. What to do? Part of the rim had broken off. There were scratches all over it. Her eyes were drawn to her father's blood, a dried dull, dark red stain on it, shaped like a weird continent on a twisted map. It looked dry enough that the lightest touch might cause flecks to come off. And where would they end up? On her clothes. A witness for the prosecution, ready to convict her. Lizzie stood again. Turning slowly a full 360 degrees, she hoped inspiration would come to her. But by the time she stopped, facing the decanter's resting place again, she still had nothing. She stared down at it. A second fear was developing. If she left it here – plan or no plan what to do with it – what if one of the Butlers decided to come and get it? They didn't know that Liam's fingerprints were on it, but they didn't need to. If they thought he did it, then they'd assume they were. What if they began thinking like she was and decided to go looking for a little insurance to keep them out of trouble? Could she take the risk and leave it here? Lizzie looked from the decanter to the stagnant pool of water. She could throw it in there. But that'd be the first place they – Butlers or police – would look. She took her hoodie from her shoulders. She could wrap the decanter in it. Take it with her, back to the house, until she could decide what to do. It wasn't a great idea. The hoodie, even if she washed it over and over, would carry treacherous clues. Removing a weapon from the scene of a crime was wrong and could only make her look suspicious. But, right now it felt safer than leaving the decanter here, hoping the Butlers wouldn't turn on them.

Decision made, Lizzie took hold of the hoodie sleeve and used it to pick up the decanter. She slipped it into the front pouch pocket. If she tied the hoodie back around her waist, the pocket facing in, no one would notice the telltale bulge. She'd be able to take it into the house without raising suspicion. Bring it up to her room without anyone knowing anything. What she'd do with it then, she hadn't a clue, but she'd think of something. Maybe she'd even show it to Liam, explain to him the implications. It might be the nudge he needed to tell her what the phones were about.

Lizzie stood, tied the hoodie around her waist. She felt the decanter in its fabric pocket swing gently against the top of her thighs. She took one last look at the gloomy space and headed back out. Retracing her steps.

Even with the decanter hitting the back of her legs like a pendulum with every step, she moved easier. She mightn't have an endgame planned but doing something felt better than just worrying about it. She crossed the undergrowth, away from the paths, back towards the folly area, and where she'd entered the woods.

In the distance she heard something.

A voice. It was getting closer.

Someone was calling her name.

27

'Lizzie!'

Through the trees, Lizzie saw a blonde head emerge. Freya. She had a canvas bag over her shoulder and a rolled up rug under her arm.

'Ah!' she cried out. 'There you are.'

'Hi, Freya,' Lizzie replied with less enthusiasm. What was she doing here? And as the concealed decanter bounced against the back of her legs, Lizzie squirmed.

Freya hurried up and joined her. She held up the bag she was carrying.

'I brought a picnic!' She beamed.

'What?'

'Your mother was worried about you. I thought, you know what, I'll grab some food and come find you. And we could have a picnic.'

'Oh, that's very thoughtful of you, Freya—'

Freya held her hands up.

'No, you're not allowed to object. I won't hear it. Your mother is right, you need to eat, but maybe it's a bit much to expect everyone to sit down together all the time. I suggested that maybe dinner tonight would be buffet style? I don't think anyone wants to sit down at the table and recreate last night.'

'That's true.' Lizzie had to agree with her. The thought of them sitting around that table had her twitching.

'Come on, let's eat this. I'll bring you to a lovely spot where the stream is a little bigger, it's very pretty up there and we can sit by the bank and dip our toes in the crystal clear water.'

'I'd really rather—'

Freya put an arm through hers and pulled Lizzie.

'I said I wouldn't take no for an answer. You'll thank me.'

A twenty minute walk with awkward conversation brought the pair of them, as Freya had promised, to a pretty part of the stream. It was wider here than down at the bridge so the sun had a clearing through which to shine. Light dappled the meandering water. After laying down the rug, Freya took off her boots and socks and sat with her feet in the stream. With Freya distracted, Lizzie carefully took off her hoodie and placed it down by the base of a tree behind them. She then joined Freya on the bank and took off her own boots and socks. As her toes entered the cool water and the sun shone down on her face, Lizzie had to admit that Freya might have had a point. This was lovely. Next to her, Freya opened the bag and started taking out little parcels, laying them down between them on the rug. Lizzie watched as cheese, salami, avocados, olives, roasted peppers and hummus were laid out. Her stomach gave an almighty growl. Freya laughed.

'I think someone is peckish after all!'

'Yeah, maybe I am,' said Lizzie, with a sheepish grin.

'Tuck in.' Freya found a couple of plates in the bag and handed one to Lizzie. A tied-up napkin came out last, full of bread. An easier silence fell between them as they loaded up their plates. Lizzie felt her belly gurgle appreciatively as she tried not to wolf it all down. She turned to thank Freya, but stopped.

'Is that salami you're eating?' she said, shocked.

'Oops. Rumbled,' said Freya, licking her lips, grinning like a naughty child.

'I thought you were a vegetarian.'

'Practically a vegan these days really.'

'I'm sorry to tell you that those don't come from a salami plant.'

Freya laughed, and then snaffled a second slice of the cured meat.

'Please don't tell Hudson,' she said with a guilty smile once she'd swallowed. 'I really don't eat meat. Just the odd cheat... sometimes I miss it, you know? Fillet steak, pork chops, sausages and bacon! Oh, Lizzie, I miss them!' and she laughed, tilting backward on the bank, face angled to the sun.

'I won't say a word,' said Lizzie. 'Not my place.'

'God, he'd be heartbroken. He's so sincere about it all.'

'If you'd asked me, I would have thought you were the driving force there.'

'Well, there's no one quite as fervent as a convert, no? He introduced me to it all. I had started dipping my toe in the lifestyle when we met at a yoga class in Martha's Vineyard. I'd been moving towards it, to a plant-based diet, a more mindful way of life, but Hudson was the push I needed.'

'That wasn't too long ago. You said something yesterday about only being together a few months?'

'Oh, no, we met a good while ago, last year. We just didn't get *serious* serious until recently. Well, he didn't get serious until recently. You've seen him, I was all in from day one!' Freya laughed.

'He is handsome, there's no denying that.' Lizzie spread some hummus on a bread roll and took a large bite. 'And he seems nice too.'

'He is, he's a good guy.' Freya licked her fingers and then pushed the salami away from her. She grabbed the hummus instead, spooning a dollop onto her plate. 'So, do you have anyone special in your life?'

Lizzie nearly choked on her food.

'Oh God, sorry,' said Freya, patting her back. She dug around in the bag and found a bottle of water, poured Lizzie a plastic cupful and handed it to her.

Lizzie sipped and got her breath back.

'No, no one serious. I, em... I've been too preoccupied with ruining my life to meet anyone, you know?'

'Ah. Yeah, I guess I can imagine. But look, you're on the right track now, you're bound to meet someone.'

'Yeah, maybe,' said Lizzie. It wasn't something she'd thought about much. She'd just wanted to get better. To get to the point where she could start making amends with Claire and Liam. Not hooking up with dealers and fellow addicts was already a one hundred per cent improvement in her love life.

'So, with all the addiction stuff... do you mind if I maybe, like, have a crafty ciggie?'

'Seriously?' said Lizzie, again taken aback.

'It's just a regular one, nothing wacky in it, but if that's out of bounds, that's no trouble at all.'

'No, I'm just surprised you smoke. But feel free, don't worry about me.'

Freya slipped out a small packet of tobacco and began to assemble a skinny rollie.

'It's like the meat: only very, very rarely,' she said, before licking the side of the cigarette paper. 'Hudson would be horrified about this too, though, so please don't tell him. He's quite innocent in his way.'

Freya smiled at her, the slim cigarette clamped between her lips. She struck a match and lit it, taking a long, deep drag.

'Ooh,' she sighed as the smoke exhaled. 'That's lovely.'

'Have you got a naggin of vodka in there too?' said Lizzie nodding at the bag.

Freya laughed.

'Actually, we do have a drink or two now and then. A nice glass of wine is allowed.'

'I'm glad to hear it – "too long a sacrifice can make a stone of the heart".'

'What's that?' Freya took another pull on her cigarette.

'Oh nothing, just a line from a poem. I'm glad to hear you two allow yourselves to relax with something.'

'Hey, we're relaxed all the time. That's the whole point of what we try to do.' Lizzie could hear the edge in her voice.

'Sorry, I didn't mean it like that. Look at me, I'm not judging anyone. They did a lot of that kinda stuff,' Lizzie waved her hand, circling it in Freya's direction, 'with us in St Brigid's. It helps. I... em, earlier, I was feeling overwhelmed, and the mindfulness stuff they taught us worked. I wasn't disparaging you. Honestly.'

'You're okay, we just get a bit of that sometimes, boring no-fun hippies, that sorta thing. But I think we're lots of fun! And, sorry to hear you were feeling bad earlier. Like, it's only natural. I'm just surprised everyone isn't totally losing it.'

So am I, thought Lizzie. And with that thought the ease she realised that had settled on them evaporated, though she did her best to hide it. The Butlers were far more relaxed, were not having panic attacks, because they'd shifted the blame to her brother. She pulled her feet out of the water.

'You okay?' Freya frowned.

'Yes. No.' Lizzie stood. Freya stubbed out her cigarette and got up. 'I'd like to go back to the house now. Is that okay?'

'Sure, sure, of course. I hope it wasn't something I said?'

'No.' Lizzie shook her head.

'Okay, let's just pack up, and go back.'

Lizzie fetched her boots and socks. But her feet were wet.

Freya was using the picnic rug to dry hers. She pointed to Lizzie's hoodie.

'You might have better luck using your hoodie. This bloody blanket is repelling water. And you don't want damp feet in hiking boots. Your feet would be all blisters by the time we get back if you do. I wasn't thinking, I should have brought a towel. That would have been the smart thing to do.'

'Thanks for the advice.' Gingerly, Lizzie went over to where she'd left the hoodie and sat down on the ground. Grabbing a sleeve she slowly dried her feet, trying not to move the hoodie any more than she had to. She shot glances over at Freya all the while, but she seemed more interested in gathering up the food and packing up, than in anything Lizzie was doing.

Finally dry enough to avoid painful blisters, Lizzie pulled on her socks and boots. Freya came over, the bag on her shoulder and the rug rolled up.

'That's a lovely hoodie, I like it. Doesn't look like you had to get it too wet,' she said and before Lizzie could stop her, Freya dipped down and picked it up. The chipped neck of the decanter stuck out of the pouch pocket. Lizzie froze. Freya stared at it. Then pulled it out. Speckles of dried red blood clung to the hoodie as it came out, others floated in the air, slowly drifting to the ground.

28

'Is this... is this the decanter that killed him?'

Lizzie said nothing. Her mind whirring, desperate to come up with an explanation that didn't involve suggesting the Butlers would turn on the O'Sheas.

Then, as if she'd gotten a massive electric shock, Freya dropped it. The decanter rolled to Lizzie's feet.

'Jesus – now my fingerprints are on it!' She stared at her hands as if they were covered in blood. 'Did you do that deliberately?' she yelled at Lizzie.

'What?' Lizzie snapped. 'Did I take the decanter, hide it in my hoodie in the hope you might magically realise it was there and touch it? Are you actually stupid?'

'Okay. I suppose.' Freya scowled at her. 'But what are you doing with it?'

Lizzie looked down at the decanter. Maybe because Freya had been nice to her, talked to her – whatever the reason – she heard the truth come tumbling out.

'Liam's fingerprints are on it.' She looked up at a confused and increasingly anxious Freya. 'But not how you think. He picked it up last night. My dad had it with him in the kitchen when I came in. And then he left the whiskey behind him. Liam was worried I'd drink the end of it and so picked it up and poured out what was left. I got worried that if the plan to walk away from all this somehow went wrong, the Gardaí would get their hands on this and wouldn't believe us.'

'Well, you're sorted, they'll be blaming me now.'

Lizzie looked at Freya with a spark in her eyes.

'Oh, now. There's an idea.'

'Gee, thanks, Lizzie.'

'No, that's not what I mean, I've just thought of something.' Lizzie hunkered down and picked up the decanter with her bare hands.

'Don't!' blurted Freya.

'Now it's got mine too. Dad, Liam, me, you, we've all touched it, it's a mess of fingerprints. It'll prove nothing.'

'Oh. I guess.'

Lizzie stood up again. Decanter in her hands. They both stared at it.

'What are you going to do with it now?'

Lizzie shrugged. She could put it back in the bathhouse, but was there any point? Maybe she'd hold on to it. Keep it safe with her things. And if the worst happened and the Gardaí did get involved, perhaps it would reflect well on her, and the O'Sheas, if she was able to hand it over? Claim she was keeping it safe for them?

'I don't know.' Lizzie looked her in the eye. She'd shared too much as it was. Freya didn't need any more of her confidence. At least this little time bomb had been safely detonated. 'Let's go, though? I'm not leaving it here, anyway.'

Lizzie shoved the decanter back in the hoodie pocket and tied it around her waist again. With a nod, they started back, stepping into the depths of the woods. The brief ease between them of the riverbank was gone, and the awkwardness of the trip back was matched with a difficult silence as they made their way out. Only the crunch and rustle of the forest floor as they walked in their ears.

They came out onto the lawn, and Lizzie could see Claire and Hudson on the terrace. Claire at the table, Hudson off to the side, reading on a wooden recliner.

'You found her, good,' called out Claire.

'I did,' said Freya, summoning a smile for Claire as they trotted up the terrace steps.

'Did you have a nice picnic?' asked Hudson, swivelling to sit on the edge of his seat. He put down the paperback he was reading. Freya looked down at him.

'Oh yes, lovely. The hummus was divine, I'll have to get the recipe from Mia.' Freya turned her head slightly, catching Lizzie's eye. A slight glint at home there.

Hudson sniffed the air. He looked confused.

'Have you been smoking?' He looked at Freya as if he'd asked her if she'd turned orange, or something equally impossible.

'That was me, don't worry,' said Lizzie before she could think about it. Freya gave her a barely perceptible nod and mouthed 'thank you' at her.

'Oh. Ah, alright. Sorry, sweetheart, I just got a fright.'

'No worries, hon. I might just go and freshen up, the smell does tend to linger.'

Freya headed into the house and Hudson picked up his book again, swinging his legs back out onto the lounger. Lizzie went over to the table, and could see that her mother was working on a large jigsaw of a cityscape. Lizzie untied her hoodie as she walked. Sitting across from Claire, she bundled it onto her lap, under the table.

'Smoking?' said Claire, the disapproval a ticker-tape parade across her eyes. Followed by a marching band of *not surprised*.

'No,' Lizzie whispered. 'I was covering for Freya.' She nodded in the direction of Hudson.

'Oh,' said Claire. Lizzie could see she didn't entirely believe her. As usual.

'Would you like to smell my breath, would that help? Proof? 'Cause I know my word isn't worth anything around here.'

Claire wrinkled up her nose.

'No. It's fine.' She laid a piece of the puzzle in place and looked up at Lizzie. 'Did you eat?'

'Yes, we sat by a riverbank, dipped our toes in the water and ate some delicious food. It was quite nice actually.'

'That's good, I'm happy to hear that. You need to eat. And it's nice you're getting to know Freya better. She seems like a nice girl.'

'Yeah, she's okay.' Lizzie lowered her volume again. 'Some bad habits she's keeping quiet though.'

'I think we probably all have some of those,' replied Claire. She fitted another piece in the puzzle.

'Yes, I guess.'

Lizzie looked around the terrace.

'Where's everyone else?'

'Post-lunch siestas. You're the only one who caught up on our early start.'

'Ah right. You're not tired?'

'Exhausted. But not sleepy.'

'Fair enough.' Lizzie stood up again. 'My hoodie got wet, I'm just going to pop it inside.' Lizzie took a few steps closer to the door and then stopped. She looked back at her mother.

'Want some help with that jigsaw when I come back down?'

'That would be nice, yes.' Claire looked back at her, not exactly smiling, but her face was at least missing its near permanent wariness.

'Right, won't be a moment.' Lizzie got up, holding her hoodie close to her. Hudson smiled at her as she passed. Lizzie smiled back but felt antsy at the scrutiny, knowing she had the whiskey decanter hidden in her grasp. She hurried to the kitchen door, hugging her top a little closer to her. But in doing so, she shifted the decanter, and before she could do anything, it slipped from its hiding place. It hit her boot with a muffled thump, before sliding into the kitchen, skittering across the tiled floor with a clatter. Lizzie dived, trying to hide it from view.

'What was that?' Claire turned around. Hudson looked up from his book.

'Nothing,' shouted Lizzie over her shoulder, from the kitchen. 'I knocked a glass.' She scooped the decanter up from where it had come to a rest at the island.

'Did something just break?' Mia appeared from the pantry, a couple of spice jars in her hands.

'Feck,' muttered Lizzie to herself, straightening up and looking at the puzzled woman. 'It was nothing. Nothing, nothing.' Holding the hidden decanter close to her she hustled out of the room. She slipped up the stairs, treading as quietly, but also as quickly, as she could. The sound of running water came from the bathroom. Freya freshening up. Lizzie shut the door of her room behind her with a relieved sigh, resting her back against the door, the decanter still bundled in her arms. She was annoyed with herself for that blunder. The idea had been to reduce the level of suspicion, not increase it. Hopefully neither Claire nor Hudson actually saw what had made the noise. Hopefully they'd been distracted by their jigsaw and book. And hopefully Mia had been too deep in the pantry to notice either. Hopefully.

Lizzie looked around the room. Where to stash it? There weren't many options, it was a minimal space. In the end she left it wrapped in the hoodie and shoved it into her rucksack. Maybe a better spot would occur to her later.

With a few calming breaths, taken standing with her eyes closed in the middle of the room, Lizzie headed back out again. Mia was gone from the kitchen as Lizzie passed through, so the fixed fake smile she'd donned was unneeded. She slipped out of the house and headed for the seat next to Claire and, with a smile to her mother, started picking up jigsaw pieces. The direct sun had left the terrace, but the heat of the day felt like it was only getting going. It was a relief right now that the trees and house cast such shade. Lizzie looked up at the cloudless sky, looking at it in sections, divided up by the strings of unlit fairy lights. Watched the carefree birds glide on the thermal updrafts, lazily surfing the blue expanse. Head raised, the corner of her eye caught movement in the attic window. Her head snapped around, looked fully at the small dormer aperture at the top of the house. A flash of a face, and the curtain was snatched across. Mia. Watching them as they sat here unawares.

George emerged from the house a couple of minutes later, sleepily rubbing his eyes. He smiled at Claire who muttered, 'Hey, sleeping beauty,' at him with a chuckle. George bent and kissed her head. A kiss from a prince to break the spell. Lizzie's momentary calm slipped away.

29

Lizzie stayed by her mother's side for the afternoon as the others came and went. They didn't chat much beyond consulting over jigsaw pieces, but it wasn't awkward either. Lizzie remembered doing similar when she was small. Kneeling on a chair, beside Claire, watching her do jigsaws that had seemed to Lizzie's young eyes to be vast and impossible. She'd been amazed that her mother had been able to finish them. Now, as she sorted pieces, making piles of greens and greys and blues, fitting them into spaces when she saw connections, she knew that all it needed was time and patience. Perhaps that was the solution for them too. Time and patience. Whether it was the solution for what was going on around her, she wasn't so sure. She'd like to fit those pieces together now. Who hurt her dad? What was up with George and Mia? With Liam? She'd like to see that full picture, now. But she didn't see how. There was no loose thread she felt safe to pull on. Telling her mother about George and Mia at the folly felt a no-go for the moment. And Liam and the phones – there was nothing to even pull at there. So she kept her head down and kept building up the puzzle picture in front of her.

As the afternoon wore on and early evening replaced it, the whole party, one by one, made their way back to the terrace. George found a pack of cards and he, Hudson, Freya and Liam played at one end of the table as Lizzie kept on at the never-ending jigsaw at the other end. Liam was looking a little better which made Lizzie happy, hopefully he'd slept. Claire had given up on the jigsaw and retreated to the lounger Hudson had vacated. She was dozing there, snoring gently.

'Will we have music?' asked Hudson, abandoning his cards in front of him, folding yet again.

'Oh yes,' said George. 'Pop on the player in the library. Just not too loud.' He nodded in Claire's direction.

Hudson hopped up and disappeared into the kitchen. A minute later the library French doors opened. The soft tones of Roxy Music wafted out with him. Singing along to the smooth melody, Hudson came up behind his wife and wrapped his arms around her shoulders. Freya laughed and looked up and kissed his cheek. Humming, he sat down. Shuffled his defunct cards. 'A full house!' declared George as he placed his hand down on the table, face-up, with a flourish. Freya and Liam threw their losing cards into the centre of the table as George crowed. With a flicker, the strings of lights above them came on. Lizzie looked at the others, laughing and smiling, bathed in the soft twinkling light, George gathering in his matchstick winnings and Freya dealing out a new hand. From the lounger, Claire stirred. She smiled a sleepy smile as she stretched.

'I'll go see what's the story with dinner,' she said, suppressing a yawn.

'Thanks, dear,' said George, picking up his cards. 'I hope you enjoyed your nap?'

'I did.'

Lizzie felt a pang. This assembled group was having an enjoyable time. Her cynical self when she'd been picked up from St Brigid's had seen this weekend as a chore, an obligation to be endured to begin the journey of making amends to her mother. But if it hadn't been for Declan's resurrection, and subsequent destruction, this would have been good, healing, restorative.

Claire came out of the kitchen.

'Lizzie, want to help me carry out the kitchen table? Mia can lay the food out there and not disturb anyone's fun.'

'Sure, Mam.' Lizzie got up.

'Let me,' said George, half standing. Claire waved him down.

'Don't worry, stay with the game, we can manage.'

They manoeuvred the table out, setting it against the house, under the kitchen window. Then, helping Mia, they brought out the buffet dinner she had prepared. There was red lentil curry, jasmine rice, coriander naan breads, garlic potatoes and salmon, salads and more freshly baked breads. Everything smelt spicy and buttery and zesty. Lizzie had to credit Mia with that at least – for a blackmailer she certainly knew how to cook. Lured by the smells, cards were placed down and plates were picked up. A small queue formed as everyone helped themselves. Sitting back down, chatter and music filled the air. Claire sat with her food beside Lizzie, telling the table about the plants in the walled garden, exotic, dangerous or more mundane. George told them all about the route the men were going to take through the estate the next day, all the areas of interest they'd hit. Yawns around the table increased as the plates emptied. The chat also slowed. Despite the afternoon naps, everyone was still worn out.

Mia delivered coffee and slices of cake to the table. No sign of the bride and groom figures this evening. As people filled their mugs and nabbed some cake, Freya stood and picked up her empty plate. She pushed in her chair and leant against the back of it.

'Everyone, I know it's only seven thirty but I am so tired.

Unlike the rest of you I didn't have a rest in the middle of the day. So I'm going to go to bed. And I want to be up early tomorrow morning. I'm thinking of heading out to the end of the estate by the south boundary wall, and taking a day of retreat. Today has been... difficult. I know you all understand.'

'I think that sounds like a fine idea, my darling,' said George.

'Thank you, Daddy. Hudson, you're going to be gone for hours with the boys, so you won't miss me. Claire, Lizzie, would either of you like to join me? I am thinking a hike, then some deep meditation. Perhaps some yoga and journaling, depending on how it goes.'

'Thank you,' said Claire, 'but I was planning on spending more time in the walled garden. There's just so much there.'

'No, worries. Lizzie?' Freya looked across at her.

'Em, I think I'm just going to hang around here tomorrow, if that's okay? I'm not feeling very introspective at the moment.'

'That's no problem at all. Will you both be alright here, just yourselves with the rest of us out and about?'

Would they be alright? Thought Lizzie. A day with no Butlers sounded like bliss.

'I'm sure we'll manage.'

'If we don't see you before you go in the morning,' said Claire, 'enjoy your retreat.'

'Thanks.'

Gradually, one by one, everyone admitted defeat. The men were also due to be up very early, so had gone inside to bed not too long after Freya. Though still bright, with only the faintest hints of sunset in the sky, the light had changed, the brightness translucent, gossamer thin. An evening breeze wandered unhurried across the terrace, rocking the curved strings of fairy lights like a baby's cradle. Claire the last, bar Lizzie, stood.

'What time is it? I appear to have misplaced my phone.' Claire patted her pockets.

'I don't know, mine's up in my room. There's a clock in the kitchen.'

'Well, whatever time it is, I'm worn out, I'm going to head up.'

She rested a hand on Lizzie's shoulder.

'Will you be okay out here? Just yourself?'

Lizzie nodded. 'I want to finish this,' she said, fitting another piece of the jigsaw puzzle in. 'I'm nearly there. Plus, I'm not as tired as the rest of you.'

'Don't stay too long, okay? Mia will be around, clearing up, but don't be out here on your own too late.'

'I won't.'

'I'll listen for your footsteps on the stairs.' She squeezed Lizzie's shoulder and Lizzie, without looking up at her, placed her own hand on her mother's.

'Goodnight,' Claire said and was gone.

The silence – not a silence at all with the vast forest sitting there just beyond her – settled around Lizzie. The breeze had lingered and encouraged mischievous tendrils of her hair to tickle and tease her. She pulled them back, running her hand through her hair. There was a flap and flutter from the treetops and then silently the barn owl Lizzie had seen last night glided across the sky, its ghostly face and dark eyes glowering down at her. She followed its path, watched as it found its way to the opening in the roof, the eerie hissing cry of hungry chicks greeting it.

The kitchen light came on, and Lizzie looked over her shoulder. Mia emerged and started picking up bowls and plates from the table under the window.

'Can I help?' called Lizzie. Mia stopped and looked at her.

'No, don't worry. This is my job.'

It was said in a neutral tone, neither friendly nor snippy, but Lizzie couldn't help but feel put off by her.

Lizzie got up anyway. Bringing over plates and mugs from the table.

'Thanks,' came the curt response from Mia. Definitely unfriendly this time.

'You're welcome.' Lizzie took the dishes inside and left them by the sink. Mia came in and began decanting leftover food into lidded plastic tubs.

'The food was really lovely, just to say.'

Mia looked up at her, bowl in hand.

'Thank you.'

'Did you go to college or are you self-taught?' Lizzie saw the irritation in her eyes at the interrogation. Lizzie felt that maybe this was a thread she could pull. Find out something about her? Who was this woman who knew George Butler? And what secrets was she keeping?

'I trained in Cathal Brugha Street, in Dublin.'

'Ah, nice. You must have cooked a lot at home, in Roscommon, before you came up to Dublin to train?'

'All my life, since I was small. But it was Mayo, not Roscommon where I grew up.' Mia fixed her a look. A look that said she was suspicious. Suspicious Lizzie had been trying to catch her out in a lie. And she was right. Lizzie had. Lizzie's brief bloom of daring withered under Mia's glare.

'Oh, my mistake,' Lizzie muttered, anxious and jittery.

'No worries.' Mia smiled at her as she transferred dishes to the sink and turned on the taps, water sluicing and splashing. Lizzie suddenly felt far away from everyone else. The main bedrooms were most likely out of earshot down here. It was just her and Mia. Or rather *Maggie*, if the argument earlier was to be believed. Indeed, what could be believed about this woman? Quite forcibly, Lizzie didn't want to be down here, on her own, with this woman a moment longer.

She looked up at the clock. Ten thirty.

'I'm gonna, em, head up now. You okay to...'

'I'm okay to lock up. Goodnight.'

Dismissed, Lizzie headed for the door. Paused briefly as she passed through to the hall. Watched Mia wash the dishes, humming to herself. Without a care in the world.

30

Lizzie stopped, one foot on the bottom step. She wasn't tired. She was only going up to get away from that woman. She looked down the row of doors to the library. She'd grab a book. No, *the letters*. She just remembered. With everything that had gone on today, they'd been forgotten.

Lizzie slipped into the library. The door creaked like a crypt as she opened it. She was met with strange shadows and shapes. In the dimness she cast her eye along the spines. Ran her fingers along them like piano keys until her fingers stopped on the fake copy of *Treasure Island* with all the Mary Butler letters inside. They might be the best reading here. A record of a strong-willed woman and her refusal to do what was expected of her. Lizzie couldn't resist – she liked the idea of reading about someone sticking it to the Butlers, even if it was by one of their own.

She put the book under her arm and headed for the door. The large photo of Grace, in shadows on the mantelpiece, made her pause. With Mary Butler, she was the only other inhabitant of both the library and the graveyard. Grace stared back at her. She imagined a young George, just as broad and as large as an oak, but maybe not quite so stocky. With even more life to him.

His hair still completely blond, not peppered with grey. She imagined him behind the camera. A young newly-wed this time. More like Hudson, perhaps. Starting his life with this woman, unaware that it would be cut short. How different his life was going to be. But none of them knew what the future had in store for them. This weekend was proof of that.

Lizzie pulled the library door gently behind her.

Upstairs, in bed, she took out the pile of letters. Her anxiety from the conversation with Mia slipping away as anticipation at the continuing adventures of Mary Butler and her attempts to fend off the impressively relentless Robert. Lizzie settled back into her pillow and picked out the letter at the top of the pile.

18th June, 1910
Ranelagh

My dearest, darling Mary,

I hope my missive finds you in better spirits than I left you. I understand that you find my persistence vexatious, but it is for your own good. Trust your father for once! It was a rare delight to go with you into Castlebar but you mustn't drive your automobile so fast! The baker's son barely had a chance to get out of the way. And I am quite sure they heard you laugh as we passed.

Taking tea with you back on Butler Hall lawn was all I hoped it would be. Your dear father seemed in particularly good form. I do hope though that he did not have as bad a reaction to the elderflower cordial as I did. I am sorry if I offended you but my constitution is not as robust as yours or your father's. It comes from growing up in the city methinks. Those who spend most of their time in the countryside like yourself are hardier speci-

*mens, I feel, than us city folk. But I am sure I will grow
accustomed to all the delicious fare on offer when I am
permanently in Butler Hall as your husband. Please do
not frown as you read these lines. I can see your pretty
face sullied by it now in my mind's eye. I know that you
have reiterated your desire to remain a spinster, vehe-
mently, but I know too that you will change your mind.*

*I will see you in a few weeks' time when I will visit you
again,*

All my love

Robert

Lizzie had to give the man ten out of ten for perseverance.
She was puzzled that he would be so keen in the face of such
obvious hostility. Mary Butler must have been very beautiful.
Men were such deluded creatures. She picked up another
letter.

*29th January, 1911
Ranelagh*

Mary,

Lizzie noticed the lack of *dearest* or *darling* before her
name. She checked the dates – this letter was seven months
after the last one she'd read. Mary was obviously wearing him
down at this stage, not, as he'd hoped, the other way around.

*Please thank your father for the brace of pheasant he sent
up to me here in Dublin after Christmas. I was sorry to
leave before the shooting began but as you saw these days*

I am too tired to do so very much. I fear my already limited appeal to you diminishes further as my health fails. Why would you, with no love in your heart, play nursemaid? That is saved for those who have true love. True devotion. You barely respect me. Why would you nurse a man whose sight is failing and is disagreeable with headaches from morning to noon to night? I am not an old man, but I feel old. Only the sight of your pretty, darling face – when you deign to come close enough for me to see you clearly – gave me any pleasure. It is not too late, Mary, to reconsider. I fear you would not have to endure my love for too long. Would that not be enough to entice you?

Relay to your father that I will take up his offer to spend a month with you in the spring. I feel the country air will do me good. And perhaps you will come to Dublin to see me in the summer? The King will make his coronation visit to us here in July – though I know you do not approve of His Majesty so much. Maybe a visit to the Abbey Theatre might lure you more? I am sure Mr Yeats or Synge will have something on show to tempt you.

All my love

Robert

Lizzie would have chuckled if it hadn't been so pathetic. She could see the scene. The anxious, desperate Charles Butler, inviting the ailing suitor down to Butler Hall for a month. Also aware that if Mary would just agree to marry him she might be a widow soon enough. Poor lovesick Robert, happy to take her even on these sad, desperate terms. And Mary, impervious to it all.

Lizzie slipped down in the bed as she leafed through the letters. Getting comfortable and despite everything, or rather probably because of everything, she felt sleepiness snuggling in beside her like a cat settling down for the night. With yawns gathering pace she read more of the letters, out of sequence, moving back and forth in time. Moving between a healthy and hopeful Robert to a fading and desperate lover and back again. And always addressing an indifferent Mary. A constant fixed mark. Never budging. As Lizzie's eyes grew heavy, and she let the pages down on the sheet that covered her, something tapped at her brain. Something in these lines, in these century-old words, was whispering to her. As sleep welcomed her to its sweet embrace she let it go, too tired to decipher it. If it wasn't just a trick of a shattered, traumatised mind. A strange hallucination. Letting all her thoughts go, Lizzie gave in to sleep's oblivion.

31

Around 6 a.m. the hushed leaving of the men disturbed Lizzie. Through the open window their whispers and footsteps floated up to her as they headed off to the outhouses and out for their day. Barely awake, Lizzie's ears paid little attention to the flutter and crumple of paper as the forgotten letters of last night got caught under her and others slipped off the bed as she rolled over. She slept on oblivious until closer to 9 a.m. when the songs of happy woodland birds gently eased her into consciousness. With a yawn and rubbing her eyes, she sat up.

This time the scrunch of paper made it all the way to Lizzie's brain. She looked down in a panic, quickly wide awake. Fumbling through the sheets she found the first creased page. It hadn't torn or disintegrated, as might easily have happened. But it was a mess. She flattened it out as much as she could, then looked around her. The entire discourse, the parrying back and forth of Robert and Mary, was scattered about her, pages on the bed, pages on the ground. She jumped out of bed, her feet finding space among the pages, scattered like autumnal leaves. She stooped to gather them up, paying no attention to which letter they came from. She straightened the sheets on her bed.

Finding the less lucky pages that had suffered through the night, at the mercy of her restlessness.

Lizzie took the pile over to the window. Grabbing the dressing table chair, she sat in close to the deep windowsill, taking advantage of the best light. She started reuniting letters with their correct pages, in the correct order. It was like a strange game of Solitaire.

On the windowsill, and in piles on the floor by her feet, she saw snippets of their sad story all over again as she sorted. Robert's ailments. Mary's indifference. Lizzie shook her head. He had been so full of life and joy in the early letters, so sure that he would win her over. But he just got sicker and sadder. Headaches mentioned on this page that she was reuniting with the rest of its letter from late 1910. Dizziness after the month's stay in the spring of 1911 mentioned in the opening paragraph of another.

Lizzie slowed down.

That weird feeling, the one she'd had just before she'd fallen asleep, was back.

What was it? She put down orphan pages and picked up the letters she'd successfully put back together. She scanned them, smoothed edges that were still bent. She read the pages over again. And again.

And then it came to her.

Robert's symptoms. She sorted quickly through the letters, grabbing at pages with any mention of what was wrong with him. She traced a finger over the looped handwriting where he mentioned a new ailment.

Headaches. Dizzy spells. Losing weight. Heart problems. Failing sight.

This exact list of symptoms, identical, was a list she'd heard in another context. From Freya, about her mother. Yesterday, in the library, Freya had talked about how Grace had died. These were the same symptoms. Had they both had the same cancer?

Both left undiagnosed and untreated? Lizzie looked out the
window as she thought. It could have happened, but what a
coincidence. Had something stacked the odds? Something environmental, something in the environs of Butler Hall that had
left these two previously healthy young people fatally afflicted,
a century apart. Lead in the pipes? Radon in the ground?

Lizzie, letters in hand, ran through theories and ideas, her
eyes looking out over the trees but not really seeing them. And
then it came to her. Her eyes snapped into focus. Back in Mary
Butler's day, when the grounds were still maintained, Lizzie
would have been able to see from here a part of the grounds that
was hidden now.

The walled garden.

And what lay within those walls?

Poison.

32

Still in her pyjamas, Lizzie grabbed the letters and raced barefooted from her room. She barrelled downstairs, through the hall and into the kitchen.

Claire, sitting at the island with a coffee in her hand, jumped at Lizzie's eruption into the room. 'Oh! Good morning, Li—' she began, coffee cup stalled midway to her mouth, but Lizzie didn't reply or slow down. With an outstretched arm she grabbed her mother's phone from the granite countertop – 'You found it, great. I'll bring it back. I'm not stealing it!' she cried, thrown over her shoulder as she went. Without losing speed she was straight out the kitchen door, across the terrace and lawn before plunging into the woods.

Panting and sweaty, she came to a stop at the flowerbed at the back of the walled garden. The flowerbed that looked like all the others but which Claire had told them was really very different.

Lizzie dropped the letters onto the overgrown grass behind her. Fumbling, her hands shaking, she unlocked the phone – how many times had she told her mother not to have 1234 as her passcode? She swiped until she found the app. The plant

identifier app. Her breathing was still coming in gasps and
shudders, but not just due to the exertion of getting here. Her
nerves kept her arms vibrating, shaking as she tried to hold the
phone steady so it could take a picture of the plants and
compare them to its database. She held her wrist with her free
arm, steadying the phone.

The first result, a pretty white flower, a thimbleweed,
could cause nausea. Then bluebell-like flowers, columbine,
could cause heart palpitations. Foxglove added confusion,
sight problems to all the others. And more and more, different
flowers, roots, berries, each causing their own chaos. Every
symptom suffered by Robert – and Grace – could have been
caused by something here. Lizzie took a breath. Was she
running away with herself? She fell onto the grass and picked
up the letters, read them again. Flicking through pages, sorting
them behind each other as she read. During the early letters
he was fine. Nothing but descriptions of a hale and hearty
man in the prime of his life. Tennis, hunting, dances and the
good life. As the time went on and as Mary continued to
refuse his advances, his health declined. And all the more
damning – every letter where Robert complained of a
symptom there was invariably, somewhere, a compliment to
Mary on her cooking or baking. Or on treats that had been
sent up to him in Dublin.

He'd been poisoned.

Whether it had been one plant or many, the problem of
Robert had been dealt with. Oh Mary, wasn't refusing him
enough? You were doing that so well. No one seemed to be
forcing the marriage on you. Lizzie looked over the pages again.
Maybe though, it hadn't been Mary? Robert detailed a particularly nasty spell of illness after Charles had sent up pheasants to
him after Christmas of 1911. Had Charles grown desperate at
Mary's refusal to marry Robert? Had he hoped she'd relent and
marry a dying man? That she would agree to such a compro-

mise? And Charles had misjudged? Killed him before Mary gave in?

And had the crimes of 1911 slithered and snaked their way down the family tree to eighteen years ago? Because, if Lizzie was right – if Robert had been poisoned – had Grace been poisoned too?

Lizzie, sitting in the warm summer morning sun, felt very cold.

In any other circumstances she'd say she was adding two and two together and getting a hundred.

But.

All the facts of the last twenty-four hours converged on her, swarming, loud and angry.

George knew all about the 'notorious' Mary Butler and her ailing fiancé. These letters – innocuous, just a collection of an ancestor's correspondence – had no reason to be hidden, but were instead kept from prying eyes, lest someone spot, like Lizzie had, the inspiration. In *his* library. Among *his* books. George was the one who convinced them all to not bring in the Guards when they found Declan dead. He was very keen to keep them out of his business. He'd made such a song and dance yesterday of not knowing the poison garden was there. Made sure they all heard. And how likely was that? George, the man who was so connected to his land, didn't know it was there? Lizzie found it hard to swallow.

And last of all.

Most damning.

George was being blackmailed. Mia knew something about him. She was from Mayo – a fact she'd been at pains to point out last night. Had she a connection to Butler Hall? Heard whispers of something bad?

Something bad – like he'd killed his wife.

Lizzie felt as dizzy with the weight of these revelations as if she had ingested something from the flowerbed beside her. What was she going to do?

'Lizzie?' A voice floated over to her from the walled garden gate. 'Lizzie, are you in here?'

Claire.

She wouldn't be able to see Lizzie sitting there on the patch of grass at the back of the garden. The overgrown shrubs were too thick and wild. Lizzie could sit here, not move, and Claire might go away. But Lizzie felt her legs unfurl. Placed her arms down on the ground to push herself up. She had to talk to Claire, and she should do it now. She might have worried about telling Claire about the folly argument yesterday, but this discovery changed everything. And unlike yesterday, there was no crowd in the walled garden now. All the men were off hiking. Freya was meditating at the other end of the estate. And here, they were away from Mia in the house. There would be no better time to talk privately.

No better time to plan how to get away from George and go to the Guards.

And she'd make her mother believe her. She had to.

Lizzie stepped out from around the shrubs.

Claire spotted her and trotted over. A look of confusion on her face.

'There you are,' she said. 'What was that all about? Can I have my phone back, please?'

Lizzie handed the phone over.

'Are you okay?' asked Claire. 'You look like you got a fright.'

'Well...' Lizzie mumbled. How did you start? How did you say *I think your new husband might have killed his first wife and is being blackmailed by the cook over it*? How did you say such an unbelievable and awful thing? Even after so many unbelievable and awful things had happened. And, how did you say that to someone who would want a second opinion if you said the sky was blue.

Lizzie stood there. Weighing it all up. Claire's expression patient, if confused. She felt a tingle in her fingertips, her heart rate picking up. She took a breath.

'Mam,' she began, then closed her eyes. Took another breath and opened them again. 'Mam, I don't think George is... I don't think he's quite who he says he is.'

Claire froze. Stared at Lizzie.

'Oh?' she managed, a quiet exclamation.

Lizzie picked up the letters from the grass. Showed them to her. Told her how she found them, about the words within. Pointed to the dangerous flowers. Told her about Freya in the library yesterday. Let the whole sorry tale tumble out. She knew it was jumbled, confused, but it was all there. She finished with the scene at the folly. What she'd heard. The threats and the blackmail.

As she talked, the look on Claire's face evolved. Confusion as Lizzie spelt out the details. Then slow comprehension. Lizzie had expected it to end by morphing into an expression that matched hers. Shock and terror. She expected the first words out of her mouth to be 'Let's get Liam and get out of here.'

But instead of fear and terror, Claire's face went blank.

'Mam... what do you think? I know there's a lot to take in, and it's all a bit incredible... but, come on, it's compelling. We need to get out of here. We need to go call the Guards.'

Claire shook her head.

'No,' she said.

'No? What?'

'Those are letters from a hundred years ago, Lizzie. You can't go accusing people of murder based on that.'

'Have you forgotten the bit about the cook blackmailing George?'

Claire didn't reply.

'Oh surprise, you don't believe me. Seriously?' The fury of indignation caught light. 'Why would I lie about something like this? I'm not drunk, I'm not high. I'm not trying to take your money!'

'Lizzie, it's not that I don't believe you... but, the cook black-mailing George? Can you hear how bizarre that sounds? You must have misunderstood what you saw.'

Lizzie stood and stared. How could her mother be reacting like this? So stubborn, so unbelieving. Would the words from someone else's lips have convinced her? Was she so blinded by her love for George, from her second chance at happiness, that she couldn't let herself listen? Where was her smart, intelligent, no-nonsense mother?

'Whatever hold he has over you, Mam... you have to shake it off.'

'He has no hold over me.'

'That's not true. The Claire I know would be coming now, with me, to the Guards. Not standing there defending him. He's given you something from this garden! You are under some sort of spell.'

Lizzie stepped around her mother.

'Where are you going?' she cried.

'The Guards!' yelled Lizzie. 'Even if I have to walk all the way to Castlebar!'

Claire grabbed her arm, her fingers digging in.

'Lizzie, no!'

Lizzie wrenched her arm away.

'I'm doing it for you, someone's got to save you! And I'm doing it for Dad as well.'

Claire blanched.

'What?'

The final piece of the puzzle. George had claimed they all had motive to kill her father. Each one of them who'd sat around that table yesterday morning. But only one of them had killed before. And gotten away with it.

George himself.

'He killed before. And he killed again. It's why he didn't want to call the Guards. Convinced us all not to. But I'm not under his spell. *Unlike* you.'

'Lizzie, please listen to me, don't go,' cried Claire, her eyes burning. She grabbed at Lizzie's arm again but Lizzie shook her off. Started to run. To get away from her mother. To go get help.

33

Lizzie pulled her dress over her head, then grabbed her boots. Her buzzing fingers fumbled with the boot laces, desperation fuelling her and hobbling her in equal measure. She snatched up her phone, barely looked at since the loss of signal, and dashed downstairs.

'Lizzie! Please!' beseeched Claire, as Lizzie sprinted for the path to the folly. But Lizzie didn't look back. She was going for the quad bike. She skidded to a halt among the trees at the moss-covered tumbledown buildings.

She circled to the front of the first shed and pulled open the door. She looked over her shoulder, checking for Claire. It would have been clear from the kitchen doorway which direction she'd headed. It wouldn't take Claire long to catch her up.

Relieved to see the key in the rusting red bike's ignition Lizzie hopped on, the decrepit suspension groaning. She turned the key. Nothing. She slapped the side of it and tried again. A splutter this time. 'C'mon!' she yelled, but took a breath before turning the key for a third time. Anxiety growing with every passing second. Expecting Claire to appear at the door at any moment. With a wheezy growl it spluttered into life. She shot forward, expelled from the shed, the jolt nearly unseating her. As it coughed and spat, and she found her balance, Lizzie sped it along a rough path that led away from the outhouse through the undergrowth. Away from the folly. Towards the path that had once been the driveway to the house. Perfect. That was the way out. She just needed to point herself straight and she'd come to the old, falling-down gates. And from there to civilisation, and safety. She patted the letters which she'd stuffed into her jeans and pressed on the throttle. And still no sign of Claire trying to stop her.

The bike jumped and jostled Lizzie as it bounced over each incline and decline. Her bones rattling. Lizzie swerved, avoiding a fallen branch which would have felled the ancient quad bike and sent her flying, breaking her neck. She turned the bike, going along the line of the side of the house. She felt it shudder under her.

'No!' she cried out, as it spat and spluttered again. And with a strangled cry it rolled to a stop. The woods quieter for the sudden silence. Lizzie climbed off and kicked the bike.

'Stupid hunk of crap!' She kicked it again. Tears rolled down her cheeks. She was going to have to walk out. All the way to the gate, a trek that had taken them nearly an hour, two days ago. She rubbed her sleeve across her face, mopping up the tears. She had to keep it together. She had to show up at the Guards and be believed.

She sucked in a deep breath and started walking, abandoning the treacherous quad bike. She followed the path, looking through the trees to the house as she went. Scanning for Claire. She peered in every window she passed. In a gap in the trees she had a full view of the house, right up to the roof. Her eyes were drawn upwards. Looking to see if there was a side window that matched the one where she'd seen Mia yesterday.

Lizzie stumbled. Stopped. Stared, transfixed.
There was indeed another window to the attic room.
Mia was there once again.
And she wasn't alone.

34

Lizzie wanted to vomit.

'Mam!' she cried out.

In the attic room, next to Mia, it was her mother she could see. And she could also see that Mia was angry. Was waving her arms in the air. Claire had her palms up, placating.

Lizzie bolted through the undergrowth, pushing back leaves and branches. Bursting out of the trees at the side of the house she skidded on a patch of mossy grass. Stopping, she looked up, desperate to see what was happening. But she was too close to the building to see anything. Heart thumping, Lizzie sprinted back around. Back to the terrace and the lawn.

In her panic she had stopped wondering where Claire was. Why she wasn't following her. Stupid, stupid mistake. Lizzie had left her alone with that woman. All in the name of saving them. How could she have been so stupid?

Supercharged by adrenaline and terror, Lizzie shot through the kitchen door, sending it crashing against the counter behind. Glasses and crockery shook, chiming and clanking in alarm. Lizzie rounded the island and pulled open the door to the attic stairs. Here wasn't like the staircase in the hall. It was poky and dark, slowing her down. Her boots pounded on every wooden step, the sound ricocheting off every surface of the enclosed space. But she didn't care if they heard her coming. She *wanted* them to hear her. She was drawn like a charmed snake to the top where she could hear raised voices. And like that snake she was ready to bite.

Two doors greeted her on the landing. Her mother's voice from the right one. She grasped the door handle and threw it open.

The two women whirled around.

'Leave her alo—' roared Lizzie, but her voice died.

Claire had her hand on Mia's shoulder. Mia was in tears.

Lizzie, like the quad bike, spluttered and stalled.

In this attic bedroom, with its sloping ceiling and two small square windows, the three of them froze.

35

Claire recovered first. She marched over to Lizzie, went past her and stuck her head out the door. With a finger to her lips, she listened for a moment, then shut it. Pushed across the small metal bolt.

'What the hell is going on here?' said Lizzie.

Ignoring her, Claire looked over at Mia.

'Sit.'

She looked at Lizzie.

'And you too.'

'Not until you tell me what's happening!' Lizzie looked from her mother to Mia and back again. Bewildered.

Mia sat at the end of the small single bed and sniffled. Lizzie stayed standing.

'What's happening, you ask...' said Claire, facing her daughter.

'Don't—' barked Mia, looking at Claire.

'I'll say what I want to say,' Claire snapped back. They glared at one another. Then Mia began to cry again. Proper, big, hulking ugly tears. Claire rushed to her, sat and put an arm around her. Lizzie watched, stunned.

'Maggie, it's okay,' her mother cooed, her words low and soothing. Words said in a way that took Lizzie back to her childhood when she'd fallen, hurt her knee, was scared of the dark. Calming, motherly. 'Maggie, I'm sorry, we shouldn't fight. Don't cry. C'mon. We're under so much stress, we need to pull together, not apart.'

'I know, I know,' the crying woman said, blowing her nose on a raggy tissue.

Lizzie stamped her foot on the polished wood floor.

The two women looked up at her.

'One of you please do me the courtesy of telling me what the absolute hell is going on here!'

'Lizzie, please, keep your voice down.'

'Mam!'

'Okay, okay.' Claire held up her hands. 'I'll explain. I will. Just be quiet. And you'll want to sit, there's a lot to tell.'

'It certainly looks that way!' said Lizzie as she dragged a wooden chair from a corner of the room to where she'd been standing. She sat down and looked at Claire and Mia. Waited.

Claire sat up straight and took a deep breath.

'Lizzie,' she said. 'This is Maggie Fitzgerald. Not Mia Casey. She's a cook, but she's from Sligo, not anywhere around here. She usually lives in Dublin now. Not far from us really.'

'I see,' said Lizzie.

'We met on a Facebook group. About eighteen months ago.'

'A Facebook group?' said Lizzie, eyebrows furrowed. 'Like how you met George?'

'Yes. Well. Facebook was the only thing it had in common. It was a very, very different kind of group. It was a support group for women who had been emotionally and financially betrayed by their husbands. It was there to help us process and deal and move on. I needed something because I wasn't coping with the fallout from Declan. You were a nightmare. Liam was only sixteen. I was on my own and angry. So very angry.'

'I was there for the same reason,' said Mia. Or rather 'Maggie' as Lizzie should think of her now. She sniffled and rubbed her balled-up tissue under her nose. 'My husband went off with all my money. My life's savings.'

'We got talking,' said Claire. 'And when we realised we lived close to each other we started to meet in real life for coffee. To help each other. To talk it all through. To talk about how stupid we felt, how betrayed. Talk about the humiliation. The business hadn't quite picked up yet and we were still struggling financially. As was Maggie. It helped to have someone there who understood it all. Who knew what it was like to get to the end of the week and have nothing in the bank and know it wasn't your fault. That a man you loved and trusted had screwed you over and left you in this position. It's not something many people can relate to. And all my friends, Lizzie? They didn't know what to say to me. They crossed the road when they saw me coming. They all fell away.'

Claire's cheeks were blazing red at the memory.

'And it was the same for me,' said Maggie. 'Nobody wanted anything to do with me. My life – our lives – were destroyed.'

'We understood each other when no one else could. Maggie, by being there, saved my life. I don't think I would have made it through otherwise.'

Maggie reached out and squeezed Claire's arm.

'I owe her so, so much.'

Lizzie looked from one to the other. A horrible jumble of emotions churned within. Guilt, her old friend, gut-punched her, hearing a side of her mother's suffering she hadn't before. And the part she'd played in it. After it was complete and utter confusion.

'Okay, I follow all that,' said Lizzie, brows furrowed, 'but I don't understand what it has to do with now? How have you gone from coffee and support to an attic bedroom in a mansion in the wilds of Mayo?'

Maggie looked at Claire. Claire nodded. Maggie closed her eyes. Her shoulders tensed, raised up a fraction as the muscles contracted.

'I asked Claire to be here,' said Maggie.

'*You*, asked *her*?' said Lizzie. 'But that doesn't make sense, surely it'd be the other way round?'

'Yes, it would look that way, but no. I asked her. I needed her. I was sick of being a victim, so I asked her to help me get my money back. To take it back from my lying thieving husband.'

'And how does coming here do that?' asked Lizzie, but with a sinking feeling.

'How?' said Maggie. 'Because my lying, thieving husband lives here. He's the lord of the manor himself – George Butler.'

36

'You were married to *George*?' Lizzie looked at Maggie, stunned.

'Yes,' she replied. 'And well, no.'

'What?'

'Sorry. It's confusing but the answer is I thought I was married to George Butler. He led me to believe we were married. But the reality is, I wasn't a big enough fish for him. The ceremony was on a beach in Thailand and he said he'd sort out all the paperwork so it was legal back at home. But he didn't and I never knew, not till the end. So, yes and no is the answer.'

'Jesus,' whispered Lizzie, shaking her head. 'When were you together?'

'About two years ago... two years, two months and one week ago, if you want to be precise. It didn't last long. Six months. All the time it took for him to pour my life savings into this money pit.' Maggie waved a hand around the room. 'This house now, this is his one real, true love.'

Maggie sighed. Ran her hand through her short hair, pulled it back off her face.

'What you have to understand is George Butler is all he says he is. He owns Butler Hall and is the descendant of all that great family. All that is true. But what he doesn't tell you, what he keeps a secret is – he's also a scam artist. Romancing vulnerable women is his canvas. And you're looking at one of his masterpieces. Sorry to be so melodramatic, but he took all my money. Every last cent.'

'George? A scam artist?' asked Lizzie. 'What?'

'I'm afraid it's true,' said Claire.

'We don't know how many women he's defrauded but we think we know of at least two others. A woman from London, and another from Cork. But people feel so humiliated afterwards. They want to never speak of it again. He's probably ruined dozens of lives.'

'Did you know all this, Mam? When you met George?' Lizzie looked alarmed at her mother.

Claire stared at her feet, eyes downcast. She said nothing for a minute. Then she looked up at Lizzie. Eyes ablaze.

'Oh, I knew alright. I knew ALL about him. The truth is I went looking for him.'

'You did what?'

'I went looking for him. As Maggie said, we decided we were sick of being victims. Sick of suffering because of awful men. We decided to take back our power. And more specifically, our money. I couldn't get a penny back from what your father lost, it's just gone. But I could at least help Maggie get hers.'

'I'd gone to the Guards when he dumped me,' interjected Maggie, 'but they said there was nothing they could do. I'd given him the cash willingly is how it looked. He was smart, he never forced me, never coerced. I gave it all to him because I loved him and this place was our dream.'

'We found out that George was coming into a little bit of cash,' said Claire. 'And unusually for him, from a legitimate source. He is phobic about selling any of the land of the Butler estate, even to pay for fixing up the house. He's driven to keep the Butler legacy intact, no matter what. He much prefers to pay for the house renovations and upkeep by scamming women. But he lost fifty acres to a compulsory purchase order; the council needed to put a road through a far corner of the estate. When we discovered that I hurried up and joined the same Facebook group where George had found Maggie, the infamous support group for young widows and widowers. Maggie's first husband died young, you see. It's her late husband's life insurance policy money George stole.

'I hung out in that group. Making a bit of noise. I knew from Maggie what to say to draw his attention. I also made sure the business's improved finances were all over the internet. So he could see how well it was doing now. Reel him in. And, surprise surprise, it worked. One cold December morning, about a week after you entered St Brigid's, he slipped into my DMs.'

37

'Soon it was coffee. Then dinner. The protestations of undying love came pretty quickly. And, keen as mustard, the marriage proposal was made by the end of the first month.'

'Bloody hell, Mam. Really? What was going to happen after you married him? What was the plan? I can't believe I'm even asking this.'

'There's no delicate way to put this. That was when the blackmailing was going to happen. Maggie wasn't blackmailing George about his first wife and whatever madness you were going on about in the walled garden. It was all part of our plan! She was pretending she'd tell me all about her and him, that he was a scam artist. We were blackmailing him, scamming the scam artist. Giving him an overdose of his own medicine. All he had to do was return her money and we'd leave him alone. Freya had been in America the entire time George and Maggie were together so we knew she wouldn't recognise her and rumble us. We did change Maggie's name to Mia, just in case George had talked about her to Freya. It seemed like a plan with no drawbacks.'

'You two were blackmailing George... Christ almighty.'

'You were never meant to find any of this out,' said Claire. 'You or your brother. I thought you'd come here for this weekend, and then Liam would be off to university in a few months, most likely heading to the UK. I imagined you'd be in Dublin and I'd be down here. Neither of you would have time to get attached to George. In a few months I'd tell you that we'd split. That we'd realised we'd married in haste. But I'd be okay, not sad or distraught, so neither of you would be too worried. That is how it was supposed to go. But the last few days have been a bit of a... a bit of a curveball. No one would have anticipated anything like that.'

Lizzie stood up. Paced about the small room. Which was feeling smaller with every passing minute. This was unbelievable. Her mother and this woman in cahoots? Trying to scam a scam artist.

George was a scam artist.

She felt a strange ball of disappointment in her belly. Despite all her fears about him, she must have been charmed by him at the same time.

God, he was good.

She shook her head. Trying to dislodge the confusion. Trying to simplify and collate everything her mother had just revealed. It seemed vast. A universe that was expanding. She needed to catch it in a net and drag it back to her. Get her head around it.

One thing came to the surface. Made no sense.

'Mam, but surely marrying George plays into his hands? Does he not have exactly what he wants – access to all your money? To the business? How is that justice?'

Claire shook her head.

'No. We played him at his own game. Again. Our wedding? It wasn't legit.'

'It wasn't?'

'Nope. I convinced him to let me arrange it all. His hubris

meant that wasn't hard. He wasn't in the slightest bit suspicious. But the officiant was an actor. Nothing we signed was legal. Our little wedding in that beautiful seaside guesthouse was a complete fiction. It was partly why I didn't want either of you there. I didn't want to involve you any more than I had to.'

Yet one more time Lizzie was speechless. She turned and looked out the window, surveyed the square of Butler estate she could see from here. The full implications of what her mother and Maggie had done began to sink in. She was appalled. She turned back to her mother.

'Mam. I'm shocked. What have you been thinking? Your judgement... Did Dad mess you up that much? I'm meant to be the screw-up. Blackmail? Fake weddings? Scamming a serious criminal? You're not thinking as clearly as you think you are! And don't ever talk to me about trust and truth again.'

Claire stood.

She pointed her finger at Lizzie, her voice dangerously low. 'Your father's actions destroyed me. Doing this has been the only thing that has made me feel in control again!'

'Listen to yourself, Mam!' said Lizzie, not angry but concerned. 'You sound like me. I drank because Dad destroyed me. I drank because it made me feel less powerless. Mam, can't you see that? And... I'm sorry, neither of you can see the danger in all of this. George Butler isn't just a serious scammer. I think he's dangerous. Very dangerous.'

'Oh, stop with that nonsense. After everything I've just told you, we're back to this?'

Ignoring her mother, Lizzie turned to Maggie. 'What do you know about Grace? Can you tell us anything?'

'Er,' Maggie looked at the annoyed Claire and then back at Lizzie, 'I don't know much. He said the same, cancer. And he was left with Freya who was very young. I saw the pictures and the grave here, when I first visited Butler Hall. But that's about it. Claire was saying you think he poisoned her? Really?'

Claire rolled her eyes.

'I found some old letters. I think someone associated with the family was murdered a hundred years ago and his symptoms were identical to Grace's.'

'You're seeing things that aren't there, Lizzie,' said Claire. 'Our actions have been making you suspicious. You'd never have come to that conclusion, otherwise. It's time to drop it.'

'No it isn't. In fact, I'm only more convinced now, after hearing all this. He's a crook. And, it sounds like he didn't just get inspiration to murder Grace from the letters. He took another leaf out of great-granddaddy Charles Butler's playbook and has made a career of marrying for money.'

'George, a murderer?' said Maggie. 'I don't know. It's a big leap from fraud to murder, no?'

'You didn't think he was a fraudster when you first met him. His whole job is to make you think he's big, innocent, jolly George. And murder makes sense when you look at the facts. If he couldn't bear to be parted with even a square inch of his land unless he was forced to, would he risk a divorce? And lose half of it? Over and over with each marriage? Never. And he clearly has a pattern of serial marriages. Spend the money, move on to the next victim. Far better to be a widower than a divorcee.'

'He didn't kill Maggie,' said Claire.

'Well he's not stupid. It's safer to walk away if he can. And he'd managed to not have to marry her. I'm not suggesting he's some kind of thrill killer, it's probably just a matter of practicalities. I bet if we look into Grace's background we'll find she was very well off.'

Claire said nothing.

'Makes sense, no? And it also convinces me all the more about Dad.'

'Really, Lizzie,' said Claire, but with a little less conviction.

'Think about it. When Dad reappeared, what did that do to George's new marriage to you? The one he thinks is legit? The one that's going to give him access to lots of money? It makes it invalid. I actually pointed that out to him! In the kitchen after Dad reappeared. I was feeling worried for you guys. Sure, there were probably some grey areas, Dad having been declared dead, but one way or the other it was going to be messy. So George saw his lovely payday slipping away. If only Dad was dead again, huh? I think that George didn't just dispatch his first wife, but your first husband too. And, at some point, you'd probably have been next.'

38

'You're playing with fire with all of this, both of you. He's a dangerous man.'

Maggie looked up at Claire.

'Maybe she's right...?'

'We're nearly over the finish line, Maggie. George is doing as he is told, he's transferring the money as we speak. We're so close.'

'He's transferring the money now? But he's out with Hudson and Liam,' asked Lizzie.

'This stupid day out? It's just an excuse to get to the outer reaches of the estate, to where there is a bit of signal. So he can make the transfer.' She turned to Maggie. 'Isn't that right, Maggie? That's what he said to you?'

Maggie nodded.

'Yeah, he popped up here yesterday when he was supposedly napping. That's what he said he was going to do.'

'The money will be in Maggie's account tomorrow. She'll be heading off the grounds to get signal to make sure it's all gone through. Come talk to me then, Lizzie, and we can see about getting you back to Dublin. I don't think Butler Hall is doing you any good.'

'Mam, come on! We need to go to the Gardaí. Not wait on a money transfer. We should be packing our bags. Now.'

'Maggie and I are going nowhere until the money is through. We've spent nearly a year planning this. We're not abandoning it at the very last minute because your imagination has run away with itself!'

'You know, I don't think Butler Hall, or George Butler, is doing you any good either!' Lizzie yelled. She turned on her heel and tore open the bedroom door. She clattered down the stairs. Her feet missing steps. Slipping. She grasped the banister, but she didn't slow down. She didn't know where she was going, but she knew she had to get away from Claire before she said anything more. Before she said anything she couldn't take back.

'Lizzie!' Claire was calling her. She didn't look back but she heard her mother's feet stomping down after her. 'Lizzie, wait!'

She caught up with her at the foot of the stairs.

'Don't be like this, Lizzie. I know it's all a massive shock. I can understand you must be reeling... but I had to do this.'

'No you didn't,' snapped Lizzie. 'She had to, maybe.' She pointed back up the stairs to Maggie's room. 'She's the one gaining everything here. She's getting her money back and all she had to do was cook a few dinners and threaten George. And all the while you're here, married to the guy! I know you said it's fake. But how fake is it really? You're in his bed every night, aren't you? Dad was wrong. So very, very wrong. But so is this. And it's dangerous too.'

'Let the money come through, Lizzie. Once she confirms it's in her account, then okay, maybe we go. I'll think about it. I'd have to tell George something, and he might put it all together, but I'll consider it. Okay? One more night, Lizzie.'

Lizzie stood there, staring at her mother. One more night? She couldn't bear the idea of one more minute.

'Please, Lizzie.'

'I don't know, Mam... I don't know.' Lizzie turned away from Claire and headed for the back door. Suddenly drained. Her fight or flight response spent, deflated.

She stepped out and felt the sun on her face. On her arms and legs. How could it be so glorious, how could the natural world just keep on being so beautiful, when all this was happening? Lizzie looked around her. She remembered the abandoned quad bike by the side of the house. She'd put it back. If George returned and saw it sitting there, he'd ask why. She wasn't as good a liar as him. And she needed some time to think about her next step.

The quad bike in, she pulled the outhouse door shut behind her and rested back against its red, painted-peeling wood. She felt flecks of paint transferring from the door to her hands. She turned her palms up for inspection. They looked like they were covered in spots of blood. She rubbed them together, trying to get rid of the paint. Tenacious red specks remained.

Lizzie heard footsteps, coming from the path behind the stone buildings. Someone was muttering and cursing to themselves. Lizzie looked around the corner of the outhouse. Hudson, on his own, marched by. Mumbling and kicking branches and leaves out of his way as he went.

'Hudson!' Lizzie called out. He stopped and turned.

She trotted over. Joined him on the path.

'You okay?' she asked, looking back down the path, looking for George and Liam. 'Where are the others?'

'Oh, now, gee – that is a good freakin' question.' Hudson, whom Lizzie had only seen with a gentle, happy look on his face, glared at her. 'I don't know.'

'Huh?'

'Yep! Not a clue. They could be halfway to China by now

for all I know.' Hudson pointed back down the path. His cheeks red, and his pupils dilated. 'Or for all I care, at this point.'

He stormed off, stomping on down the path.

'Hold on, Hudson!' cried Lizzie, running after him. 'I don't understand. I heard you all go out together this morning.'

'We did. And it was fantastic.' Hudson threw his hands up. 'George took us miles and miles out. But two hours ago, we're hiking through a particular dense part of the woods and – poof! – he's gone! I turned around and no sign of him. He was there and then he wasn't.'

Lizzie fixed her expression of concern. She had a pretty good idea where George had gone. He'd ditched the lads for a bit of privacy to transfer the money. But where was Liam? She felt her heartbeat begin to gear up again.

'But why are you on your own then? Where is Liam? Surely he didn't disappear as well?'

'Funny you should say it but he did! We spent ten minutes looking for George and then, just like my father-in-law, he was gone! Vamoosed! The pair of them abandoned me like some kinda frat house prank.' Hudson's voice was getting louder and louder. He was shaking with anger. 'Lizzie, I don't care what this family thinks is funny... I've been walking around and round in circles, getting more and more lost, just trying to find my way back here...'

'Hudson, I don't think this sounds funny either. Especially considering recent events.' Lizzie glanced back down the path. And all around, peering as far as she could into the dark woods. She couldn't see anything. She looked back and Hudson had taken off again, powered by indignation. She scurried after him. Where the hell had Liam gone? She knew what George was up to, but why was Liam AWOL? She was scared to her core knowing he was out there somewhere, with George.

Lizzie caught up with Hudson on the terrace. He lashed out at a chair, sending it rocketing back across the ground.

'Humiliating,' he spat.

'Hudson. Please.' Lizzie kept her distance. The normally gentle and soft man was freaking her out. She looked around, towards the kitchen, for her mother.

'I'm sure it's all just a misunderstanding.'

He looked at her.

'Ha! Yeah, they think it's funny and I don't!'

'You've got to calm down. You're not helping yourself, being so worked up. Think of your yoga breathing, mindfulness. I'll just go get you a drink. Stay put.'

Hudson scowled but said nothing.

Lizzie hurried over to the kitchen. Maggie and Claire were at the door, drawn by the raised voices and noise. Lizzie whooshed them back inside.

'What's going on?' asked Claire.

'Hudson is back but George and Liam aren't. They ditched him and he is pissed off! We know what George is up to, but Liam? Where is he?'

Claire's eyes widened. She threw a look out the door, out to the trees.

'Maybe he got lost... he doesn't know these woods.' Fear filled her eyes.

'I hope that is all it is. I really hope. I'm going to go look for him. But you need to come out and get Hudson to calm down, he's losing it out there.'

Lizzie grabbed a glass and filled it with water from the tap. She rushed outside again. Claire followed.

Lizzie dropped the drink on the table. Hudson was still buzzing angrily, like a wasp trapped in a glass.

'Calm down, Hudson!' commanded Claire. 'Take a deep breath.' Her tone, a verbal slap, so familiar to Lizzie, worked instantly. He stopped, surprised, as if she'd actually touched him.

'Sit down.' He did as he was told. 'Now, tell us, what's happened.'

His anger not entirely extinguished, quietened to a simmer. He took a sip of his water then recounted the same details he'd given to Lizzie.

'Which way did you guys go?' Claire asked, looking left and right. 'Liam doesn't know these woods, he's not like George who knows this place like the back of his hand.'

Hudson opened his mouth to speak, but a familiar booming baritone blasted from the far side of the house. Followed near instantly by its owner, shotgun resting on his shoulder. Lizzie and Claire turned and looked. A beaming George appeared. And beside him was Liam.

'Fear not, my dear,' sang George, in flying form. Lizzie stood there, stock-still. Relief flooding through her to see Liam back, safe. But each cell in her body sparked with fear at the sight of George. It was like one man had gone into the woods this morning and a different one had come out.

'I have your dear Liam here for you. He took a wrong turn, but I found him. You don't need to rush off and rescue him.'

They rounded the low pillared wall and climbed the couple of steps up to the terrace. George made straight for Hudson.

'There is that fine son-in-law of mine, thank goodness! We lost you too! Please no one tell my daughter, I will never be forgiven!'

Hudson stared up at him, saying nothing.

Lizzie hurried over to her brother, giving George as wide a berth as she could without looking suspicious. George's rambunctious tones filled the available air behind them. *Sorry, old chap, not sure what happened there. A pheasant enchanted me and I went in pursuit...*

Lizzie placed a hand on Liam's arm, stalled him. She fixed him with a stare.

'Are you okay?' she said in a hushed voice. A quick look at George over her shoulder.

'Why wouldn't I be?' he said, and took her hand off his arm.

'Where did you go? Hudson said you ditched him.'

'He's just an idiot.'

'Don't be flippant, Liam. He's not an idiot. And neither are you. How could you take a wrong turn when Hudson said you were there one moment and gone the next?'

'I just did. They're big woods. Everything looks the same.'

'Liam, I was worried and scared. So was Mam. There's things—'

'It happened. Okay. Drop it. I'm here now, amn't I?'

Liam stepped around her and walked over to the table, placed a hand on Hudson's shoulder. She heard him mutter 'Sorry'. He then walked over to Claire. He hugged her and Lizzie could just about hear his quiet apology to her too. *Really sorry, Mam, the last thing I meant to do was to worry you.*

Lizzie watched Claire draw him in close. Her precious family, they were worrying the hell out of her. She looked at George, picking up the fallen chair and chatting to Hudson. Working his charm. Hudson looked less enraged already. It was fascinating to watch. Lizzie nearly gasped, seeing a smile emerge on Hudson's face. How did George do it? It was like magic.

A bad, twisted magic.

39

Late in the afternoon Freya strolled out of the woods, slow and lazy, a glowing advertisement for her day of meditation and nature. Dumping her yoga mat and bag by her feet, she sat beside Hudson. She leant over and kissed him, tickling a lock of hair by his ear with her finger. Lizzie listened as George told her about the morning's misadventures. Lizzie stared at him as he spoke. Transfixed by his total ease. He'd transformed this morning's tensions between the men so they'd spent the quiet afternoon hours playing cards, laughing and talking. As George dealt Freya in, the tale of Hudson alone in the woods had morphed into a funny anecdote that had them all doubled over in fits of laughter.

Lizzie had rebuffed all efforts to include her in the card playing. It wasn't just her horror at who this man really was, but she feared he'd read the truth in her eyes. That he'd see how she could see him properly for the first time. She was amazed at how cool and convincing her mother and Mia were. As good actors as George himself. But they'd had time, she supposed. Had planned for this. Not just been dropped in it like Lizzie had. She'd spent the afternoon avoiding everyone. Keeping her distance. She'd emerged now, to sit on the lounger on the terrace, hiding behind a book, so as not to look too suspicious with her absence.

But it was hard. Could she give her mother one more night here? Let Claire see the money transferred before they ran? She felt crazy to be even considering it. To have this information about who George really was, and not do anything. How could they just sit around, playing cards and eating food – food Maggie, his ex-wife it turned out, had yet again prepared – and do nothing? But, as the hours passed, that was exactly what happened, and she didn't get up and leave.

As the light changed and evening emerged, Claire came over to her. The others had grown tired of playing cards some hours ago and Freya, head resting on Hudson's shoulder, had dozed off. Liam was idly moving about. Fitting in pieces of the jigsaw that still sat at the end of the table. Occasionally looking up and saving moths who were drawn to the fairy lights, whooshing them away to safety. George had dug out a cigar from the library and was now standing on the edge of the terrace, smoking and contemplating his domain. The earthy scent of the tobacco mingled with the night air. Lizzie stared at him. Transfixed. Scared.

Claire sat on the end of the lounger. She looked at Lizzie. She laid a hand down gently on Lizzie's leg.

'Any good?' she asked, nodding at the book in Lizzie's hands.

Lizzie looked at the cover of the book she'd taken from the library earlier.

'So-so.'

'It's good to see you reading, you always loved to read. Before... you know. We always had that in common.'

'I had a lot of time in St Brigid's. I got back into it,' said Lizzie, eyeing up her mother cautiously. This was the friend-liest interaction they'd had in years.

'So,' Claire lowered the volume of her voice, 'do I take it by not leaving, you've made a decision?'

One of Liam's moths fluttered and dived around their heads. Lizzie swatted it away. She stared at her mother, suppressed a desire to scowl. This sudden appearance of open, unresentful Claire wasn't as organic as she was trying to make it look. Claire wanted her to play ball, not ruin her plan. Lizzie felt she was looking in a mirror. A mirror into the recent past. Claire had been manipulating her. Just like Lizzie had when she'd been in the deepest thrall to her addictions. Manipulating her mother into second chances, into accepting excuses, into believing her lies. But the tables had been turned.

It had been in increments. The concessions Lizzie had been making for her mother. First agreeing to come to Mayo, to meet this new man George. To make nice about the marriage despite her misgivings. Then, against her better judgement, agreeing to the foolhardy plan to let a dead Declan stay dead. And now, Claire was asking her to stay, when they should be running away as fast as they could. The tables were well and truly turned. And Claire didn't even seem to be aware of it. That her behaviour was just as messed up as Lizzie's had ever been. And had the same root cause. Declan had done a number on her just as much as he had on Lizzie.

'Are you really, really sure you won't go?' Lizzie whispered back.

Claire shook her head. 'No.'

'You know that you are consumed by this insane scheme. You're as bad as I ever was. And like me you can't see it.'

'Don't, Lizzie, please. That's not true.'

Lizzie could feel anger bubble up within her. That Claire was just as guilty, just as weak, after acting so high and mighty. But much like how, despite everything she'd thrown at her mother, Claire had never given up on her, had always made sure she was safe, Lizzie realised she would do the same for her.

She couldn't leave her here, at risk. While she was blind to the danger of the situation, Lizzie wouldn't leave. Nor Liam. Not with that man. No way.

Lizzie sighed.

'Okay,' said Lizzie. 'I'll stay. For you, because you stayed with me at my worst.'

Claire leant forward and grabbed Lizzie, drew her into a hug, a hug Lizzie couldn't remember happening between them in so very, very long. Lizzie clung to her like a drowning man.

'Ah, my dears,' George's voice rang out. 'That is so lovely to see, you two getting on better. I love it.'

Lizzie woke early the next morning, nature's alarm clock rousing her from a restless sleep. Birds singing. Wind through the trees. She got out of bed and pulled on shorts and a T-shirt, and padded softly downstairs. Hoping not to disturb anyone who slept on.

Maggie was in the kitchen, cooking sausages and rashers.

'Your mother's in the drawing room,' she said.

'Okay, thanks.' Lizzie turned around and walked back down the hall. She pushed open the drawing room door. She hadn't been in here since the first day they'd arrived. She shut the door behind her.

Claire was sitting on one of the brocade sofas, coffee mug in her hands. Someone had tidied away the blanket and pillow her father had used. There was no trace left that he'd been in here.

Lizzie stayed standing, looking down at her.

'Morning, sweetheart,' said Claire. 'Sleep well?'

'No. Unsurprisingly,' Lizzie replied. She'd tossed and turned the whole night. Disturbing dreams when she was asleep, disturbing thoughts when she lay awake, staring at the ceiling.

'I'm sorry to hear that. If it helps, Maggie's going to go check soon.'

'Good.'

'She'll have to walk out to the edge of the estate to get a signal, and then come back. But we'll know by noon, latest, if he transferred the money.'

'Fine,' said Lizzie. 'Come find me then.' She turned and left the room and walked back to the kitchen. Maggie looked up at her, eyebrow raised. Lizzie grabbed a mug and poured herself a coffee.

'Noon, latest,' she said.

'Of course,' replied Maggie.

Lizzie headed for the kitchen door. It was early so the terrace was still in shade. It held on to a little of the night's cool-ness, but Lizzie welcomed the chill. It suited her mood much more than the vivacious, optimistic heat. She made for the steps to sit with her coffee. As she crossed the terrace she saw some-thing beyond it, on the lawn, by the edge of the trees. Mounds, brown and dome-like, on the ground. One large, one small. Her brain couldn't make sense of what the shapes were. She moved closer. Placing her mug down on the table as she passed it. By the steps she was beginning to understand what they were. She moved faster. Down the step onto the lawn, she was running now. She knew what she was seeing.

'Oh God, no!' Lizzie cried, coming to a shuddering halt at the collapsed doe and her fawn. The two creatures lying on the grass on their sides. Lizzie fell to her knees beside them. The baby was already dead, Lizzie could tell. Its large black eye glossy and blank. Heartless flies already buzzing around it, undisturbed.

'Oh no, no no,' Lizzie repeated, fat tears falling from her onto the distended belly of the mother. The teardrops dark-ening the coat of the animal where they fell. The doe was barely alive, Lizzie could see that she was struggling. White froth gathered at the side of her mouth.

'What's happened? What is that?' Lizzie looked up. Maggie was at the edge of the terrace, frowning.

'The fawn, it's dead. Her mother's dying.'

'Oh God,' said Maggie, her face drained pale in horror. She ran back to the house, calling for Claire. Claire came running, emerging at the kitchen doorway, panic in her eyes. Then confusion. They hurried to Lizzie on the lawn.

'What on earth?' asked Claire, looking down at the dead and dying animals.

'This isn't natural. Someone has killed them,' cried Lizzie between tears.

'Why?' breathed Claire.

'I don't know.' Lizzie, distressed, looked up at her mother, then over to Maggie. 'You tell me.'

'Why would we know?' asked Claire. 'And be quiet, Lizzie. We don't need to be overheard.' She looked back at the house.

'*Mia*, you might want to go for *your walk* now. You have two hours, and if you're not back, I don't care. I'm leaving. And you'll be coming with me, Mam.'

Lizzie got up. Stalked across the lawn, shouldering past her mother and Maggie. She stormed into the house and went back upstairs.

Sitting at her bedroom window, in turmoil, Lizzie watched. Maggie, doing as instructed, sloping off with furtive looks left and right. Lizzie checked the time: 9 a.m. She had until eleven, and that was it. They were getting out of here.

Lizzie saw her mother come into the house, a minute later heard her footsteps on the stairs. Out on the landing Claire knocked on doors, rousing the men. Lizzie heard the soft murmurs of conversation as Claire told them about the dead animals. After a few minutes they emerged outside. George, Hudson and Liam. She watched as their sleepy heads, Liam in pulled on jeans, barefoot and askew hair, the other two a little more awake, crossed the lawn and examined the situation. Freya had emerged too. Her blonde hair mussed, a cream shawl over her shoulders. She stood there crying, looking down at the beautiful creatures.

'They must have gotten into the walled garden, gotten at those poisonous plants,' Lizzie heard George say, his words carrying up to her.

George headed towards the path to the outhouses, returned with a roar unbefitting of the morning on the quad bike. And the shotgun. The doe twitched on the ground. Lizzie shuddered, understanding what would soon happen. They hogtied the animals, like the spoils of a day's hunting, and hefted them onto the back of the creaking bike. George then climbed onto the machine and disappeared into the woods. Lizzie got up from the window and went over to her bed. She lay down, contemplating the ceiling. Waiting to hear the distant sound of an animal being put out of its misery. She counted down the minutes until eleven. When she could be put out of hers.

Even with spells of exhausted dozing, the time passed excruciatingly slowly. Lizzie turned her head and finally saw the crawling slow hand had reached the top of the dial on the small brass clock. The small hand at eleven. It was time. She swung her feet off the bed and got up. Her heart picked up pace. She left her room and went downstairs, at every step her heart rate increased a further increment. She met an equally anxious Claire in the kitchen.

'There you are,' said Claire. 'How are you?'

'How do you think?'

'God, it was awful. But they've been dealt with.'

'I saw. Where is everyone now?'

'George and Hudson are outside. Liam went back to bed. Freya was so upset she went for a walk to clear her head.'

'And Maggie?'

'I haven't seen her yet. But it's only just gone eleven, Lizzie. Give her a little more time.'

'Mam...'

'Let's just give her some more time.'

'Oh, for the love of—' Lizzie didn't bother finishing her sentence. Instead she went to the window and stood there, staring out.

'Lizzie, can you try to be less obvious...'

'No one cares about me staring out the window.'

Claire sighed and shook her head.

The clock ticked behind them. And Lizzie watched.

Another fifteen minutes passed. Lizzie turned to Claire.

'She's coming,' said Claire.

'We had a deal, Mam.'

'Maybe she's nervous about being spotted coming back, let's go outside and check for her.'

Lizzie sighed.

'Okay. Fine.'

They trooped outside, nods and smiles for George and Hudson as they strolled oh-so casually around the house scanning the woods for a lurking Maggie. They saw nothing.

'Let's try the front again,' said Claire and Lizzie reluctantly agreed, doing another circuit. Nothing. No sign of her. With mutters of 'more coffee' as they passed the men again, they stepped back into the kitchen.

Freya was back. Pale and quiet, she was at the counter, pouring hot water into a mug. The smell of chamomile scented the air. She looked up at the arrival of the pair of them.

'How are you doing?' asked Claire.

'Oh, you know. I'll be fine. It was just... a bit...'

'I know, hon.' Claire went over to the girl and gave her a hug. Freya looked at her with a teary smile.

'I'll be fine,' she sniffled. 'I'm going to go and lie down with my tea for a bit.'

'That's a good idea,' Claire replied.

Freya left the room, blowing on her mug. Claire and Lizzie stood in silence, listening for her feet on the stairs.

'We should check Maggie's room,' whispered Claire. 'We might have missed her coming back.'

'You think?'

'Maybe.'

They took the narrow stairs to the attic.

Maggie's room was pristine. And empty. The bed made. The furniture straightened up. No personal possessions out on show. It looked like no one had stayed here recently.

The only hint otherwise was the note.

40

'What's that?'

'I have no idea,' said Claire.

They crossed to the bed. Claire picked up the folded sheet of paper. Her name was written on it. She opened it and read.

Claire,

I'm sorry. I'm scared. Maybe Lizzie is right and George is even worse than we thought he was. I didn't sleep a wink last night just going over and over and over it all in my head. No money is worth this. I've made up my mind. When I set out this morning to check if he has transferred the money, whether he has or not – I am not coming back. But I don't want to tell you in person. Because I know I am letting you down. I know that you were doing this for me. But this is all too big, too dangerous. Promise me you won't try and confront him now, by yourself.

I'm sorry.

Maggie

'She's gone!' yelped Lizzie. 'I knew it! She's got what she wanted and is gone. She used you to do her dirty work for her and she's off to enjoy the spoils! She's a bloody scammer too!'

'She's not a scammer!'

'Did you learn nothing from Dad? Fool me once, shame on you, fool me twice... Christ, Mam.'

'She is not a scammer,' hissed Claire, her cheeks blazing red. A faint noise from down below in the kitchen shut them both up. Claire strode over to the door and shut it.

'I had her checked out. I'm not stupid, Lizzie. She's genuine. And she's my friend. The worst thing I can say about Maggie is she's lost her nerve. But, I did this for my own reasons just as much. I haven't been taken advantage of.'

'I don't mean to be triumphalist, Mam. I'm just scared. Scared for all of us.'

Claire sat on the bed. The letter in her hand. She stared at it.

'I hope he's transferred the money at least,' she said.

'Can we leave now?' asked Lizzie. 'Can we go to the Gardaí?'

Claire fanned herself with the letter in the stuffy attic room and looked up at her daughter. 'Early on, Maggie and I talked about going to the Gardaí, after we got the money back, to try and stop him from doing all this to any other woman.'

'Scamming vulnerable women is the least of the worries about George.'

Lizzie waited for Claire to rubbish her fears that George was more than a thief. But she said nothing.

'Are you beginning to believe me about him?'

'I don't know. But you scared Maggie. She took you seriously.'

'I'll try not to be offended that you're listening to me because of Maggie and not just taking my word for it.'

'Oh, Lizzie, it's not that.'

'Isn't it?'

'No, I'm just not arrogant enough to be intransigent when you've convinced someone else there might be a case to be worried. I'm open to considering there is more going on here than I thought there was. And the fact of the matter is, what if you're right? What if George has been up to worse things than scamming women out of their money? Is that a bet I'm willing to take? If I don't have to? Good sense would suggest it's safer to err on the side of believing you.'

'Does that mean we can go?'

'I suppose it does.'

'Oh thank God. Right, we need to get our things together. I'm going to bring the letters with me so I can show them to the Guards. George needs to be locked up! I won't ever feel safe if he's not... and Dad, Jesus, as terrible as he was, he deserves some justice.'

'Lizzie, I don't want to seem negative, but if you're serious about that, I don't think those letters will be enough. I'm willing to be more cautious and get out of here, but you're going to risk sounding like a crazy woman to the police. You need something irrefutable.'

'Like what?'

'I don't know, you're the one with the wild theories! Financial evidence, maybe? An internet search on poisons? A signed confession? Lizzie, I don't know—' Claire stopped. She stood up. Lizzie saw fear creep onto her face.

'Actually, you need it to be watertight.'

'I do? Why?'

'Think about it, Lizzie. If you can't find something undeniably suspicious about Grace's death, then the only nefarious death that has taken place on this estate that the Guards will pay any attention to is your dad's. And without something definitive pointing to George's involvement in Grace's death – if we don't have a big arrow pointing at the guy who has killed before – then Declan's body implicates any of us. Like George argued around the dining room table after we found your dad dead. If you go to the Guards about Grace's "murder" without watertight evidence, what's to stop George turning the tables and making something up about Liam, or you or me? To give them an equally plausible suspect? He could so easily say he saw one of us argue with Declan, or heard one of us threaten him. Stack the evidence against us. George has made a career of being convincing. If he's going down he'll take us with him. You want to be damn sure about this, Lizzie. Otherwise we might all pay the price.'

'Oh,' said Lizzie. Her mother was right. There was no room for error here. It was all or nothing.

'And there's another thing.'

'What?'

'Leaving here isn't that simple.'

'It is! We can just grab our things and go!'

'Lizzie, you're a smart girl. Think about it. Getting out of here means walking all the way out to the gate and then on down that mud track. Then we'd need to hitch a ride to town or hope a taxi can find us in the middle of nowhere.'

'We can do that.'

'Of course we could try to. But all that before George starts wondering where we are? You think that's doable? Even if we call the Guards the minute we hit signal, that'll still be about forty plus minutes that we're missing. If he realises we're gone he'll know exactly what's up. Then what? He'll come after us. We'll have no mobile signal, no transport, and unlike George we don't know the land. We'll be sitting ducks. He'll understand Maggie's disappearance, she's got her money, she's gone. Us, he'll know we're onto him.'

Lizzie said nothing in response. He would try to stop them. He had everything to lose by letting them go.

'But we have to try, don't we? What other choice do we have?'

'Well, there is another option.'

41

'And what option is that?'

'Waiting.'

'Waiting? What?'

'I think we should wait until tomorrow to go.'

'No, Mam! We have to get out of here. Now.'

'Listen to me. The taxi is coming back for us all tomorrow anyway. It's ordered. We just sit tight till then, act as if all is fine. Then we all walk off the estate and get to Castlebar as planned. There we can get away from him. We'll be in civilisation, our phones will be working, the Garda station will be right there. Think about it, Lizzie.'

'Oh, God, I already agreed to stay here one more night to give Maggie the chance to get her money. I don't want to stay a moment longer!' Was this how it had been like with her? At her worst? Taking, taking, more and more. Pushing Claire to her limits?

'You're forgetting something.'

'What?'

'You need that watertight evidence; you need something else to convince the Gardaí of your theory. I was being flippant earlier, but maybe there is something here that you can use? Staying means there's time to find it. I could help? If the safety of this family and making sure George pays for his crimes is what you really want, this is the way to do it.'

'If we do that... What now then? We just go down there and pretend everything is fine? I don't know if I can do that. Even if it is the best option.'

'We can do it. I believe we can. George isn't suspicious of us, we're not in any immediate danger.'

'What will we say about Maggie? Won't it be weird that she's just gone?'

'I'll come up with something. I suspect George will be so happy she's gone he'll listen to anything I have to say.'

Lizzie looked about the room. Was she really going to agree to stay yet one more awful day? Reluctantly she admitted it was the best way. If, as her mother had said, she really did have her family's safety, and justice, as her motivation.

'Fine.' She went to the door. 'Fine.'

Lizzie and Claire trooped back down the stairs. Halfway down, they looked at each other and put smiles on their faces. They came out into the kitchen. George was standing by the fridge, peering in. He looked up at their arrival.

'Ah! That's where you got to.'

Claire walked over to her husband and kissed him on the cheek.

'Sorry, sweetheart. I was just checking that Mia hadn't forgotten anything.'

'What?' George furrowed his brows.

'From her room.'

'I'm confused.'

'Oh, I thought she said she was going to talk to you as well.'

'About what?'

'She wasn't feeling great. I told her not to worry, to take it easy upstairs until she felt better, we'd look after ourselves. But she said that if she wasn't going to be well she preferred to go home. So she took off. To be honest with you, I didn't think she looked that bad. Felt a bit like an excuse...'

'Oh right, oh, I see,' said George. 'Right. I thought she was looking a bit peaky. But maybe don't hire her again, not very reliable...'

'No, I'm not impressed.'

George's shoulders relaxed. Lizzie could see what her mother meant. George's body immediately loosened. His eyes, always bright, beamed as if someone had just turned the dimmer switch all the way up.

'Well, it's coming up on lunchtime,' said Claire, turning and heading towards the fridge. She squeezed Lizzie's hand as she went. 'I will pull something nice together for us. It's not my first rodeo.' She looked at Lizzie and George and smiled.

'And then Freya and I can do dinner tonight, too!' said George. 'That will be a bit of fun for our last night.'

'I think that sounds great, don't you, Lizzie?'

'Definitely,' said Lizzie, smiling as best she could. An Oscar would never be in her future, but hopefully she could manage some level of fakery for the next twenty-four hours.

'Excellent, excellent.' George clapped his hands and practically did a jig about the kitchen. Then he stopped and frowned. Lizzie and Claire looked at him.

'What's up?' asked Claire.

'We might be eating inside tonight, though. I heard the forecast on the wireless. A summer storm might be on the way.'

The three of them looked out the kitchen window at the clear blue sky. Not a cloud to be seen.

'Really?' said Claire.

'Forecasts are always wrong. But even if it isn't, getting to eat in the dining room will be a treat. Especially for our last dinner for this visit. It'll make it special.'

'It will,' said Claire. 'That's a lovely idea.'

'Okay, we have a plan! Great stuff,' said George. He looked around the kitchen. 'Let me help you with lunch, darling. We'll have it rustled up in no time.'

Claire beamed at George. Lizzie was amazed at her mother's ability to seem so unperturbed. As if nothing was going on beneath the surface. She'd never have guessed. The Oscar might be heading her way. Lizzie watched her for a few moments. She was *very* good at this. Acting. Pretending. Had been the whole time they'd been here. Lizzie felt an uncomfortable twist in her belly. The thought was unsettling. Claire had also managed to get Lizzie to agree to stay yet one more night. Manipulation an addict would have been proud of. Using family love and loyalty like a crowbar to open her box of needs and desires. Her mother was meant to be unimpeachable. The safe harbour in every storm. Where was Lizzie without that? Adrift in a tempest, that's where.

A quieter affair than most of the meals, lunch passed with subdued chatter. The incident with the deer had upset everyone. Lizzie could pass off her own troubled mood as having the same root as the rest of them. No need for as much pretending as she feared.

George passed a carafe of water down the table. Lizzie watched as it moved from hand to hand. It made her think of the whiskey decanter, up in her rucksack. Evidence, but the wrong kind. She needed to search for something that would point away from her family and towards George. What did that look like? There was no internet here, so there wouldn't be any incriminating internet searches. Might there be a suspicious book about poisonous plants? A careless bookmark left at just the most incriminating page, a note scribbled in the margins? Unlikely — George would never be so careless. This wasn't a stupid crime novel. More promising maybe would be looking for evidence of Grace being wealthy. And what happened to this money if it existed. Or some hints at the other women Maggie had mentioned. She could search George's private files in the library. She'd have to dig.

Lizzie felt a cooler breeze bite at her bare arms. She looked at the sky beyond the trees and saw the first hint of clouds gathering in the distance. The forecast looked like it had, in fact, been correct. That crackle of electricity in the air that accompanied an impending summer thunderstorm seemed to dart through the air around her. She felt it in her own cells too, throughout her body. She felt jumpy, full of charge, a dangerous current in her fingertips, sparking.

Lizzie wanted this all to end. She stared at the carafe of water on the table. Part of her thirsty for a biblical miracle where it changed to wine. She shivered again, but this time not due to the breeze. She'd been horrified at her temptations earlier, repulsed by the impulse. But not quite so much now. Wishing water into wine. The change in her restraint horrifying in itself.

'Can I pass that to you?'

Lizzie jumped as Hudson's voice intruded on her thoughts.

'What?'

'You were staring at the water, can I pass it to you?'

'Oh. Right. No, no thanks. I was just miles away.'

'No worries. Understandable.' He scooped up a forkful of salad. 'What are you going to do with yourself this afternoon?'

'I don't know,' Lizzie said. *Look for incriminating evidence on George, most likely.* 'Read another book, perhaps?' she said instead.

'Good idea.' He smiled and then looked across the table. 'Claire, what about you?'

'I might grab a last little bit of time in the walled garden. It'll be a few weeks before George and I get back down here, so I want all the time I can get.'

'That sounds like a nice plan.'

George coughed.

Everyone looked at him.

'Hudson, you've put me in mind of something we need to talk about. That we haven't and probably should have sooner.' He looked around at everyone, lingering on each face. 'We're leaving tomorrow and there is something we have to do this afternoon. And if it's going to rain, we shouldn't put it off any longer. We need to bring our... guest in the icehouse... and lay him to rest in the family plot. I'm going to need a few volunteers. I'm sorry to ask.'

'I'll help,' said Hudson immediately.

'Me too,' said Freya, who had been uncharacteristically quiet all meal. Her eyes had flicked back to the lawn a number of times during lunch, Lizzie had seen her. Looking at where the deer had died.

'It'll be hard, physical work, my dear,' said George, softly.

Freya flexed her right arm, her bicep bulging. 'I'm yoga strong, Daddy. Trust me, I can help.'

'Okay, thank you, dear.'

'I'm coming too.' It was Liam.

'No. And I mean it this time,' said George.

'He's my dad. I need to do this.'

George looked at Claire, his eyes searching hers.

'Mam,' said Liam, turning to look at her. 'I'm doing this.'

'Okay,' she said.

'Right, then,' said George. 'But neither of you are allowed.' He pointed at Claire and Lizzie. There was a heaviness, rock hard, in the pit of Lizzie's stomach. She was out of tears for her father and for herself. Perhaps they would come back later. Right now her emotions were all about survival. Getting through the next twenty-four hours. She would take George's pass on that grim task.

Everyone finished up their food without ceremony. Eyes

flicked to the skies continuously, anxious about the coming rain. George stood, and pushed in his chair. The grave-digging party followed suit.

'Hudson, help me with shovels first, okay?' Hudson nodded and the pair of them headed to the outhouses. With a funeral hush, Claire and Lizzie brought the lunch dishes in. When they emerged again, George and Hudson were back with their tools, looking like sentries with their rifles, standing to attention on the lawn. Liam and Freya joined them.

'We'll see them off,' said Claire to Lizzie. Like troops off to war.

'Sure.'

They followed the mute procession as they entered the woods. The grey clouds that had been in the distance before lunch were advancing quickly, their effect obvious even here, beneath the thick leafy canopy. The light was lower, gloomier. Reflecting the mood.

Claire and Lizzie stopped, watching as the others kept going, off into the distance.

Lizzie looked up. Above her she heard what sounded like the beating of a thousand drums.

The storm was here.

42

'Now's your chance, Lizzie, they're all out of the house and they're going to be some time. You couldn't have planned it better. Go get some evidence.'

'But what about the rain? Will they stick to the plan if it gets too wet? What if they decide to do it later when the rain stops?'

'I think they'll just get on with it, it has to be done. But I'll wait here for a while and keep an eye out in case they return. I'll come warn you if they do. So, go, hurry, we don't know how long you might have.'

Lizzie looked towards the house, along the dim path. She could see the rain fall beyond it. She started to run.

'I'll help you once I'm sure they're not coming back,' called Claire after her, shouting to make herself heard as the rain beat down, heavier and heavier.

'Thanks,' cried Lizzie over her shoulder.

Reaching the edge of the forest, the trees thinned enough that raindrops found their way through, falling on Lizzie. And as she dashed from the edge of the lawn, up the terrace and in through the kitchen door, she was soaked. Dripping onto the kitchen tiles, she pulled her plastered hair back off her face. She grabbed a tea towel from beside the sink and dried her face. She was soaked through and needed to change before she could do anything.

Lizzie headed upstairs. In her room she opened the wardrobe and pulled out her bag, which she'd left sitting there at the bottom. She crossed to the bed and pulled it open, dipping in for a new T-shirt. Expecting to feel the decanter wrapped up at the bottom. Her fingers went deeper than she expected. In fact, the bag felt lighter than it should. Upending it, dumping the contents on the bed, they all tumbled out. The hoodie was there. Flecked still with her father's dried blood. But the decanter was gone.

Lizzie stood and stared.

Someone must have taken it. Freya knew she had it. But hadn't she dropped it where Hudson, Claire and even Maggie could have seen it too? And if they had, well, then George or Liam could have been told about it. She could hear the hushed tones – 'Would you believe what I saw Lizzie with?'

'Dammit!' Lizzie yelled. She spun around, as if the decanter might just be in the room. That she'd forgotten she'd taken it out and put it somewhere else. But she knew she hadn't. She'd have to search for it too, as she looked for the evidence against George.

And not worry too much that someone else had a plan.

Pulling on fresh clothes, she stepped out onto the landing. Looked at all the doors. She'd look about George's room first.

Everything was white and teal in George and Claire's room. What little that was in here. Another minimal space. Two bedside tables with one drawer each and a small wooden wardrobe. A bed. That was all. She checked the bedside tables first. Nothing. Just the usual creams, earplugs, tissues. Nothing strange or useful. Then the wardrobe. But it held even less. Claire's clothes and George's. Nothing more. No evidence nor whiskey decanter secreted away. She stepped back out onto the landing. Crossed over to Freya and Hudson's room.

She stood in the open doorway. Surveyed the space. Neat, with sea green the chosen tones in here. Hints of the teenage Freya remained. Photos stuck to the mirror of her dresser. A poster on the far wall. Would George really have hidden something important in here, in his daughter's room? It felt unlikely. But Lizzie still checked drawers and wardrobes. Any nook or cranny. Saw nothing to raise her suspicions. And there was no decanter here either. She pulled the door to behind her, then headed for the stairs. The library was far more likely to yield something useful anyway.

Lizzie paused as she passed Liam's door. If there was nothing in Freya's room, what were the chances there was something in this, one of the guest bedrooms? Probably not high, but at the very least she wanted to check for the decanter.

She went in, finding the room just as messy as her last visit. Even though she knew Liam was smarter than that, she still went first to the chair with the pile of clothes from yesterday. Of course the phones weren't still there. She searched the rest of the room. Her brother's bags, the furniture in his room. Nothing. No decanter. No smoking gun with regard to Grace's death. But weirdly, no burner phones either. Anywhere. It felt like Lizzie had imagined that meeting in his room, the phones hidden under a dirty T-shirt. Puzzled, but under pressure, Lizzie left the room and headed downstairs.

To the library. George's domain. She felt that surely, there, she would find something.

She stepped into George's sanctum. So dark, the storm clouds acting like blackout blinds. She flicked on a lamp, but not the full ceiling lights. Lit up, those French doors would give too clear a view of her inside as she searched. And if someone came back unexpectedly, she would be on full display.

Lizzie surveyed the room. Where to start? There was the

desk under the window, and all the shelves. Seeing as he'd hidden the letters in a fake book, this was where Lizzie went first. On tippy-toes she ran her fingers along the top rows of books, pushing every book in turn, waiting to feel the telltale lightness of a hollowed out edition. Then the next row down. And then next. Speeding through all the shelves, she stopped at one or two, but she was mistaken. They were just the same as the others beside them. It took time but she came to the last book and there was nothing.

She moved to the desk. Sat in his wooden swivel chair. It was an oak pedestal desk, a drawer unit on either end. Turning to the left set, Lizzie pulled the first one open. Papers. Lots of them. She riffled through them. Bills. Invoices. Quotes for building work. Nothing leapt out at her as strange. She moved to the next drawer down. A deeper drawer. Nothing here either. Just stationery. Catalogues. A few copies of some magazine about renovating old heritage buildings. Nothing to do with anything other than George's obsession with this house and grounds. As she closed that drawer she swivelled around, checking again that there was no one out there, watching her go through George's private papers. The rain was coming down now as if it was the end of days. Bouncing off the terrace surface like pipes below had sprung a leak. Lizzie wondered how much protection the trees in the graveyard were giving the others.

She swivelled back around and turned to the drawers to the right. Again she searched the top drawer first. Rubber bands. Staplers. Post-it notes. A collection of biros. It couldn't have been more mundane. She slammed it shut. Dragged open the last, her irritation driving her. Here there were suspension files. She rooted through A to Z, finding slightly more interesting fare – George's birth cert was one. He was a few years older than she had imagined, fifty-nine, a stray thought that he looked well on it passed through her head. Next to it was Freya's cert. Lizzie scanned it quickly. She stopped at the entry for mother's name.

It wasn't Grace Butler. Instead, it listed Grainne Ann Butler as *Mother*. But Lizzie shook her head. Grace was just the anglicised version of Grainne. People went by different versions of their names all the time. It said Elizabeth on her own birth cert. This wasn't the brilliant clue to help unravel it all. In a fit of temper Lizzie slammed the drawer shut.

She looked up. Looked over at the fireplace and the photo of Grace looking back at her. With that half laughing look on her face.

Don't laugh at me, Grace, I'm trying to help you.

Beside the photo, on the mantel, was a dark polished wooden box. Lizzie stood up and went over to it. There was a small brass keyhole in the front but when Lizzie tried to open it, she found no resistance. It wasn't locked. This spot was the darkest part of an already dark room. She took the box over to the window to see what was inside properly. Laying it down on the green leather inlay of the desk, she lifted the lid.

She took out a tiny silver bracelet. Then a couple of photos of a chubby blonde baby. Following them came a piece of blanket, a soother, a downy soft blonde curl. The opposite of a smoking gun. Something utterly innocent. This must be Freya's baby memento box. Lizzie slumped down in the desk chair. Disappointed but somehow soothed by the innocence of this trove. She picked up the curl, wound it between her fingers. She heard a sound from outside, and turned. Claire, from the trees, making the dash towards the kitchen back door. Lizzie gathered up the baby items, started to put all them back in the box. The curl went last. Lizzie paused. Stared at the curl as it rested on top of all the other baby memorabilia. Hair... hair was often used as evidence. Wasn't it? They could tell a lot from it. They could tell if you'd been doing drugs, couldn't they? She'd heard some of the inmates talk about that at St Brigid's. How worried families had tested them that way. Were able to tell that they'd been using. And what they'd been using. Evidence. Solid, irrefutable evidence.

Drugs.

Poison.

Same difference, no?

43

Lizzie placed the box back on the mantelpiece and looked at the photo of Grace. It had been eighteen years since she'd died. What were the chances there was any hair left somewhere in the house? A hairbrush young Freya had kept as a memento? A lock of hair snipped and saved by a 'grieving' George? And if such things existed in Butler Hall, where would they be? She'd already searched the house, and areas most likely to have those things. And she hadn't spied anything.

Lizzie sank into the wingback chair that sat with its back to the door. She'd been excited for a moment, about Grace's hair evidence. Thought she'd come up with something smart. But the only place she knew for certain that there was likely a crop of Grace's hair was out there, in the graveyard, where the others were now. Perhaps they could do her a favour, and bring Grace up as they sent her father down. Lizzie shivered at the gruesome thought.

She should search the house again. Not just for hair, but anything. Lizzie reminded herself that she hadn't found the decanter yet either.

The door opened behind her.

'Lizzie? Are you in here?'

'Jesus!' Lizzie hissed. 'Mam... don't do that to me!' She peered around the chair at Claire, who also looked a little startled at her appearance.

'Sorry, hon.'

'Are they coming?'

'No, no sign. They must be going for it despite the conditions.' Claire rounded the chair and sat down opposite her. Her hair was damp and dripping.

'Have you turned up anything?' she asked Lizzie.

'No.'

'Keep looking, they'll be a long while yet. It's a big job. And it's so wet.'

They looked outside and watched the rain. Soothed by its soundtrack.

Lizzie sighed.

'I thought I had some inspiration, to find some of Grace's hair – in a keepsake, hairbrush, anything. That it could be tested and show she was poisoned. But I didn't notice anything on my sweep of the house that might have some. I wasn't looking for it then though... I'm going to look again, specifically. And I should go through everything in here again, in case I missed anything.'

The first roll of thunder rumbled outside. An angry shaft of lightning lit up the sky. The library was illuminated by a crisp white light, brighter than it had been at any other time.

'I think George is going to get away with it,' said Lizzie.

'Don't,' said Claire. 'You'll look again, you'll find something. And I'll help, I'm here now.'

'And I mean all of it, Mam, too. Not just Grace. Dad. Unless we find something I don't think we could even go after him on the scams.'

'Why not? We've plenty of evidence on that.'

'Remember what you said about him lying about one of us arguing with Declan? He might pull that out to punish us if we try to get him on the scams, if we can't find anything on Grace. If he's going down for the women he swindled, due to us, what's to stop him deciding to drag us down for murder? He could turn the tables on us.'

'Then we'll definitely have to find something on Grace. Let's not give up hope just yet.' Claire hopped up. 'Right, where do you want me to start?'

Lizzie followed her lead and stood.

'Okay, you check the bedrooms? Looking particularly for anything with hair. I'll go through everything in here, again.'

Claire hurried out of the room. Lizzie headed for the shelves and this time took the books down one by one. Inspected them all individually.

Claire reappeared forty minutes later. Put her head around the door. Shook her head.

'Nothing, I'm afraid.'

Lizzie put a book back on the shelf and shook her head too.

'Still nothing here either.'

The pattern repeated itself for the next hour. Searching the entire house. Every room. The living room. The drawing room. They even checked the half-renovated spaces in case they were hiding something.

They found themselves in the kitchen. Lifting pots and pans. Looking into the darkest corners of the presses and drawers.

They looked at each other. Neither willing to admit defeat. Neither willing to acknowledge that leaving the house as things stood right now – empty-handed – meant George got away with it. Got away with everything. And, he would be free to keep doing what he was doing with no repercussions.

A flash of movement caught both their eyes. They looked out the kitchen window. Freya was making a break for it across the grass.

'Freya!' said Claire.

'There's nothing more we can do,' said Lizzie.

Falling through the door with a gasp, Freya bounded in, soaked through. Muddy splashes on her bare legs. Dirt under her fingernails.

'Wet!' she yelped. 'So wet out there, guys.'

'We noticed,' Claire said with a smile. Like a switch being flicked, Claire was ready for the cameras to start rolling again. Lizzie ignored the gnawing tug in her belly at the sight of it.

'How is... everything?' asked Lizzie, throwing Freya over a tea towel. Trying not to look at the signs of digging and disturbed earth on her.

Freya dried her face and, catching her breath, looked at Lizzie.

'Yeah. They're getting there. Nearly done really. I've come back to make a start on dinner. So it's not too late. I suspect the others will be along in half an hour or so. Right, I'm going to have a shower and then come back down and get chopping vegetables.'

Leaving a wet trail behind her, Freya left the room.

Lizzie stared out of the window, watching the rain batter the glass. Once the others were back, that was it. They could try to keep sneaking around and keep looking. But they'd had the house to themselves all afternoon and turned up nothing. They'd been over everywhere multiple times. And found nothing. There was no smoking gun here. Lizzie had been naive. George wasn't that stupid. He'd been careful.

Lizzie thought about the evening as it stretched out ahead of her. A slap-up meal to celebrate the end of their weekend. George at the head of the table, laughing and joking, full of the joys of life. And she'd have to sit there and take it.

44

'Sit! Sit!' George said as he placed more dishes down on the already laden dining table. The glorious smells mingled oil and water with Lizzie's misery.

Lizzie tried not to clench her jaw and scowl at George. She could barely stand to be in the same room as him. He was going to get away with this and all the while he would never even know he was at risk. Without a clue how close to the precipice he was. No idea that Lizzie was privy to his dark secrets.

The door pushed open. Newly showered and cleaned up, Hudson and Liam appeared.

'Welcome, young men! Join the party.' George hustled over to them and, arms outstretched, directed them to their seats. The dining room door opened again, this time Freya appeared. Wisps of her blonde hair mussed at her hairline, and her cheeks rosy from the warm kitchen and hot cooker.

'This all looks amazing, sweetheart,' said Hudson.

'Oh, it was Daddy just as much as me! I can't take all the credit.' She placed a bunch of serving spoons down on the table, in between all the bowls of food. 'Hopefully it tastes as good as it looks, now.'

'I am sure it will.' Hudson grabbed her free hand and kissed it. Freya giggled and blushed. George looked on, soppy-eyed.

'C'mon, Daddy, let's bring in people's mains.' Freya trotted out of the room, a wink at her husband as she left, George in tow.

Claire passed them at the door.

'Everything smells fabulous, Freya,' she said.

'Thank you, Claire,' said Freya as she disappeared.

'I helped too!' said George, pretending to be offended.

'You're brilliant, darling, don't worry,' Claire said and George laughed, kissing the top of her head as he passed. Lizzie gripped the table, her tummy lurched watching George touch her mother. The Butlers left the room.

Claire walked along the table. Stopped at Lizzie and rested her hand on her shoulder. She pulled out a chair next to her – an empty space between Lizzie and George – and sat.

'Hang in there,' she whispered.

George and Freya bustled back in, placing plates in front of diners.

'That one's for Hudson,' said Freya, directing George. 'It's one of the vegan ones.'

'Okey-dokes,' said George, placing the correct plate in front of his son-in-law.

One more round trip to the kitchen and everyone had their dinner in front of them. Freya dipped out of the room one more time. When she came back a moment later, Lizzie could see that she was hiding something behind her back. Sure enough, as she rounded the table, Freya produced two bottles of wine. Lizzie's heart plummeted. Freya addressed everyone, but looked at Lizzie.

'Guys, so, Hudson and I picked these bottles up at duty-free on our way over, before we knew the situ, and that we would be keeping a dry house for the weekend. Obviously we're super respectful of that, and Lizzie we really admire your strength of character and how you've overcome all your challenges. But we were wondering, seeing as it's our last night here, and it's been a pretty tough day for everyone... We wondered if maybe you'd be okay if the table had a glass or two? Anyone who wants one. But, Lizzie, it's entirely your call. If you aren't comfortable, I will put them away again.'

Lizzie felt all eyes on her. Most of them disguising their desire for a glass of wine behind a thin curtain of concern for her. Lizzie didn't care. She didn't care about anything much right now. Everything was going so far wrong, what difference if all around her, her dinner companions drank? She was tempted to suggest that they strike up a joint while they were at it. Under the table, Claire sought out her hand and gave it a gentle squeeze. Lizzie looked down at her plate and straightened her knife and fork. Moved her napkin so it sat at a perfect right angle.

Claire spoke up. 'Freya, you're so good but—'

'No, Mam,' Lizzie interrupted her. She took a deep, slightly shaky breath. 'It's okay, everyone have a glass, if you'd like.'

'Are you sure?' asked George, frowning. 'We don't want to force you. And you seem out of sorts this evening.'

A devil was now sitting on Lizzie's shoulder. A reckless creature, a product of her misery. He was a companion she'd grown very accustomed to over the years. He whispered the secrets of the old destructive patterns in her ear. She remembered him from when she wanted to punish herself. When she felt bad. It had taken a weekend for the good work of St Brigid's to come undone – though Lizzie felt hard pressed to think of a scenario more stressful than the last few days here. She'd a feeling that if she ended up back in rehab and explained the situation to her therapists, they'd all be 'fair enough'.

She could see from the corner of her eye an anxious Claire. Lizzie squeezed her hand back.

'Don't worry,' she whispered. *Do worry*, said the voice in her ear that only she could hear, *worry about everything*.

With a pop, a cork was extracted from one of the bottles. Soon the old familiar glug of alcohol being sloshed into glasses joined the soundtrack of chat and laughter and rain lashing against the windows. The heady, potent aroma of red wine began to entwine itself with the cornucopia of scents from the meal. But even in the mêlée of smells, Lizzie could pick it out clearly. She watched as glasses were raised to lips. Bowls of hot delicious food were passed around. Each dish more appetising than the last. Around the table there wasn't a sense that wasn't stimulated and Lizzie fought a dizziness from the overload. She kept her breath even and a smile on her face.

George tapped the side of his glass and stood. Chatter quietened and everyone turned to look at him. He held his wine in his hands.

'So. I just wanted to say a few words.' George cleared his throat. 'This weekend, it hasn't been quite what any one of us thought it was going to be. And if there were prizes for understatements of the century, that might just get the gold. But, despite the challenges, it has been a joy. To be with you all. To be here with my darling new wife, Claire. To meet and get to know your two amazing kids. And my own dear Freya, home again after so long. And bringing a bonus son with her. My cup runneth over.' George clasped his glass with both hands.

'I will keep this short,' he continued. 'I don't want anyone's food to go cold, Freya has done such a good job.'

'You did too, Daddy!' she called from her seat. George smiled down at her.

'Just the donkey work, you are the clever cook. But before I let you tuck back in, I wanted to raise this glass to you all. And I want to raise this glass to Declan as well. Yes, I know. We spent a good amount of time this afternoon, getting him sorted out. It was a hard, physical job. But I know for some people around this table, they've had to do hard, mental work. I just want you, Claire and Lizzie, to know that he is resting peacefully now. It was very dignified. We said a few words for him to the man upstairs. And, if either, or both, of you want to say your good-byes before we go tomorrow, you don't need to be afraid. It's not scary there now.'

Lizzie bowed her head. She couldn't look at him. Fear and rage battled inside her for dominance. She gulped. Feeling a tidal wave of tears surge in her belly. Claire grabbed her hand. Gripped it.

'Thank you, George. Everyone.' Claire looked around the table. Her own eyes, glassy, feverish with controlled tears.

'To you all!' George held his glass aloft. The others lifted their glasses, clinked their neighbour's glass.

'So,' said Claire, still gripping her daughter's hand. Lizzie still battling to control herself. 'Let's talk about happy things. What is everybody going to get up to once we leave? George and I are looking forward to the beach in Mauritius.'

Staring at her food, a new terror occurred to Lizzie. One more horrible layer to this mess. How was Claire going to get out of this? She and Maggie had planned all this before the complication of Declan. Before they knew how dangerous George really was. When they could walk away, victors, without a worry of any serious consequences. But now... Was Claire actually considering going to Mauritius with him? To play for time as she tried to come up with a new, safer exit strategy? And if she did go, would she come home?

45

'To heck with the beach, my dear! I can't wait to visit the Black River Gorges National Park!' chipped in George.

'Always the forests and nature for you, Daddy!' Freya grinned and treated her father to an affectionate eye roll. She then looked at Claire. 'Hudson and I are going to tour the country. I'm going to show him what an amazing land we have here.'

'Lucky you two,' said Claire, smiling.

'Lizzie and Liam, what are you guys up to next?' asked Freya.

Lizzie looked at her brother.

'Getting ready for college,' he muttered, eating another over-full fork.

'Super,' replied Freya and she then turned to Lizzie.

'Lizzie?'

She shrugged. Could say nothing. Too upset for words.

'Job probably?' said Claire, looking at her. Eyes downcast, Lizzie nodded.

'Sounds fantastic. New starts for everyone, it sounds like.'

Chatter took over the table as the wine and good food did their job. All Lizzie could do was eat, try to act normally, and not break down. After what felt like an eternity, the diners finished gorging themselves and one by one pushed finished plates away. Lizzie stood quietly, began to gather the empty plates to the left and right of her. Anything to get out of this room, even if it just meant two minutes' relief in the kitchen.

'Oh, Lizzie, don't worry about those,' said Freya, half standing from her seat.

Lizzie held her hand up.

'No,' she forced a painful smile, 'you cooked. Coffee, anyone?' Making coffee would give her another a brief respite.

Hands went up around the table. Freya requested a peppermint tea.

'Why don't we have our coffee in the drawing room,' said George. With murmurs of thanks to the chef and a couple of yawns induced from overeating, the party all stood and headed for the adjoining double doors to the drawing room.

Claire stood but didn't follow them.

'I'll help you,' she said as Lizzie stacked plates. Lizzie shook her head.

'Thanks, Mam, but I could use space. This is all... overwhelming.'

'Are you sure? I'll just be in there.' She pointed towards the living room.

Claire followed the others, looked back, worried at Lizzie.

Lizzie started hauling plates and dishes and cutlery into the kitchen. Now with only the driving rain, and occasional far-off rumble of thunder, as her soundtrack. The quiet helped but not quite enough; she could still feel the horror of everything in every part of her. And she was going to have to go back in there with the coffees.

In the kitchen she filled the kettle and put it on. Rooted around in the cupboards for a cafetière. Moving. Keeping busy. Relieved by the lack of people. She opened a press, looking for sugar. In front of her a third bottle of wine. It was open too, for some reason. Had Freya added some to the food while cooking? She shook herself, like a wet dog in from the rain. Shook off the visceral reaction she had to the dark liquid within the green glass. The kettle clicked. Furious steam billowing from it. The cafetière sat ready beside it. She took a step towards them. Looked back at the wine. Then, she snatched it. Tore the cork out of the bottle's neck. Put it to her lips and poured the deep red liquid into her mouth, tilting her head back, funnelling it into her as quickly as possible. Barely tasting it. Dribbles of wine, like blood from a thirsty vampire's fangs, rolled down each side of her mouth, down her chin.

She slammed the bottle down. Didn't bother to wipe away the streams of red dripping from her. She stared at the bottle. The astringent alcohol burning her mouth, her gullet, her stomach. Her hand wavered, reached out, to take it again and drink it all. To welcome sweet release. This was how it had worked, this was what she used to do. She snatched it up. Drank again.

With a crack and crash the sky outside lit up. The lightning flash illuminated the entire garden. She put the bottle down. Looked out. For a bare moment she thought she saw the dead fawn. Alive again. Stepping back into the woods.

Lizzie looked at the bottle of wine on the counter.

The spell was broken.

With a grief-soaked cry Lizzie fled from the room. Dashed up the stairs and threw herself into the bathroom. She snatched up the toilet seat lid and bent over it. She rammed her fingers down her throat and made herself sick. The wine and dinner came back up, Lizzie heaving, violently expelling her mistake. Wave after wave.

Eventually, her stomach completely empty, Lizzie collapsed beside the toilet, beads of sweat on her brow, bile and stomach acids stinging her mouth. She tore off some toilet paper and wiped her lips. And then she began to cry. Disgusted at herself.

Horrified to be once more sitting hugging a toilet, her mistakes her master.

But as she tried to calm herself down, staunch the flow of tears, a new emotion forced itself to the fore. Anger. She wasn't here, on this bathroom floor, because she'd been weak. The horror of the past few days was more than anyone would be reasonably expected to cope with. It had been like, in some ways, the horrible days after her father had died the first time. She was here in the same position, literally, as she had back then.

No. No way. Not again. Anger raised its fist.

And she'd been put in this position because of one person.

George.

Her hard fight to reclaim her sobriety, threatened by him. Her father murdered by him. Grace too. Maggie scammed. Her mother now at risk.

Lizzie pushed herself off the floor. Rubbed a towel over her face and stared at her pale reflection in the mirror. Staring at her blotchy face, her long black hair behind her ears, her brown eyes, red-rimmed. Saw the fury in her eyes.

Lizzie realised there was one way.

One way to get that irrefutable evidence.

Get it from Grace herself.

46

Lizzie marched past the drawing room door, hearing the sounds of chat and laughter behind it.

She was going to dig up Grace.

She didn't care how awful that sounded. It was the only way.

Hair lasted a long time after you died. She'd get what she needed if she could bear to do this. Lizzie went into the kitchen, heading for the back door.

'Ah, there you are,' said Claire who was in the kitchen with the kettle in her hand, pouring the hot water into the cafetière. 'Where'd you get to?' She looked up and saw Lizzie's pale but determined face.

'You're not doing well, love. Hang in there. We can get home, so soon. And maybe we'll think of something.'

Lizzie stopped.

'Funny you should say that. I have.' Then she kept on, towards the door.

'Where are you going?' said Claire, alarmed. 'What are you doing?'

Lizzie looked back from the door, looked at her mother and

then around her out the door to the hall. There was no one there.

'I'm going to dig up Grace and get some of her hair for the Gardaí to test.'

Claire stared at her, speechless. Then she laughed.

'I'm not joking.'

Claire's face fell. She looked down at the bottle of wine on the counter. Pointed at Lizzie's T-shirt, where giveaway speckles of wine stains had settled.

'Lizzie. Have you been drinking? Are you drunk? Is this what's making you say this?'

'I've never been more sober.' Lizzie turned back to the door and opened it. The rain had eased, the storm much calmer, as if assuaged by Lizzie's grisly resolve.

'Oh my God – you're actually serious?'

'It's the only way.'

'Jesus, Lizzie. Don't.' Ignoring her, Lizzie stepped out the door. 'Lizzie!'

Claire ran to the door, grabbed Lizzie's arm, stopping her.

'How can you even—'

'It has to be done.'

'There's got to be another way.'

'There isn't. You know there isn't.' Lizzie took a step away from Claire, shaking off the grasp on her arm.

'Wait!' cried Claire. She turned and looked back into the house. 'Let me give them their coffee. I'll tell them you need a breath of fresh air. I'll go with you if you're determined.'

Lizzie said nothing, but stopped. Claire looked at her, then dashed back into the kitchen. She frantically placed the cups and the coffee pot onto a tray, spilling some as she went. With another glance back to check that Lizzie was waiting, she disappeared out of the kitchen.

Lizzie felt the light rain land on her. Felt cooler out here. She had to do this. She breathed deep into her lungs, feeling them expand at her righteous resolve. She heard hurried foot-steps and Claire came back into the kitchen. She followed her out onto the terrace.

Lizzie began to walk in the direction of the outhouses. The men would have returned the shovels there not that long ago.

Claire trotted behind her, trying to keep up.

'Lizzie, we can convince the Guards, come on. This... this is too horrible. We can't go digging her up! You've lost the run of yourself.'

'*I've* lost the run of myself?' said Lizzie, shooting her mother a look over her shoulder. 'I'm not the one who married a murderer in some misguided attempt at revenge. And got us into all this!'

'Lizzie, that's not fair...' Claire stopped.

'Not fair?' Lizzie laughed and dashed for the cover of the trees. Claire followed her.

The dark clouds still covered the sky. Keeping under the canopy it was darker still, as if summer's bright 9 p.m. had swapped with its winter counterpart.

'Yes, it's completely unfair,' Claire continued. Lizzie stopped and turned to face her.

'Can you hear yourself, Mam?' Lizzie pointed her fingers at her ears, growled. 'Can you? That's my line. When you called me on my shit. "That's not fair! How could you accuse me of taking money from your purse!"; "That's not fair! I didn't promise to go to rehab". You've gotten as bad as me! I didn't say anything last night but, honestly, this is getting ridiculous!'

'You're actually accusing me of being like you?' Claire's face screwed up in indignation. 'After what I had to cope with? After how little you cared about what you were putting me and Liam through! The danger you put him in!'

'Oh my God, Mam! Switch the names there! It stands up – this whole bloody situation is just as bad. Have you seen the state of Liam? Have you? And I'm doing just great, wouldn't you agree? How can you not see it?'

'It is not the same! How dare you, Lizzie, how dare you!'

'Christ, was I this deluded? I can only apologise,' Lizzie spat. Storming off down the path. They got to the outhouses and Lizzie pulled open the red wooden door, nearly ripping it off its hinges in her temper. The smell of dank earth hit her nostrils, the shovels, wet and mucky, were leaning against the wall, just inside the door. She tried not to think about what they had done. And were about to do.

Claire stood outside, saying nothing.

Lizzie emerged with a shovel.

'Lizzie, this is an awful plan.'

Lizzie looked back at the shed.

'There's another shovel in there, if you want to help.'

'Dammit,' spat Claire and she stomped into the outhouse and retrieved a second tool.

Lizzie walked, led the way through the trees, towards the graveyard.

They marched on in silence, the occasional raindrop finding its way through the leaves and branches overhead and landing on them.

They came to the small wall of the family plot. The headstones and crosses casting dark shadows. The thinner tree cover here let the dreary light of the stormy evening through. And also the rain, which was getting heavier again. Lizzie pulled open the decrepit metal gate and entered the Butlers' ancient resting place. Rain fell on her, quickly plastering her hair to her head and face, soaking through her thin summer clothes. Claire followed. Getting just as wet. In the corner they could see the fresh grave. Both snatched glances at it, but turned away, tried not to look at it.

'The rain will make digging easier, soften up the ground,' said Lizzie, her mouth a grim straight line. They followed the overgrown path down the small number of rows. Stopped where the newest headstone sat.

Lizzie turned and walked down the grassy path until she stood in front of it.

Grace Butler 1968–2004 Mother, Daughter, Wife. Beloved and Missed she could just read in the gloom.

Lizzie stepped on the foot of the grave. Held the shovel in front of her.

Sorry, Grace, she thought. Forgive me.

Then Lizzie sank her spade into the soft earth just beyond the halfway point. She'd try and just dig up around the top of the grave. See if she could dig down there, create a crack in the coffin lid. Retrieve what she had to that way. Not see too much.

The shovel sank in easily. Lizzie carefully placed the removed earth to the side of the grave. Claire stood and watched Lizzie in her grim determination.

And again. The spade went in, sinking into the dark earth, beetles and worms squirming as she added to the freshly turned pile.

In again. Deeper. Lizzie was thankful for the six months at St Brigid's where they worked on the farm, hard physical work the prescription for what ailed them. Freya wasn't the only one strong and able. Lizzie was used to digging. Used to using her body, her muscles and ligaments, her lungs and heart to find peace of mind. Which was what she was doing now. Just a different kind of peace of mind and a different kind of digging. She was planting nothing. No new life would come from these actions.

Sweat mingled with rain as she went deeper. She wiped her arm across her forehead, leaving a streak of mud there. The spade went in again. Methodically clearing a three foot square. Claire stepped up. On the other side of the grave. And as Lizzie placed the removed earth down, Claire took a shovelful of her own, leaving no moment free from digging. Her efforts weren't as deep or effective as Lizzie's, but they sped the process.

Half an hour passed and neither woman had spoken. Just dug. Getting wet. Being slashed with dirty rain where it mixed with the earth. Despite Lizzie's strength and Claire's help, it was slow going.

'We're taking too long, Lizzie,' said Claire, stopping a while, wiping the sweat and rain from her face. Breathing hard.

Lizzie glanced up at Claire but said nothing. Kept digging.

'We've been gone for a good while already. They'll get suspicious. They might come looking for us. How will we explain the state of us? And if they catch us here! There's no explaining this away.'

'We'll dig for another twenty minutes and then decide.'

'Fine,' said Claire with a sigh. And resumed her part in this macabre dance, scared with each shovelful that it would be the one to reveal their goal.

Returning to silence, only the thud and suck of each sod removed, and the tender tap of raindrops on the leaves above, filling the space around them.

And then a different noise. A thunk as Lizzie's shovel hit something solid. She felt the reverberations all the way through her hands and wrists up her arms and to her shoulders. Claire paled and looked away. They weren't nearly down deep enough yet. Not if they had to go the full six feet. But maybe, thought Lizzie, in a private plot it was different. Shallower.

Lizzie closed her eyes and took a deep breath. Trying to compose herself. She could feel a tremble of horror grow from her toes to her fingertips. The reality of what she was doing somehow only now became really real.

Slowly opening one eye, and then the next, she looked down.

Lizzie frowned. Her racing heart stilled. She stood there, staring down.

'What is it?' asked Claire, puzzled at Lizzie's inaction.

Ignoring her mother, Lizzie took hold of her spade again and started scraping away at the soil in the hole. Then she stopped, looked up behind her, and then once more looked back down into the hole.

'Lizzie?' asked Claire. 'What's going on?'

'Even more lies, Mam. That's what's going on.'

Lizzie threw down her spade and stormed out of the graveyard.

47

'Lizzie! Where are you going? Wait for me!' The squeal of the metal gate swinging on its twisted worn hinge a plaintive addition to Claire's cry.

Lizzie didn't slow down. Even with Claire's frantic footsteps in her ears she marched on through the trees. Claire caught up with her.

'Lizzie, slow down. Tell me what's going on!'

'I'll tell you when I know myself,' said Lizzie, not breaking her stride.

Her mother shadowed her all the way back to the house but Lizzie didn't say another word. She wasn't going to until she was sure. As they stepped out of the woods the screech of the barn owl, ready for a night's hunting, filled the air. They both looked up. The bird glided, a dark outline against the cloudy incoming night sky, swooping soundlessly, searching for prey. Though it had stopped raining, it was still cooler than the previous two nights. The air was thick with the earthy scent of rain on the dry ground and the lingering of ozone after the earlier lightning.

Claire stifled a small groan and wrapped an arm around her middle. This, finally, made Lizzie pause.

'Are you okay?' Kinder words, a truce after their bad-tempered exchange.

'Just indigestion. All of this,' she waved her arm around, 'is churning me up.'

'Hang in there... bear with me.'

They climbed the terrace steps, and Claire turned towards the kitchen door. Lizzie took her wrist.

'No, this way,' she whispered, putting a finger to her lips, directing Claire towards the library doors. Lizzie opened it and they went inside. She switched on the lamp that sat on the drinks side table. A soft umbrella of light illuminated that corner of the room. She turned to the large photo of Grace on the mantelpiece. Walked over and with dirt-caked hands, picked it up, flipped the frame over. She slipped back the three catches that kept the back and stand in place. Lifted it off.

'Ha!' she spat. She shook her head slowly and turned the frame so that Claire could see what she was looking at.

'What?' asked Claire, utter confusion in her eyes. She touched the exposed back of the photo. They both stared at the columns of text on the rear of Grace's image. Lizzie read a few words. It seemed to be an article about some kind of skincare product.

Claire picked the photo out of the frame. Except it wasn't a photo at all. But a page from a magazine. She held it by a corner, its flimsy paper rippling as it hung there.

'Lazy,' said Lizzie, shaking her head.

'Lizzie, now. What the hell is going on!'

'Props. Fakes. That's what's going on. You better put that back.' She held the frame open and Claire put the fake photo back in. Lizzie closed it up and replaced it on the mantel.

Keeping her voice low, she continued.

'I hit roots. In the grave. Large, old, long-term roots. Roots that showed no one had dug up that ground in a very, very long time. Did you notice the old oak tree behind the grave? The one that most definitely didn't just grow there in the last eighteen years?'

'I guess,' said Claire. 'There's a lot of bloody trees around here.'

'The grave is empty, Mam. It's a fake. Like these photos. Like Grace herself.'

48

'Seriously, Lizzie?'

'Yep. All props to support his tragic backstory. How many heartstrings – and then purse strings – did he pluck standing all grief-stricken in front of that "grave"? Mooning in front of these "photos"? Big, vulnerable George and his dead wife. It's pretty smart.'

'So, what, Grace just didn't exist? She's a complete invention?'

'Yeah, that's what I think.'

'No murders? No poisonings?'

'Nope. I'm an idiot. You were right. It was just my wild imagination. All I've done is maybe solve a murder from a hundred years ago. That's it.'

'But there's Freya, she didn't just spontaneously appear, and we've seen her birth certificate, she's a Butler.'

'We also saw her mother had a different name. Similar, yes, but that just means George borrowed the English version of her actual mother's name for his fictional tragic wife. Just like he borrowed her fatal symptoms from the letters. He's obviously not that creative and dug about as deep as that grave for her backstory.'

'Christ, Lizzie.' Wide-eyed, Claire shook her head. Stared at the picture of the smiling blonde woman in the picture. Just some random model, it seemed. Claire looked back at Lizzie. 'Does Freya know?'

Lizzie shrugged.

'Who knows what stories George could have told her? We know she's his daughter because we've seen the birth cert. But we've no idea what became of her actual mother, this Grainne Butler. If she took off when Freya was a small child, who knows what George has been saying to her all these years? You heard what she said at the grave yesterday – that she wasn't sure any more what's a real memory or one she's invented. But, Mam, it doesn't matter. Grainne Butler could live next door and Freya could know all about George's carry-on. It doesn't matter. I've been chasing a poison-giving wife-killer. Who killed Dad. I've been terrified that we are all in danger. Scaring Maggie away. Scaring you. But you can't kill an imaginary person. He's no wife-killer. And that was the foundation upon which I built my theory that he killed Dad.'

Lizzie slumped down into a wingback chair. Felt her damp shorts stick to the leather. Claire sat opposite her.

'No Grace and no wife-murder,' said Lizzie, 'then no reason for me to think he is any more likely than the rest of us to have killed Dad.'

'But someone did still kill Declan,' said Claire. 'And, your reason for suspecting George – that it invalidated our marriage – it still stands and is strong.'

'Yet, to go from scam artist to murderer? It's such a big step.' They both heard it, each using the arguments they'd tried to convince each other with only yesterday.

'No one else has such a strong motive,' pressed Claire. 'I know originally when this all kicked off, George argued we all had motive. But in comparison they're weak. Freya, Hudson? George's reason for them was a bit of a stretch. And it wasn't you, me or your brother either. None of us have done anything suspicious. I know Liam went to the icehouse, but he just needed closure. Nothing more than that.'

Lizzie didn't reply this time. Claire didn't know all the other strange things Liam had been doing.

Claire looked at her, eyebrows furrowed.

'What is it, Lizzie?'

Lizzie let out a trembling sigh. She sat forward in the chair and with two hands pushed back her damp hair from her face. A streak of mud was drying across her forehead.

'There's been odd stuff going on with Liam.'

'What do you mean??'

'I can't believe he's capable of hurting anyone. But I don't know why he's been doing what he's been doing. I haven't any explanations. But...'

With a hesitant guilt she told her everything – the weirdness of him on the first afternoon staring into the woods, the going out into the dark forest that night Declan came back, the burner phones. With the ditching of Hudson and disappearing again in the woods, it painted a strange picture.

Claire stood and turned towards the library door.

'We're going to get to the bottom of this.'

Claire grabbed hold of the top of the wingback chair, winced again. Her other arm hugged her stomach.

'Ah, Mam, you're not okay.'

Claire waved her off.

'I'm fine. I'm fine. C'mon, let's get this over with.'

Lizzie followed Claire. They went out to the hall. They could hear the chatter still coming from the drawing room. It was quieter now, more mellow. Lizzie felt anything but mellow herself. She hadn't thought this nightmare could get any worse. But it just had.

'I'll get Liam, and we can talk to him upstairs. Give him a chance to explain.'

'Okay.'

Claire stuck her head into the drawing room. Hiding as much of her mud-stained self as she could behind the door. George's boom of 'there you are!' and a forced chuckle from Claire followed.

'I got caught in the rain, would you believe. I'll be right back once I get changed.' She pulled out of the room, but then stopped and stuck her head back in. 'Oh, Liam, hon, could I just have you for a minute.'

'Sure, Mam,' Lizzie heard her tired sounding brother reply. Claire looked at Lizzie, her mouth poker straight. Liam emerged and saw both their faces.

'What do you want?' he asked, looking from his mother to Lizzie and back again.

'We'll chat upstairs,' said Lizzie and turned for the stairs.

'What have you been doing? You two look as bad as we did after earlier in the graveyard.'

'We'll explain.'

In silence the three of them walked upstairs, like two Guards leading a condemned man.

'We can talk in my room,' said Lizzie, leading the way. She sat in the dressing table chair and Claire sat on the end of the bed. And though she patted the space beside her, Liam stayed standing.

'What's this all about? You two are acting weird.' Neither Lizzie nor Claire spoke.

'Seriously, what's up?' Liam tried again.

Lizzie began.

'It's about Dad.'

'What about him?' said Liam slowly, looking from one of them to the other.

'You've been behaving strangely.'

'He was killed. We should be behaving strangely. I'm the only normal one by behaving strangely. You're the weird ones being so calm about it all.'

'It's not that.' Lizzie listed all the odd things that she'd observed. Liam's face drained of what little colour it had left. He stood mute and terrified-looking.

'Liam,' Claire spoke. 'My darling child... if there's anything you need to tell us, anything at all, you know you can. Don't you?'

'Anything,' repeated Lizzie.

They watched his expression speed through a reel of emotions, like how they said your life flashed before your eyes before you died. It eventually stopped and settled on despair. His face crumpled. Collapsed. He began to cry big fat ugly tears.

'Oh G-God, you're right... I am responsible. It's my fault. He's dead because of me.'

49

'What?' Lizzie gasped. Her head snapped around to Claire. Had she heard the same thing? Her mother sat there, frozen. They'd come up here because of his strange behaviour, but still Lizzie hadn't expected this. A confession. So bluntly. Lizzie was breathless with disbelief.

'Liam... you can't have?' Lizzie pleaded.

Liam rubbed the backs of his hands across his face, his chest shuddering. Grabbing juddering half-breaths.

'It's... it's all my fault,' he kept repeating. Over and over. More gulps and trembling, Liam teetered on the edge of convulsive tears again.

'You can't have killed Dad. You wouldn't hurt him like that, strike him with that crystal decanter. You just wouldn't. You save earthworms from puddles...' Lizzie croaked out the words.

Claire remained horrified and frozen.

He sniffled. 'I didn't hit him. That bit wasn't me. But I might as well have.' Liam began to wail again, snotty, spittle-flavoured tears.

Lizzie crossed the room and grabbed him by the shoulders.

'What do you mean, you didn't hit him? That bit wasn't

you? You either killed our father or you didn't. What is going on with you, Liam?'

'He'd still be alive if it wasn't... wasn't for m-me,' spluttered Liam. 'Th-that's what I mean.'

Claire stood, joined her children. She took Liam's hand, stroked it. She spoke slowly.

'Tell us what you know. Just tell us.' Liam looked down at his mother. For all his height and age he looked like an over-whelmed toddler. He tried some deep breaths, but only managed gasped shallow inhales. But with each attempt he took in more air and gradually calmed down. He tried a few words.

'He... He t-turned up outside sch-school three months ago.'

'He did what?' Claire gasped. Liam nodded.

'I sorta d-didn't recognise him at first.' Liam rubbed his eyes again. 'I couldn't believe it was actually him.'

'Three months ago?' More nodding.

'What did he want? Why didn't you tell Mam?' asked Lizzie. Liam had known for months that their father was still alive? She couldn't believe it.

'He told me he'd seen the engagement notice for you, Mam, in the paper. He told me he was sorry for disappearing, but he'd only gone so that he could make everything better with the busi-ness. He didn't me-mean to be gone so many years. And he didn't want Mam to marry G-George, he wanted us all back together.'

'Oh Lord,' gasped Claire.

'I was so happy he was alive. And he was so happy to see me. Like, before, we never really got on, not really. And here he was, picking me to reappear to. I felt special. He acted like he actually saw me, like he never did before. I was such an easy target.' Liam started to cry again, quieter tears this time. Lizzie put her arms around him. And he let her. A moment of close-ness, the first time he'd let her touch him since she got out of St

Brigid's. Liam's chest heaved and he stepped back, rubbing his eyes.

'You told him this is where we'd be, is that it?' Lizzie probed gently. 'Is that why he turned up here on Friday?'

Liam nodded.

'Yeah, I sent him messages, until the data gave out.'

'That's what all the looking back was about on the way in and why you went into the woods before dinner on Friday?' said Lizzie. 'Looking for him?'

'When I'd no mobile signal, I didn't know if he'd got my last messages.'

'But what about all the rest?' said Claire, looking at Lizzie. 'Those other things you said, Lizzie?'

'Like what?' asked Liam.

'You've been doing so many odd things. The strange phones. Going into the woods again, late on Friday, and you disappeared during the day out with Hudson and George... and you went back to the icehouse... Plus I saw the phones are gone. Why?'

Liam hung his head.

'I destroyed them. Dad gave me one outside school that day. It was just for us to communicate. When I saw how upset everyone got when he showed up at dinner, I smashed up my SIM. I got worried 'cause I led him here. I didn't want to get in trouble. That's what I was doing out there that night, Lizzie. But then... when he got killed, I got scared. Scared you or the police or someone would see that I led him here. I was afraid they'd think I did it. So I got Dad's phone off his body in the icehouse.' Liam began to tremble at the memory. 'I tried not to look at him, I didn't want to see him like th-that...' This time quiet tears rolled down his cheeks. He shook his head. 'He looked like he was asleep. Then I smashed up his SIM card, buried the phones when George took us hunting. That's what I was doing.'

'Liam, my darling,' said Claire, reaching up and stroking his face. 'Why on earth did you say you killed him? You did nothing of the sort.'

'But he wouldn't be dead if I hadn't led him here, Mam. If-if I hadn't he'd still be alive.' And the tears began to flow again.

'You've been manipulated, you're not responsible.' Claire gathered him to her and rubbed her arm up and down his back, hushing him, soothing him like a small child. She looked at Lizzie over his shoulder with sad eyes.

Lizzie watched her mother hold her brother, her brother whose kind heart was riddled with grief, a twisted grief that saw the fatal actions of others as partly his fault.

'Liam,' said Lizzie. He lifted his head from his mother's shoulder and peered around at her. 'This is no way your fault. And Dad would have found a way here if he really wanted. I imagine if I wasn't locked up in St Brigid's he'd have tried me too. And he'd have succeeded. Don't blame yourself. Really, little bro, don't. You're guilty at most of being too forgiving, too kind.'

He nodded and sniffled. A faintest hint of a softer expression played across his face. But then a dark cloud came after it.

'He'd... he'd no injuries.'

'What's that, hon?' asked Claire.

Liam straightened up. Talked quietly.

'On his hands. And his face. I had to look when I was getting his phone from his jacket. There were no scratches, or bruises. He didn't get a chance to defend himself. George is wrong, it w-wasn't a fight. Someone came up behind him and hit him.'

Claire and Lizzie exchanged glances.

Liam groaned.

Lizzie looked at him, her eyes narrowed. He held his stomach.

'You too?'

'Me too what?' he said, grimacing with pain.

'Mam's stomach was at her. You feeling bad too?'

He shrugged.

'Dunno, it just hurt now. Oooh.' He groaned again. A few beads of sweat pricked at his brow.

Lizzie looked at Claire who was looking paler than she had ten minutes ago. Beads of sweat were beginning to form on her forehead too.

'Did either of you feel unwell before dinner?'

Claire and Liam thought about it and then shook their heads.

'Mam, did the pain you were feeling feel like normal indigestion or did you just say that because it was the only thing that seemed to make sense?'

'Well, I suppose it wasn't the same as normal, but the food tonight was very differ—' Claire's lips parted in shock. Understanding why Lizzie was asking these questions.

'Oh God, Lizzie,' she gasped.

'What? What?' asked Liam, snapping his head from his mother to his sister.

Lizzie looked at him. Nearly as pale as them now.

'I think we've been poisoned.'

50

'Poisoned?' said Liam, frowning. 'Why would we be poisoned?'

'We haven't, Liam, don't worry,' said Claire. 'This is your imagination, again, Lizzie. Look where the last flight of fancy took you.'

'Maybe,' said Lizzie.

'And we've only just decided that George wasn't a poisoner.'

'No, we decided he wasn't a *wife killer*. He's still a criminal. And we've also just ruled out the only other person who was acting suspiciously.' She looked at Liam. 'Sorry, Liam. You were acting odd.'

'That's okay, I was,' said Liam.

'Someone still killed Dad,' Lizzie continued. 'And with what Liam observed about Dad's body – that he'd no defensive injuries – that means he was murdered.'

'Lizzie, come on now... not again...'

'No, Mam. It's true. We still have a murderer on our hands. Look at this – George learns he's got a poison garden yesterday. Which you'll remember he was very excited about. And now today we're sweating, nauseous, cramping? I don't like how this sounds. Do you?'

Claire didn't reply.

'But whatever about the who and why. We don't have time for that. We need to get out of here. We've got to get to a hospital.'

'You thought George was a wife killer? What, Lizzie?' said Liam. Lizzie looked at him. Of course, he knew nothing. Was in the dark about everything. But this wasn't the time to unravel it for him.

'Later, Liam. I'll explain it all. Now we need serious medical attention.'

Claire grimaced again and held her stomach. Lizzie put her arm around her until the pain passed. Claire, pale and clammy, looked up at Lizzie.

'Have you any pain? You seem fine. We can't have been poisoned if you're okay, we all had the same food.'

'I'm fine, but maybe not for long, I don't know,' said Lizzie.

'You didn't have the wine. Maybe there was just something wrong with it? And that's all this is.'

'I didn't have any wine either,' said Liam, 'and I'm sick.'

The wine.

That was it. She'd come straight up here and made herself sick. Vomited back up whatever had been hidden in their food. Her slip might just be what gave them all a chance to survive. Because surviving this wasn't a sure thing. She'd read all the descriptions of what those plants could do to you. Some of them didn't have an antidote. She'd have to pray whichever they'd ingested did. And that the doctors could work out which one it was in time.

'I made myself sick, Mam, after dinner. The splatters of wine you spotted on my T-shirt, you were right, I caved, I drank some. But I regretted it immediately and ran up here to the bathroom and threw it all up. That's why I'm fine. And it gives us a chance to get you two out of here. So, c'mon, while you still can!'

Liam and Claire looked at her with wide-eyed panic. Lizzie grabbed her phone from the bedside table, the charge was low, but there was enough for when they got beyond the estate boundaries to call for help.

Claire groaned once more, her eyes screwing up in pain.

She looked at Lizzie when the wave had passed.

'This really isn't indigestion.'

Lizzie shook her head. 'I honestly don't think it is.'

'If you're right and we've had something from the poison garden. Those plants, Lizzie...' Her eyes widened. She looked at Liam, pale and sweaty. 'Some of them are really bad.'

'I know,' said Lizzie.

Claire didn't move. Her eyes seemed to lose focus.

'This is all my fault,' she said in a quiet voice.

'Mam, come on,' said Lizzie. 'We've no time for epiphanies!'

It was as if Claire didn't hear her.

'We are here, poisoned – poisoned! – because of me and my insane plan. How did I think it was a good idea?' She looked at Lizzie. 'I thought I was getting some sort of revenge on your father. As if sticking it to George balanced up every-thing Declan did to me, to us. But you're right, I've been no better than you at your worst. Worse even, 'cause I've been judging you. And all this time you've been trying to save us. Trying to talk sense into me. You've conquered your demons, and then had to contend with mine. You didn't give up. Lizzie, I am so sorry, and I am so proud of you. I am disgusted with myself.'

'Dad messed us all up.'

'How can you ever forgive me, Lizzie? If we'd got out, like you wanted, we wouldn't be poisoned.'

'Mam, seriously, shut up. You can punish yourself later, I have some tips if you want them, but right now we've got to run!' She grabbed her mother's arm. Dragged her towards the door. Liam followed.

Lizzie opened the door and the three of them crept out. Claire coming round enough to understand what they had to do. Lizzie heard muffled groans from the pair of them as they descended. She kept going. She had to. She had to get them out of here.

At the foot of the stairs, they paused. It was quiet behind the drawing room door.

With a whoosh, the door opened. The trio froze.

'Ah, there you are!' said George, filling the doorframe. 'I was wondering where you got to. It was getting quiet in here. He's nodded off,' George stepped back and pointed in at Hudson who was out cold on the sofa, 'and Freya went off to powder her nose. Poor old George is feeling abandoned!'

'We were just going to do the dishes...' said Lizzie, pushing Claire in the direction of the kitchen.

'Oh nonsense, they can wait, come in here.' He put an arm around Lizzie's shoulder and guided her into the room. Pale Claire and Liam followed. Lizzie threw a panicked look at her mother. They needed to get out of here.

'I thought you were getting changed?' said George, addressing Claire, looking her up and down. He looked closer at Lizzie too, noticing her mucky dishevelledness. 'And what happened to you? Running in sandals again!'

Spinning out from under George's arm, Lizzie dashed to the grand, stone fireplace. The time for pretending was up. They didn't have a nanosecond to lose. Claire and Liam had to get help.

Lizzie dipped down and grabbed a brass poker. Like a fencer she thrust it in George's direction.

'Get back!' she yelled, waving it. George stared at her, frowning. Lizzie gathered Claire and Liam behind her. Never taking her eyes off George. 'Your plan hasn't worked. You might have succeeded in poisoning Mam and Liam, but you didn't succeed in poisoning me! I'm getting them out of here, and there's nothing you can do to stop us!'

George's eyes narrowed further.

'Sorry, what now?'

'Don't play the innocent with me, George. We know all about you.'

'I would hope you do! I'm married to your mother!' George sniffed the air. Leaned closer to her, still smelling. He pointed at her T-shirt. At the drops of wine from earlier that were splattered there. Interspersed with the muck and dirt from the graveyard.

'Lizzie,' he said, 'have you tumbled from the wagon? Do you need some help? Your sponsor if you have one?'

Lizzie cheeks reddened. But mostly from anger. She jabbed the poker in his face. Ignored his accusations.

'Don't try and deflect. We know all about you, George Butler. The *real* you. The unreal Grace. The *imaginary* Grace. The empty grave. Maggie Fitzgerald. And who knows how many others. I'm talking about your scams. We know all about them.'

'Oh now, what is this nonsense?' George blustered.

'George, don't play the fool,' said Claire, anger forcing its way through the pain.

'Claire, my sweetheart, are you all feeling unwell? Maybe you need to go to bed.'

'Don't sweetheart me,' Claire bit. George's face fell. His perpetual bonhomie stalled.

'Claire?'

'I've known since day one. Since before day one. Maggie and I hatched the whole blackmail plan together. *Together*. To get her money back. You've been had, George Butler. You've been beaten at your own game.'

'W-what?'

'And, just so you know – you and me? We're not actually married. That minister was an actor. It was a sham ceremony. Something Maggie told me you're quite familiar with.'

George's mouth flapped open and shut but no words came out.

'Your marriage wasn't real,' spat Lizzie, encouraging Liam and Claire backwards. Back towards the door. 'That means you've poisoned everyone and killed my father for nothing. You can't get your hands on a single penny.'

George looked at Lizzie, stunned. From behind her Lizzie could hear Liam whisper to their mother, 'What? Is that true?' Claire hushed him. Muttered, 'Later.'

George took a step closer to them. Lizzie waved the poker and he stopped.

'Poisoned everyone?' he said. 'What are you talking about? And, what, kill your father? I certainly did not!'

'Don't deny it,' said Lizzie.

'But I didn't, you silly girl! I didn't kill him. Where have you gotten this idea? I'm many things but, by God, I'm not a killer!'

'Why on earth would we believe a liar and a conman?'

'Why indeed, but a stopped clock is right twice a day. And sometimes an inveterate liar tells the truth.' George studied the O'Sheas closely, then stepped back. He sat down, returning to where he'd been on the sofa, next to the sleeping Hudson. He took a deep breath. Intertwined his fingers. He looked at Lizzie.

'Okay, you got me.' He sat back and crossed his legs. He smiled and looked at Claire. 'I'm impressed. That was very clever of you and Maggie. I probably deserved that.'

'Probably?' spat Lizzie. 'You deserve a lot worse for killing my father. I know he was an awful man but that didn't give you the right to kill him!'

'Cut that out!' shouted George. Lizzie flinched at the forceful reproach. Claire and Liam took a further step back. Hudson remained oblivious. 'Where have you gotten this idea that I killed that bloody man? The worst I had planned to do was to pay him off. When I was removing him from the estate. I reckoned he was back for cash and cash would get rid of him. I'm sorry to say it but the person who killed your dear daddy was him.' He unfurled a finger, pointing at Liam.

A grey and sweating Liam shook his head.

'I didn't,' said Liam.

'It wasn't my brother,' said Lizzie.

'Of course you'd say that,' said an irritated George, waving his hand at her. 'But it had to be! It wasn't me. It obviously wasn't you either, you were so bloody keen to go to the cops. Claire never left the bed that night. I was on edge due to your father's reappearance so I slept so poorly. I'd have known if she'd gone off to do the deed. And, I heard someone on the stairs during the time frame when your father was killed. If it walks like a duck, talks like a duck... it had to be him.'

'You're making it sound like the O'Sheas were the only people other than you under this roof two nights ago.'

'My daughter and Hudson had no motive to harm your father, so leave them out of this!'

She looked over at the sleeping Hudson. Well, that was something they could all agree on.

'It wasn't Liam. I would risk my life on that.'

'Well, aren't you—' George stopped. Because Lizzie wasn't listening to him. She'd looked back at Hudson.

'What?' said George, looking over at the sleeping man and then back at Lizzie.

'How long has he been asleep?'

'Oh. Five, ten minutes?'

Handing the poker to Claire, Lizzie dashed over to the sleeping form of Hudson.

'He hasn't stirred and we're being loud. Shouting,' she said, crouching down in front of him. She took the mug that was still in his hands and placed it on the coffee table. She then took his arms and shook him. Nothing. He stayed asleep. She shook him vigorously a second time. No reaction.

Lizzie turned and picked up Hudson's mug. She smelled the contents.

'Who made this?'

'When you guys didn't come back Freya offered to go make another round of teas and coffees.'

'So – Freya made it.'

'Well, yes,' said George slowly.

Lizzie looked over at Claire and Liam. Then at George. And back down at Hudson.

'He's been drugged.'

51

'He's been drugged. And we've been poisoned.'

'What?' said George.

Lizzie looked down at Hudson. Unconscious on the sofa. Unaware of what was going on around him.

...unaware of what was going on around him. Okay, maybe there was one other person besides herself who hadn't been up to something awful or underhand this weekend.

She met George's newly anxious eyes.

'George... Where's Freya? Really, where is she right now?'

'Like I said, she's in the bathroom.'

'No she's not. We were upstairs. There was no one in there.'

'But... but she probably just... stepped out for some fresh air?'

Lizzie stood up. Looked around at her mother and Liam.

'What is it?' Claire asked.

Lizzie looked back at George.

'You know what, George? I think I believe you. Maybe you're not a killer.'

'Thank you. That's what I've been saying!' His smile faded. His brows knitted. 'Why've you changed your mind?'

'Because you're wrong about something.'

'I am?'

'Yes. You said Freya didn't have a motive to hurt my father. But the truth is she did.' Lizzie sat down beside Hudson. Picked up his wrist and felt for his pulse. She felt a flood of relief when she felt it strong and regular. She stared at George who was waiting for her answer. 'Freya had quite a few motives to kill my dad. I'd say, maybe even *millions* of them.'

52

'I don't like what you are suggesting here, my girl!' George stood up. Puffed out cheeks. Eyes blazing.

'Oh, cut it out, George. She's joined the family business, hasn't she?'

George blustered and paced but said nothing.

'It makes perfect sense. Hudson's a scam. Isn't he, George? She's doing to him what you did to Maggie, and thought you were doing to my mother. What you've done to countless others. She's doing what you taught her to do.'

George looked down at the sleeping man.

'He is so very, very rich,' he said quietly.

'My fraudster father probably saw the two of you for the crooks you are. It takes one to know one, as they say. A big fish like Hudson is motivation enough to get rid of the guy who might put it all at risk.'

'No, Lizzie, my Freya couldn't kill someone. She couldn't.'

'I don't think you know your daughter as well as you think you do. She's drugged Hudson. And she's poisoned us with dinner. She's not content with just getting rid of my father, she's trying to get rid of all of us.'

'I can't believe it,' said George.

'You can believe whatever the hell you want, George, I don't care. But we're getting out of here. I need to get Mam and Liam to hospital. And you're not going to stop us!'

'Why would I try to stop you!' George held his hands up. 'I'm a thief. That is all. I absolutely don't want blood on my hands.'

'It's the least you can do to redeem yourself.'

Lizzie ran back to Claire and Liam, grabbing their arms, pulling them towards the door. Paler by the moment, Lizzie saw Claire try to hide a contortion of pain that flashed across her face.

'Let's get out of here.'

She threw a quick look over her shoulder at George, who stood in the middle of the room, as Lizzie, Claire and Liam slipped into the hall. Lizzie glanced upstairs as they passed. Freya had said to George that's where she was going, but they'd been upstairs — there hadn't been anyone in the bathroom. Freya was somewhere else. Doing something Lizzie was sure wasn't something they'd be happy about. Like her father, Freya Butler wasn't who she made herself out to be. Wasn't the perky yoga Insta hippy. Instead, it seemed she had been like many a younger generation brought into the family business. She'd seen bigger opportunities. Seen new ways to do things. Been more ambitious, more willing to take risks...

Through the kitchen, they opened the back door, trying to avoid making any sound. They crept out into the night. It was just after ten thirty and apart from a hint of daylight tangled in the uppermost branches of the trees, it was dark.

'We'll get the quad bike,' whispered Lizzie leading them across the terrace, where lights from windows in the house lit their way. They raced as fast as they could across the lawn and into the trees in the direction of the outhouses. Once in the woods Lizzie switched on the torch on her phone. Running nearly blind, only a wild beam of light from the phone that bobbed and weaved as they ran, they fled single file down the path to the outhouses. Panting, they stopped at the flaking red door of the large outhouse.

'How are you doing?' she asked the others.

'Okay,' said Liam, an assessment which to Lizzie's eyes seemed overly positive.

'Me too,' said Claire, but a wave of pain came over her and she fell against the side of the building, clutching her middle.

'Hang in there,' whimpered Lizzie, pulling the door open. They had to keep going. They had to get out of here. She shone her torch in. 'Dammit!'

It was empty.

No quad bike.

Liam came round the door and looked into the outhouse.

'Where is it?' he said. Lizzie shook her head in the darkness. 'Maybe it's in the other outhouse?' She shut the door and the two of them went to the door of the second stone building. Claire leant against a tree, and even in the dark Lizzie could tell she was looking paler and sicker than she had only moments ago.

'Just hold on,' beseeched Lizzie. Liam pulled at the door of the second outhouse. Unlike the first, it had a padlock on it.

'Shine the torch here,' he said, pointing at the lock. Illuminated, Liam forced his fingers through a slight gap between door and frame. He then pulled with all his strength. Splintering, the door cracked and the lock came off. It swung open.

They stared into the darkness. The quad bike trailer was here. But that was it. No bike itself.

'Oh God,' Liam whimpered.

Lizzie looked at him.

'What?'

He pointed to the trailer. Lizzie, still holding the torch, moved it to see what he saw. She shone the beam of light into it.

It wasn't empty. Something in it was covered by an old painting sheet. But it wasn't covered completely.

A foot.

Poking out from a corner. A white, trainer-wearing foot.

Lizzie, heart pounding, stepped forward. She gripped an edge of the sheet and threw it back.

53

Maggie.

Dead. Rigid and cold.

Lizzie shone the torch on her rigored face. Eyes staring, caught terrified in death.

'What's wrong?' asked Claire, pain in her voice.

Lizzie stared down at the body, unbelieving. Shook her head. Felt tears well. Gone, but not how they'd thought. Had she actually been coming back this morning? And been intercepted?

'It's nothing, Mam, nothing.' Lizzie gulped, battling to contain her shock. They didn't need to add grief and guilt to Claire's burdens. She turned to Liam, held her finger to her lips. He didn't need much prompting to remain speechless. Lizzie leaned over and checked the still, stiff wrist for a pulse. She knew she wouldn't find one. It was clear Maggie was beyond saving and had been for some time.

Lizzie turned away to leave, the beam of her phone bouncing about the interior.

'Gimme the phone, Lizzie,' said Liam.

She looked at her brother. Lizzie handed it to him. He held

the beam of light up and shone it into the back of the space. He let it stop on a metal cabinet on the side of the wall. The door of which was open. Liam was staring at it.

'What's wrong?' she asked, following his gaze.

'That's George's gun cabinet. And it's empty.'

'Shit,' said Lizzie. She could see that the lock was busted. George would have no reason to force open his own gun locker.

They backed out and pushed the door shut behind them.

'What's going on?' rasped Claire. 'Gun, did one of you say gun?'

'Don't think about it, Mam. There are more pressing things to worry about.' Lizzie shook her head. 'The quad bike is gone. Maybe we've gotten lucky and Freya has left the estate for some reason. But wherever it is, we need to start walking and get out of here.'

Lizzie linked her mother's arm, and the three of them started down the path towards the front of the house. Jumpy, their eyes kept darting, following any noise. Any rustle or movement in the dark undergrowth, their heads snapped around. Lizzie sped up, dragging her mother a little. Guiding them towards the way they'd come in on Friday. The phone torch illuminating the way ahead.

The trees began to thin, they were close to where the path would disgorge them by the side of the house. There was another noise in the undergrowth. Louder than all the others. The trio stopped. Each took a backwards step, huddling close together.

Out of the darkness of the trees, a figure emerged. The weak light from the house silhouetting them. Their face in darkness.

Lizzie could feel Claire quiver next to her.

'Going somewhere?' a sweet voice called out to them. Lizzie shone the torch above them, lighting up the area.

Freya.

And she was pointing the shotgun directly at them.

54

'Freya,' said Lizzie, trying to keep the tremor out of her voice. 'Please, is that necessary?' She pointed at the gun.

'I think it is. I can't believe you were going to leave without saying goodbye.'

'Freya, it doesn't have to be like this—'

'Really? I moved the quad bike in case you tried to do a runner. Seems I was right to be cautious.'

Lizzie shook her head.

'We saw what you left there instead,' said Lizzie.

'Ah… She left me no choice. I ran into her as she was coming back. She told me all about you two.' She looked at Claire. 'Very clever, I was impressed. She thought I didn't know about my father's schemes. She thought she was warning me.'

'Did you write the note?'

'I did. I didn't want you to get worried and go looking for her. It was a risk, but no one knows anyone's handwriting any more, in this digital age. I took a gamble.'

'Lizzie, what's she talking about?' asked Claire weakly.

'I'm sorry, Mam, but she killed Maggie. I didn't want to tell you.' Claire looked from Lizzie to Freya, aghast, terror and rage added to the pain in her eyes.

'You play with fire, Claire, what do you expect?' said Freya. 'Anyway, enough. Let's get back into the house. I need you all in your positions.' She waved the long barrel of the gun.

'Positions?' said Lizzie.

Freya shook her head. 'Don't worry about it.'

They shambled slowly back towards the house, Liam shivering, Claire leaning on Lizzie. Lizzie heard the sniffle of quiet tears from her mother. 'I'm so sorry, Mam,' she whispered.

'She is right though,' stammered Claire, 'we were fools. Didn't know what we were doing.'

'Don't, Mam. Don't beat yourself up,' said Lizzie gripping her arm even tighter.

They rounded the house and headed for the terrace steps. Encouraged on by Freya and the gun. Lizzie's eyes darted around. Looking for any chance to escape. But there was nothing. The only thing she thought of was to act sick, like the others. Freya didn't know she'd avoided the poison. Even the slightest edge might help. She mopped her brow.

They stopped at the kitchen door. Lizzie would keep trying to reason with her.

'Let us go, please, Freya. We can tell the Gardaí that all this isn't your fault, that you've been manipulated by your father since you were a child.'

Freya snorted.

'Manipulating me since I was a child? What makes you say that?'

'You know, from Maggie, that we know about George and his scams. But we also now know about "Grace". That she wasn't real.'

'Do you? Well done, that's impressive work for a washed-up junkie.'

Lizzie clenched her jaw, holding back a bitter response.

Right now Freya could say what she liked, they'd have to take it.

'Good old "Grace",' Freya sighed. 'She's served us well. I grew to quite like her. But you don't have to worry about me, Lizzie, in case that's what you're implying. I was well aware that my mother wasn't the oh-so tragic Grace. My mother is Grainne Butler. Well, so-called mother. I think she's on husband number five now, so I suppose she hasn't been Grainne Butler in a long time. Grainne Metcalf, I think she is – I don't know, I haven't had a postcard from Australia or Kuala Lumpur or like, wherever, in some time. Pretend Mummy Grace was always much nicer.'

'I'm sorry you didn't have a good mother, Freya. But I had a pretty crappy father and I'm not holding people up at gunpoint. Or poisoning them.'

'Ah, so you worked out about the poison in the dinner too? I have underestimated you. But not that much. You ate it. Can you believe we've had a poison garden at Butler Hall all this time and we never knew? Thanks for that tip-off, Claire. Turns out it was perfect timing. I really felt the universe was guiding me when I heard that. And then the serendipity, when I had to get rid of Maggie, that it meant I could help make dinner. I didn't have to find a surreptitious way to get the poison into you. You all yummed it up. I couldn't have planned that better.'

'What have you given us, Freya?' Claire gasped. 'Oleander? Foxgloves? Belladonna? Freya, some of these are fatal! Please, tell me! Before it's too late.'

'What would be the point of poisoning you if I just turned around and told you what it was? I don't need you hopping off to the walled garden to grab a natural remedy or whatever. Defeats the purpose.'

'And what is that purpose?' asked Lizzie.

'That would be telling,' said Freya, tapping the side of her nose.

'Please,' pleaded Claire.

'No, I'm sorry. And you've only yourself to blame. If you hadn't left your phone lying around I wouldn't have been able to borrow it to check them all out.'

Lizzie remembered her mother's missing phone on Saturday night, when she couldn't check the time. The night Freya had gone to bed before the rest of them. She must have taken it and then slipped out to the walled garden.

With a nudge of the shotgun she directed them all into the kitchen.

Back inside, Lizzie could see how awful everyone was looking. Liam now seemed to be deteriorating quicker. His face was shiny with sweat, his eyes glassy. He and Claire were leaning against the counter to keep themselves standing.

The weirdest thing was, in the bright kitchen light, Lizzie could see that Freya was looking ill too. Her usually glowing complexion was a mottled mess. Strands of her blonde hair were sticking to her forehead. Her eyes, like the others, were dilated with pain. She wiped her free hand across her brow, soaking up a sheen of sweat. If Freya wasn't pointing a shotgun at them she'd think George had double-bluffed them. Lizzie saw her grimace and hide a grab at her stomach.

'Are you feeling okay?' Lizzie blurted.

Freya glanced at her but said nothing. Just moved to the other side of the kitchen, beside the island, watching them all.

'Freya, darling! Is that you? I need a word—' a familiar voice cried out from the hall and George bounded into the kitchen. He stopped mid-stride. Taking in his daughter and the gun pointing at everyone.

'What... What on God's dear earth is happening here? Freya?' He looked fixedly at his daughter. 'Put down that gun, immediately!'

'Oh, hi, Daddy,' she said, returning his intense stare. 'What's happening here? Good question. I'll tell you what's happening here. I'm cleaning up your mess!'

55

'Mess? What are you talking about?' George came further into the kitchen, closer to the island and his daughter.

'This bloody awful fuck-up of a weekend! You are a disaster. Maggie Fitzgerald and blackmail? And everything else that's happened this weekend because of your stupid actions? Sound familiar? That's the giant mess I'm talking about.'

'I was handling it.'

Freya laughed a harsh, rasping laugh. 'Really? Is that what you thought you were doing?' She threw her free hand up and sighed. 'You've been on the back foot from the beginning. I saw the panic on your face when Claire introduced you to "Mia".' Freya looked over at Lizzie.

'You saw that too, right?'

'Em.' All eyes were on Lizzie. 'Yeah. I did.'

Freya looked back at George.

'You see? Sloppy. I knew something was up then, but I never imagined you'd done something as stupid as marrying her and never mentioned it to me! Ridiculous.'

'It wasn't ridiculous. And I never properly married her. Everything was under control.'

'No it wasn't, Daddy, not even slightly. You can't bluff your way here, I know what you were doing to "handle it". You were giving them everything they wanted! I've been following you. First to the folly, where I heard all about how Maggie was black-mailing you. I saw you there too, Lizzie. You had a ringside seat.'

'You were at the folly?' said Lizzie, surprised.

'Yes, and I got back beside Huddy, just in time to see you fall. That would've been awkward if he'd opened his eyes and I wasn't there.'

'And that's why you were so insistent on going with me to Mam in the walled garden. I couldn't tell her what I just saw if you were there. Didn't you think I'd just tell her later?'

'Oh yes, probably, but I needed time to think, work out what the hell my idiot father had been up to during my absence the last few years. Being an ocean-going, fur-lined idiot, it seems.'

'Come now...' George spluttered.

'I followed you on your hunting trip – I wasn't on some stupid self-retreat. I heard you talking to your broker. It was all over a measly ten k. Oh, Daddy. All this mess for ten k.'

George looked at his feet, didn't meet her eye.

'The roof needed fixing, I thought it would just be a quick one...'

'Well, the roof might be fixed now, but you've been leaking our secrets left, right and centre! And I've been mopping up! Do you know what's at stake, Daddy, do you? Hudson's family is worth nearly thirty million dollars! Thirty million! Remember all our plans for this place? That we used to talk about for hours and hours? Well, I did my part. I stayed in America for nearly three years! Seducing Yanks until I found one rich and stupid enough to marry me. And then I come home to this. You, sloppy and impatient! All I had to do was romance Hudson around this beautiful place for the weekend, and there'd have been a blank cheque for Butler

Hall. We'd landed the big one, Daddy. But you had to mess it up.'

Freya waved the shotgun around, her brow florid with illness. Everyone flinched at the gun's careless pass.

'Please, put the gun down. I didn't raise you to hurt people.'

Freya threw back her pale face and laughed.

'Didn't raise me to hurt people? What are you talking about? I've been helping you scam vulnerable women out of their money since I was five years old! Remember Laura? I liked her. She was nice to me. Trusted you because of me. How much did you get out of her? Twenty-five k? Cleared her out, if I remember correctly. And that Norwegian woman, Frida. Your first ever scam. Always wanted a child, wasn't that it? I was bait. Dangled in front of her. You think she ever trusted anyone again after you? She's led a long and lonely life because of you, I'll bet. And an impoverished one as well! We've her to thank for the drawing room, no? And then all the others I helped you with. I think we can most certainly say you raised me to hurt people.'

'I never resorted to violence.'

'Oh, stop acting as if that somehow makes everything okay, that you're somehow noble for only making off with their cash. And you couldn't even do that right. You do one scam without talking to me about it first and all this happens! And even when it comes back to haunt you, you don't tell me. You should have. I mightn't have gone to talk to Declan on Friday night then. I might have stayed away.'

'Oh, my darling... No. You didn't... did you?'

'Yes, of course I killed him. Who else? We went for a walk. To talk about things. I suggested we stroll to the bathhouse. Nice and out of the way. No one would hear us down there. I grabbed the decanter from the draining board on the way out. Just for safety. Who was this guy? I wasn't planning on doing anything with it.'

Freya turned and looked at Claire. 'We walked and talked. You know, he was telling the truth when he said at the table that he was back for you, and not your money. He was genuinely sorry. When he told me how much he still loved you, and the kids, I knew that was worse than if he was back for money. We couldn't pay him off. And worse still, he was sharp. He had your number, Daddy. He hinted he came back to save Claire from you. Which is funny now, in hindsight. You were the one needing saving! Typical, arrogant men. Thinking they know it all. If either you or Declan had actually talked to the women in your life before doing something, none of this would be happening! Stupid men.'

'Why did you kill him, then?' said Claire. Taking a few steps closer to her on shaky feet. Glaring at her with a ferocity that scared Lizzie. 'Why didn't you just let him take us away? Everyone would have been happy.'

'Yeah, why?' joined Liam. Claire put her arm around him.

'Because, unlike my Daddy, I don't like to leave myself open to blackmail. Your father was a loose thread and a loose cannon.'

'Freya, Freya...' George looked at his daughter as if he didn't recognise her.

Freya shrugged.

'I realised we wouldn't be safe while he was alive. Whether he landed you in it, or decided to blackmail us if he discovered how rich Hudson was – and he would have discovered it – he was going to be a problem. We couldn't risk it, just as we finally landed the big one. What timing. And it was all so neat. When everyone got up the next morning and he was gone – well, he'd just decided to leave, hadn't he? Gone back to being dead. I'd have gotten Daddy to help me dispose of the body later, everything would have been fine. If it hadn't been for you,' Freya pointed at Lizzie, 'and your dogged insistence he had gone nowhere.'

'Sorry I made things hard for you after you killed my father,' sneered Lizzie.

George continued to stare at Freya. Silenced for once.

'Why do you look so shocked, Daddy? What else could I do? You left me with no choice when you didn't tell me about Maggie. I was working with half the information. This is the mess I am talking about!'

'Don't blame me, you shouldn't have done all this,' George groaned, shaking his head. 'Yes, I should have talked to you, especially when it was going wrong. I was embarrassed! My girl, you know I'm a proud man. And I was making it right. I love Butler Hall. It is my everything.' He took a step closer to Freya, his hands outstretched, palms upturned, pleading. 'I've always been desperate to save it. Not let the forest consume it whole.' George looked around the kitchen, making his case to this stricken jury. 'If that selfish bitch Mary Butler had saved this place a hundred years ago everything would have been different. All she had to do was marry that stupid man and the family wouldn't have been ruined. I wouldn't now be the foolish lord of a half-made house, and a relentless forest. Scrabbling around for pennies to save it.'

'Oh God, Daddy, there you go again, blaming Mary Butler for all the family's problems! But if you hadn't found those letters all those years ago you'd never have had the idea to marry for money. You owe her that, at least. She was your inspiration!'

'Her daddy, Charles, was my inspiration. He found the rich sucker.'

'Whatever. Anyway, fat lot of good it did us in the end. I did what she didn't. I've married the rich sucker. And you've put it all at risk. Ironic, no?'

'Sorry to interrupt this Butler thing you've got going here,' snapped Lizzie, 'but can't you see this is all madness?'

Everyone turned and looked at her.

'What?' said Freya, irritated at the interruption.

'There have to be other ways to clean up this mess. Declan's arrival deeply upset us all. You panicked. We understand that. I'm very sure everyone will be happy to stick to the original plan and just walk away. And whatever you've done, putting poison in everyone's food,' said Lizzie. 'We can just tell the doctors it was an accident. I'm sure George will take the blame for it too. It happens.'

'I will! It does happen. Come on, old girl!'

'It's not too late to walk away, Freya, to stop this.'

Freya closed her eyes and held her stomach. She wiped her brow. Took a heavy breath.

'It's obvious you've accidentally poisoned yourself too. Your plan has let you down. You need help like the rest of us. If we go now, we can get to a hospital before it's too late.'

'Well, thank you, Lizzie, for your concern. You've forgotten the little matter of explaining away Maggie too. I'm not sure if we could manage that. But you don't need to worry. Because you're wrong. I didn't take the poison by accident. My plan is fine. In fact, it's going exactly as I hoped.'

56

'You poisoned yourself – deliberately?' said George, bewildered.

'Yes,' confirmed Freya.

'You've lost it, my child!'

'The plan only works if the slate is wiped clean.'

'Wiped clean? What does that mean?' he asked.

Freya didn't elaborate.

'George,' said Lizzie. 'I think that means she's planning on killing everyone.'

'No! Surely not...?' said George.

'Yes,' Freya nodded. 'If you're going to be so blunt.'

'Sweetheart...'

'I don't actually want to do this, Daddy,' she said, looking at him. The shotgun pointed in his direction. 'I really don't see I have any other choice, though. I'm doing it for Butler Hall. Which I know you'll understand and approve of. Things have just been getting worse all weekend. I've been thinking and thinking. I even meditated on it. That stuff isn't bad, I'm going to keep it up. The plan came to me then, in a moment of transcendental clarity. I needed to just rip the band-aid. Go big or go home. And I realised the job's already been done. It needs a little staging, but all the pieces are here. It's really so neat. It feels like the universe sent it to me. Listen, tell me what you think, I'm sure you'll agree it's perfect...'

'I have my doubts,' muttered Lizzie. She glanced back at her mother and brother. Both struggling. 'But do tell us.'

'This is how it went down.' Freya pointed the barrel of the gun at George and then over at Claire. 'Declan has shown up, causing a huge problem with you two, the newly-weds. He's convinced you, Claire, to try again and go back to Dublin with him. Leaving my poor, dear father devastated. Consumed with anger and jealousy.'

'Freya, please...' said Claire.

'Don't interrupt. Daddy decides he won't take it! He kills Declan. Claire finds out what he's done and she's horrified, she is leaving him now for certain. But Daddy has plans for her too. If he can't have her, then no one can. And he's not leaving anyone else behind either! He'll take everyone out with poison in the dinner. Though sadly for him, he won't get away with it. Claire – or maybe Liam, I'm not sure – will have the last word.' Freya nodded at the shotgun. 'Would you like to be the one, Liam?'

Liam's eyes flared with anger. He took a shaky step forward, but Claire grabbed his arm. Freya gave them a flash of the shotgun. Liam stepped back.

'The Gardaí are seeing more and more family destruction situations these days. It'll look just like one.'

'But that's an awful plan, Freya,' said George, bewildered. 'Not sent from the universe! Why does everyone have to die? It makes no sense.'

'I suppose I left out one detail,' Freya leaned back on the counter behind her. Sighed. Coughed and pulled her hair back. 'Hudson and I aren't actually going to die.'

'That definitely makes more sense,' said Lizzie. Freya managed a little smile.

'It does, doesn't it? I've only given Hudson and myself enough to make us convincingly sick, but not enough to kill us. I've no intention of dying. And I don't want rid of Hudson just yet, that'd be far too suspicious. And he's had something to knock him out, as well as the poison. Again, courtesy of the garden. I want to keep him ignorant and out of this. I was so impressed when I worked it all out, the pieces all fitted. Especially when Hudson and I survive and can fill in the gaps. This is why it's such a good plan. Hudson doesn't even have to be in on it to help. He can confirm the Declan turning up part. And he doesn't know who actually killed him or why. He's missing all the 'revelations' now as he snoozes. So, lucky me will pull through, as will Hudson. We'll live to tell the police the sorry tale.'

'You'll be the only survivors. History is written by the victors,' said Lizzie.

'Yep,' said Freya. 'That's the idea.'

'That's quite the risk to give yourself the poison too. How can you be sure you haven't given yourself too much?'

'I have my ways.'

'How... oh,' said Lizzie quietly. 'The deer.'

'Yes, exactly. I didn't want to do it. They looked at me with their big gorgeous eyes.' Freya teared up. 'It was awful. But that doe, I reckoned she was probably about 100–120 pounds, in and around my weight. She was perfect to test it on. But I gave her too much. She was too sick. I don't want to get that bad. Just bad enough that it's clear we're victims too. But, like, I don't want to need a new kidney or anything.'

'Are you forgetting something?' said George. 'A flaw in this dreadful plan! You can't kill me! I'm your father. You love me.'

'I do love you, Daddy. Very much. But I've thought about it and thought about it, and no other solution is so neat, so close to perfect. This is a big gamble, I need it to work.'

'There's got to be another way,' George repeated.

Freya welled up again. Tears started to slip down her face.

'I know you won't get to see it, but I promise you I'll return Butler Hall to its full glory. Hudson's millions will bring the dream alive. Restore the Butlers to their rightful place.'

Freya opened a drawer and pulled out a packet of tissues. Awkwardly managing the shotgun she took out a tissue and dabbed her eyes. Then blew her nose.

'Freya,' said George, and stopped. Freya took out a second tissue. Then, keeping the gun pointed at them all, she ducked into the pantry for a second. Coming back out before anyone had a chance to move.

She was holding something. She walked around the island, closer to George and stretched out her hand.

It was the missing whiskey decanter. It gleamed, sparkling clean, though the continent-shaped bloodstain was still there, as if someone had taken great care to sanitise every inch but that spot. Freya held it by the neck with the new tissue.

'Here,' she said, handing it to George.

Confused, George took it from her. Turned it in his hands, looking at it, puzzled.

'Thanks,' said Freya, snatching it back.

'Oh, George, you fool!' yelled Claire from the other end of the kitchen. 'What did you do that for?'

Freya put the decanter away again, as realisation dawned on her father.

'Did you just make me put my fingerprints on the murder weapon?'

'Sorry, Daddy.'

Liam groaned. Freya looked at him.

'I'll wait till you've passed out to work out how to get gunshot residue on your hands. It'll be easier then.'

'I won't let you,' he said.

'You won't have much of a say in the matter, I'm afraid, Liam.'

'Is that what's next?' asked Lizzie. 'Are we going to wait now until we die? Or do you have any other prep?'

Freya's eyes focused on Lizzie. Her head tilted to the side.

'No, I think that's it. Just waiting.' Freya looked over at Claire and Liam. 'If I've gotten it right you should all be getting very weak, very soon.'

Liam groaned again, as if prompted by Freya's words. He looked at Lizzie, fear along with the pain in his eyes. He lowered himself onto the ground. Sitting with his knees bent, his back against the wall.

Lizzie stared at her brother. Both of them with rising panic in their eyes. Lizzie forced herself to breathe deeply. Forced her lungs to accept more air. She saw Claire do the same as Liam. Slowly ease herself to the ground. Claire then moved closer to Liam. Put her arm around him. Lizzie felt a tiny bit of relief. Her mother had gone down, not from weakness, just yet, but to comfort her brother. Lizzie was struck. Maybe this was how they got out of here? Do what Freya thought was going to happen? Pretend to give in to the poison. Freya hadn't questioned Lizzie's health so far. Panic and terror doing a similar job to her face as the poison. But what if Freya thought she'd succumbed? Was too weak to fight back or flee? Lizzie started to lower herself onto the kitchen floor. Sinking to her knees. She mouthed 'I'm okay' to Claire, her words hidden from Freya by a well-timed turn of her head. She issued a low moan while she mopped her brow.

'Oh, bloody hell, my girl, look at them. You've got to stop this!' George cried out.

Freya didn't reply. Through pretend drowsy eyes Lizzie watched her come over and look down. Lizzie felt the cold nudge of the shotgun's metal barrel on her side. Lizzie groaned. She was sure Freya would be happy to adapt her plan and shoot her too, if needed. Especially if she realised Lizzie wasn't poisoned. Lizzie groaned again and grimaced. It wasn't hard to sound ill, she felt enough horror in her bones not to need to act.

'Freya, stop this nonsense! I beg you!' Lizzie watched George through her half-closed eyes.

He took a step closer to his daughter.

'Stop right there,' she said, shaking her head. She moved back around to the opposite side of the island.

George took another step forward. Freya kept a close eye on him.

'I'm sorry,' he said. 'You're right. Everything you said. I messed up. This is, indeed, all my fault. But this is a gamble too far for you. I'm not saying that just because you are threatening to kill me, but because I care. You'll end up in jail, for certain. There's no way you can pull this off. It's too big a con.'

'I think you underestimate me, Daddy.'

'I probably do. Maybe I should have realised you were all grown up. I should have trusted you and opened up to you. About everything.'

Not the focus of Freya's attention, Lizzie shuffled a few inches closer to Claire and Liam. And the back door.

Freya stepped left and came out from behind the island. Nothing stood between her and George now but a metre or two of tiled floor and a vast gulf of disillusioned disbelief.

Lizzie inched closer still to her family and the door.

'Kill them all, fine. But you don't need to kill me. I'll disappear. Leave you to it.' George had entered the bargaining stage.

'I thought about that, Daddy. But the problem is the plan doesn't hold together without you. My hands are tied.'

'For God's sake, child!' George roared, slamming his hand on the island. The fruit bowl shook.

In a flash, George bolted at Freya. His two hands outstretched, grabbing for the barrel of the shotgun.

'No!' screeched Freya, rearing back, fighting her father for purchase on the cold, dark metal. Seizing the opportunity Lizzie dived across the last space between her, Claire and Liam.

'Mam,' Lizzie gasped, 'help me if you can.' She grabbed one of Liam's arms, Claire the other.

A thunderous roar exploded behind them.

A blast that shook the walls. The smell of gunpowder fell on the room like debris. They all turned and stared. A massive smoking hole in the wall over George's shoulder gaped at them as if in shock. The shot rang, deafening, in Lizzie's ears. Reverberating like chimes of doom. Everyone froze, stunned, like none of them had believed it was a real gun, capable of such damage. George and Freya, both still holding the gun, stared at the damage. Freya looked dazed, as if the hole in brick and plaster was the first hint of the reality of what she was planning.

'This is real, my girl,' said George, gently. She looked him in the eyes.

'I know.' As suddenly as they'd stopped, the struggle began again.

'GIVE IT TO ME!' roared George, pulling the gun.

'NO!' Freya grunted and screeched, pulling it back.

'Now, Mam!' hissed Lizzie, pulling on Liam's arm. They threw themselves towards the door. Lizzie kicking it open.

'Stop!' roared Freya, twisting as she struggled, seeing them half-stumble, half-run from the kitchen. Snatching a glance back at her, Lizzie saw the contortion of desperation on Freya's face as they fell into the night.

57

Out on the terrace, Lizzie helped Liam, his legs like a newborn foal, weak and new. Freya's cries of rage and frustration echoed after them.

'C'mon, c'mon, hurry,' said Lizzie, urging them on. Claire grabbed Liam's other arm. They crossed the terrace, then down the steps to the lawn. Claire slipped on the wet grass, nearly taking them all down with her. With a guttural cry she got up again. Desperation giving her strength. They made it to the trees and stopped, panting. Liam rested back against an angled tree trunk. He gave a low, pained moan. Lizzie gasped for breath. Her heart beating at full throttle. Rain from earlier fell on them from branches and leaves, mixing with the sweat of terror and poison on their faces.

'What are we going to do, Lizzie?' said Claire. 'We're in no fit state to get out of here.'

'We've no choice, Mam. We're just going to have to try our best.'

A boom erupted from behind them, in the house. Lizzie and Claire's heads whipped around. Even Liam turned. That was a second shot. Another hole in the wall? Or had one of them succeeded in their struggle? Had one of them come out on top?

Lizzie looked at Claire and Liam. Huddled closer to her mother. She didn't say a word, but knew they were thinking the same thing. This nightmare could be all over now. If George had succeeded.

They each held their breath. Stared at the house through the gaps in the branches.

A figure appeared in the doorway.

58

'Dammit,' whimpered Claire.

The victor in the doorway didn't take up all the space. Didn't fill it like George would have.

Freya, the shotgun held across her body, stood there, triumphant.

She looked back over her shoulder into the house. The kitchen lights illuminating her face. Even from this distance Lizzie thought she could see the wildness in her eyes. The adrenaline coursing through her after what she had just done. The spatter of blood on her face.

Lizzie watched as she cracked the shotgun and dumped out the old shells and fed in two new cartridges. With a snap she shut it again. Then she called out.

'Don't make this harder than it has to be, O'Sheas!'

Lizzie's pulse quickened further. Freya had grown up in these woods. She knew their every nook and cranny. Unlike the O'Sheas who could barely find their way in the daylight.

'Poor George,' whispered Claire. 'He didn't deserve that.'

'C'mon, Mam, don't think about it. We've got to go. She's coming for us.'

Lizzie reached for Liam's arm.

'No,' he said.

'What?'

'You have to leave me here,' he said, his voice weak. 'I'll slow you down. I'm getting weaker, Lizzie. Go on without me.'

Claire suppressed a sob behind her. Lizzie looked back at her mother, her face obscured by the dark of the night woods. Light from the house behind them filtering through the surrounding trees, creating a halo around her.

'No!' cried Lizzie this time, her anguish clear despite her hushed tones. 'I'm not leaving you.'

A shot pierced the still night air.

'I've got more where they came from, the plan can adapt.' Freya's voice rang out in the night. Closer.

The cold, hard knot in Lizzie's stomach tightened. How much ammunition did Freya have? Lizzie drew in a deep, shaky breath. She reached for Liam's arm, pulled him to her.

'No one is left behind.'

Dragging her brother, they plunged deeper into the darkness. The forest, dim and murky in the daylight, was now barely more than a nebulous void. The indistinct trees loomed like a malevolent crowd. What little light the stars and moon could have cast was hidden by the thick tree canopy. The only stars Lizzie was aware of were stars of rising panic before her eyes. She pressed on, Liam's arm around her neck, his body clammy against her, his heavy gasping breaths in her ear. She stretched out her free arm into the darkness in front of her. Batting away the low and small branches smacking her in the face as she moved, frightening her each time. Night insects buzzed and dive-bombed, surprise attacks on her unseeing eyes. She was desperate for the torch, but left her smartphone in her pocket, afraid of alerting Freya to where they were.

'I can't see anything,' breathed Claire, right behind her, touching her back as they moved. Lizzie could hear the same roots of panic in her voice. Felt her worried words warm on the back of her neck.

'I know, it's so black. But I think we're going in the right direction.'

The frantic thump of her heart was getting louder in her ears. Deafening her, leaving her afraid she wouldn't hear Freya, and they'd stumble upon her. Liam leant on her more, his feet dragging louder through the forest floor carpet. Lizzie fought to keep the panic at bay.

Another shot cracked. Just above their heads.

'Closer,' mumbled Liam.

'It wasn't,' lied Lizzie through gritted teeth.

Lizzie felt the lack of Claire's body heat. Heard her shuffle slow. She looked back. Her mother was dropping behind.

'Mam, you can do it.'

Lizzie stopped. Claire nodded, dragged her arm across her forehead, staunching the cascade of sweat. She tried to move quicker. Lizzie reached out a hand, but Claire stumbled. Fell into the soft, wet, sweet rotting mulch of the forest floor.

'Mam!' she cried quietly. She turned to Liam. 'I'm letting go of you for a moment. Hold on.'

She took Liam's arm off her shoulders. Leant him against the nearest tree. Turned to her mother, whose dark outline she could just make out. She took tentative steps back. Putting out her hands she found Claire's arm. She helped a panting Claire up again. Hugged her.

Claire pressed something into her hand. Lizzie felt its smooth rectangular edges in her palm.

'It's my phone,' croaked Claire. 'Keep it safe. The app... it might show what plants she looked up. If... if we get to safety, maybe it'll help the doctors...'

Lizzie shoved the phone into her pocket. *If we get to safety.* Her mother knew how grim the stakes were.

There was a sudden rustle behind them. Lizzie whipped

round. To where she'd left Liam. She could see his outline, shivering, stepping away from the supporting tree.

'Liam, what are you doing?' she hissed. Lizzie took a step away from Claire and closer to him

'You've a better chance without me.' His voice weak and frail, no need to keep the volume down, it had no power left.

'Liam, don't!'

'You n-need to help Mam get out. I forgive you, Lizzie, for everything. It's okay. Save Mam.'

He turned and fell into the pitch black.

'No!' cried out Lizzie, dashing forward. Arm outstretched.

Another shot fired. Shattering the night air.

A red-hot arrow of pain sliced through Lizzie's left bicep. She howled, fell forward. Grabbed her arm as she hit the ground. Felt her fingers overflow with blood where she grasped. She stretched her neck and looked and saw the stumbling hint of Liam disappearing into the void.

'Liam,' she cried out, 'Liam!'

Claire fell to her knees beside her.

'You've been hit, no, no!' Claire scrabbled for her, sobbing. Looking up at the direction Liam had gone as she felt for her daughter. Lizzie let go of her wound, took Claire's hand with her bloody palm.

'It's okay,' she inhaled sharply. 'It's okay.'

'Was that a cry I heard?' Freya's voice called out, her words swooping and gliding about the night like the barn owl. 'Come on, O'Sheas, let's just get this over with. It's time to die!'

59

Lizzie rolled onto all fours. Face contorted with the pain as she put her weight on her injured arm. She felt the damp of the forest floor soak her palms, knees and shins. Claire tried to help her up. But it wasn't clear who was helping who. Lizzie could feel her mother getting worse. She was weak and getting rapidly weaker.

'Oh, Lizzie,' Claire jabbered. Lizzie brought her head – light and dizzy with pain – in close to Claire's. Held a finger to her lips. Hushed her.

'Liam,' Claire whispered back, the name infused with anguish.

Lizzie shook her head. They'd never find him. They could barely see one foot in front of the other.

And Freya was coming.

Claire swayed, Lizzie grabbed her wrist. Pulled her mother's arm around her shoulder. A flash of white hot pain radiated from Lizzie's wound. She suppressed a gasp. With her other arm she pulled Claire's waist closer into her.

Lizzie started again. Taking a step or two, then stopping.

Listening. Begging her perfidious heart to quieten so she could hear Freya's approach.

Claire clung to her, letting Lizzie shuffle her forward. Panting and dizzy, Lizzie felt her knees weaken, leaden, just as she needed them most. Like Liam before her, Lizzie felt Claire's feet begin to drag.

'Stay with me, Mam, stay with me,' she cried into Claire's ear.

'Lizzie,' she whispered back.

Lizzie gave in to the hot tears that had been begging to start. Already nearly blinded by the night, they blurred what little vision she had left. The trees closed in around them.

Everything conspiring to obscure a fallen branch on the forest floor.

They tumbled. Lizzie gasped as the air slammed out of her lungs. Flat on her back, she stared up at the overhead branches, seeing a tiny gap among the treetops. A star, just visible, twinkled at her. Mocking her. Lizzie made a wish. *Let us get out of here alive.* Summoning her last reserves, she pushed herself over, pain searing through her wounded arm. Lizzie stretched out, feeling for her mother. Listening for her. She crawled towards Claire's pained mumbles, feeling the forest floor squelch and ooze through her fingers.

She found her mother in a heap, put her hands under her arms and dragged her up against a large tree; using touch and smell to find a way in the all-consuming dark. Lizzie leant back against the damp trunk and hugged her mother to her. 'So s-s-sorry,' Claire said, quieter still. Holding her, Lizzie traced her fingertips down Claire's arm to her wrist. Felt the faint, slow, thump, thump, thump of her pulse. So weak.

If they didn't get to a hospital soon, she knew Claire would die. And Liam too. Wherever he was. And that was even if they could get away from Freya. Which itself seemed an impossible task. Lizzie let her tears flow unchecked. Silently.

She heaved her mother up again, getting little help from her, her chest shaking with her noiseless tears.

A sound. Nearby.

The crack and clunk of metal. The shotgun being reloaded.

Lizzie felt woozy. Her own strength wavering. The treacherous alchemy of adrenaline and panic was turning her limbs to fool's gold. Filling them with lead. Each step became harder and harder. The flow of blood from her arm streamed down to her wrist, soaking Claire's waist where Lizzie held her.

But she was beginning to see the ground in front of them a little more clearly. With every step, the trees close to them thinned. Were they getting closer to the road? Lizzie's heart leapt. Could they really be there already?

But they weren't. Lizzie's tears stung harder. Instead they came out into a small clearing where light from the night sky snuck in through large gaps in the canopy. She could see again. She looked at Claire's face. Even in the moonlight it was deathly pale. Her eyes were nearly shut.

Lizzie caught a movement ahead of her. She pulled Claire closer. She moaned and Lizzie shook and nearly buckled under her dead weight.

A flash of metal glinted in the moonlight.

Stepping into the open, into the night's spotlight, a blonde head. A sad, but triumphant, smile.

'Told you I'd find you.'

60

Freya waved the gun at her, the dried blood on her face a spatter of over-sized freckles in the dark. She swayed a little.

'I'm surprised you're still standing,' she said to Lizzie. 'I've poisoned you, I've shot you. You're a modern day Rasputin.'

Lizzie said nothing. Clutched Claire closer to her.

'Your neat little story is ruined now, Freya. It's time to give it up.'

'I don't agree with you. It just needs a little rewrite. That's all.'

Lizzie felt Claire go fully limp in her arms. She looked down at her, her eyes were shut.

'Won't be long now,' said Freya, following Lizzie's gaze. 'So, what, are you bulimic as well as an alcoholic? Is that it? Fed the dinner to the dog? How'd I not get you?'

Lizzie said nothing.

'Cat got your tongue?'

Freya's sneer faltered. She began to retch. Lizzie took steps backwards, dragging Claire with her, away from Freya as she was bent over.

'Stop!' Freya yelled as she righted herself, swaying, rubbing her hand across her mouth. Pointing the gun back at them.

A noise in the distance made them both look about. Growling and rumbling. Getting louder quickly.

It sounded like an engine, Lizzie thought.

'What's that?' said Freya.

'It's the Gardaí,' blurted Lizzie.

Freya's clammy head shot up.

'No, it's not! There's no way.'

The engine got louder. Nearer. A beam of headlights flashed through the trees. Lizzie thought quickly.

'I asked Maggie,' she bluffed. A bolt of inspiration hitting her. 'When she left the estate to check her bank balance, I asked her to tell the Gardaí to come find us if we didn't make contact by tonight.'

'No you didn't! She'd have told me.'

'Over here!' Lizzie cried out. 'We're over here! Help!'

'Liar! Who is that?' Freya swung around. Pointed the shotgun in the direction of the vehicle. Lizzie threw herself and Claire down, terrified of being shot again.

The engine was roaring now. The headlights bouncing all around like a light show.

The quad bike came bursting through the trees. Careering wildly, as if driverless. Freya fired at it as it hurtled towards her.

Lizzie heard a cry from the bike but it didn't stop.

With a nauseating crunch and scream it ploughed into Freya.

It skidded and stopped. Bucked from the seat, the berserk driver was thrown to the ground. Landing askew, close to the stricken Freya.

Leaving Claire lying on the ground, Lizzie leapt up, ran to them.

Looked down.

Beside an unmoving Freya lay George. A wound deep and

fatal in his belly. A fresh injury to his leg. His eyes flickered. Lizzie collapsed to her knees.

'Oh God, George. I thought you were dead.'

A faint chuckle then a groan. His face flickered between agony and a hint of a smile.

'So, so did... did she.' He coughed and Lizzie winced at the death rattle. 'But she forgot... I am a conman. And a good one despite... what she said.'

Lizzie took his hand.

'I'll get you help. I'll get you on the bike.'

Lying there, George shook his head.

'No.' His voice growing weaker. 'There's no room f-f-for me. I'm, I'm only glad I knew where she'd hide it. Get your mother. Brother. Go. Go.'

Lizzie hesitated.

'Go,' he mumbled. 'We... Freya and I, we deserve this.'

Lizzie placed his hand down. Reluctant. Got to her feet.

She turned and jumped on the quad bike. Revved the throttle and rode over to her mother. Picking Claire up she laid her in front of her, wedged in by the handlebars.

Lizzie looked back at the Butlers, bloody and supine on the forest floor. George's eyes closed now. Lizzie saw his hand creep across the forest floor, searching for, then taking, Freya's hand. Then all was still.

Lizzie took one last look at them, then turned the bike and rode away.

EPILOGUE
THREE MONTHS LATER

Lizzie looked at the sheet of paper in her hand. A cold wind was whipping at it. She grasped the other side to hold it still. A map, and a number ringed in red pen – 604. There would be a small marker, with the number, and a sapling planted there. She looked up again. The leaves were mostly gone from the trees now. She was happy about that. Autumn was her new favourite season. The bare branches, the view of the sky. That's all she wanted these days. This place wasn't too bad though. The trees were some way back off the path, keeping their distance.

She shoved the paper back in her pocket and tightened the yellow scarf around her neck. Pulling her woolly hat down over her ears, she started down the path again. Going the way she thought she was meant to. Looking left and right, reading the small pegs in the ground as she went by: 306, 307, 308. It was probably lovely here in the spring, when the wildflowers started to bloom. The grass borders a sea of yellows and blues and whites. Small birds singing and swooping overhead. She'd come back then. This place was wild, but in a managed way. Not like... she shook her head. Forcing out intrusive flashbacks of a frantic night-time dash through woods, the desperate wait for an ambulance, the questions over and over, the terror. She shoved her gloved hands into her pockets. Her fingers finding the green chip in there. Green for three months sober. If she hadn't had the wine that night she'd have the purple chip. No one had said she couldn't have it. The denial was all hers. But right now three months felt right. She turned it over and over in her fingers as she walked.

She checked the map again after a while. Checking the route. She was nearly there... 546, 547. She followed the path around, keeping the tangled hedgerow to her right. Keeping to the path as it snaked to the left. She slowed as she approached the spot. Her feet heavy with the weight of her emotions. With the feelings that seemed to have replaced everything inside her. Her organs, her bones, every nerve and sinew were instead fear, sadness, regret, love...

She stopped. 604. An elm sapling planted here. This natural graveyard had no headstones. No tended rows, plastic flowers or gravel. Just resting places among nature. Part of nature. Lizzie looked down at the gentle mound of disturbed earth.

'Hey,' she said. 'I hope you like it here. It's a beautiful place.' She gazed about at the immediate surrounds. The wildflowers would be rampant here next year. 'I hope you approve of the choice. I know it's far from home, but I'll come visit. As often as I can.'

A sudden gust of wind lashed across the meadow, tossing and tangling the strands of Lizzie's black hair that fell below her hat. She shivered. Pulled her coat closer around her.

'I miss you.'

Lizzie turned, and began the long walk back to the car.

She saw no one else as she left. Her car was still the only one in the car park. People didn't like to visit graveyards at the best of times, when the sun was high in the sky and there was hope in the air. Perhaps impending winter brought with it too much gloom to visit the dead too.

She pulled open the passenger side door of her lonely car. She sat in.

'Everything go okay?'

Lizzie looked over at Liam at the wheel. He placed his phone in his pocket.

'Yeah. Yeah,' she sighed heavily. 'It's all as it should be. Where it should be. It's lovely. You sure you're not up to going to see it?'

Liam shook his head. He still looked a little gaunt. He'd be himself again by the time the wildflowers came up. They'd come back then; maybe he'd be more able for it in the spring.

'No worries. No pressure.'

Liam turned the key in the ignition. The car rumbled into life. Squinting, Lizzie pulled down the sun visor against the glare of the low autumn sun. She looked at the postcard she'd slipped into the visor pocket. A happy Buddha smiled at her. She smiled too, thinking of the words Hudson had written on the back of it. He was doing well, she was relieved to know. Much better now. It had been touch and go for a while. It hadn't been the poisoning that had left the lasting effects – Freya had judged that right and he'd been fine. It had been the emotional fallout that had done the most damage. He'd inherited the lot. George and Freya had been the last Butlers, and unlike Claire and George's marriage, his and Freya's had been completely legal. He'd been handed the keys to Butler Hall. A legacy he didn't need and certainly didn't want. When they'd met last at Maggie's funeral, mere weeks after everything had happened, he'd been pale and worn, and she'd still been in shock, her bandaged arm in a sling. They'd talked. He'd told Lizzie he had a plan. He was going to track down all the women George had hurt and swindled and use the proceeds from the sale of Butler

Hall to give them back their money. He was going to make sure some good came out of all of this mess.

Lizzie looked over at Liam.

'You sure you're feeling up to driving? It's not the shortest drive back.'

'Yes, I am, don't worry. And it's not as if we've any choice though, right?'

'No, I guess not.'

'When do you get your licence back?'

'Not for a while.'

Lizzie's phone rang. As Liam pulled out of the car park she hit answer. She turned on the heater with her free hand.

'Hi,' she said, phone to her ear, raising her voice over the quiet hum of the engine.

'Hi, darling. Well, how'd it go?' Claire's voice filled Lizzie's ear. 'Did they put him somewhere nice? Would I approve?'

'You would, Mam. It's a beautiful spot. I think Dad will rest easy there.'

'I'm glad to hear that. Thanks so much for going. I'm just...'

'You don't have to say anything.'

'Did your brother go and see it?'

'No.'

'But that's okay, maybe next time.'

'Exactly.'

'Thanks, love. Anyway, I've just put a roast in the oven. Potatoes and stuffing and carrots are going on soon too. It'll all be ready in about an hour and a half. Will you be back by then?'

'Definitely.'

'Good. Don't dally, I don't want to overdo it.'

'Don't worry, Mam. We're on our way. I'm coming home.'

A LETTER FROM TRÍONA

Dear Reader,

I want to say a huge thank you for choosing to read *The Party*. It really means so much to me that you did. If you enjoyed it, and want to keep up to date with all my latest releases, just sign up at the following link. Your email address will never be shared and you can unsubscribe at any time.

www.bookouture.com/triona-walsh

The idea for a book can come from anywhere. *The Party*'s spark came from an image on Facebook. A friend posted an aerial photograph of a forgotten mansion, a place called Moore Hall in Co. Mayo in the West of Ireland. It is ruined and lost deep in a vast forest. It didn't take much to be intrigued by this very real place. What would it be like if someone still lived there? Among the trees and nature, cut off from the world around them? Would it be claustrophobic, these trees encroaching and looming over everything? And if something bad happened... how would anyone know? A perfect setting for a murder mystery, I think you'll agree. All I had to do was people it with some interesting characters. And have a few themes, like trust, truth and redemption run through it. Lizzie is a good person who has had bad things happen to her. She's human and got things wrong. And that's life, none of us are perfect! It's about doing our best, admitting it when we've got things wrong and trying to be better next time. Oh, and not murdering anyone either!

I hope you loved *The Party*, and if you did I would be very grateful if you could write a review. I'd love to hear what you think, and it makes such a difference helping new readers to discover one of my books for the first time.

I love hearing from you – get in touch on my Facebook page, through Twitter, Instagram or my website.

Thanks,

Tríona

www.trionawalsh.com

facebook.com/TrionaWalshAuthor

twitter.com/thetrionawalsh

instagram.com/trionawalsh

ACKNOWLEDGEMENTS

To Jayne, my editor, who had to hit the ground running. Thank you for making the process so easy, and for all your brilliant work on *The Party*. Though we mightn't quite agree on what could kill a man, it's a pleasure and privilege to work with you!

To everyone at Bookouture, the biggest of thank yous. You're a fantastic team who has made this author feel supported and valued every step of the way.

The Mammy and Papa, to give you your proper names, this book is dedicated to you. And deservedly so. Quite apart from being my first readers, returning invaluable advice on plot and character, you do all the other heavy lifting. Encouraging me when I think it's all total rubbish. Telling me when it *is* total rubbish. Diligently answering the unhealthy number of text messages I send. Never failing to keep me going. I love you, you're the best.

Harry, my eldest child and now a member of the first readers club, and unlike your grandparents, trapped here with me for 24/7 free feedback. Lucky you. Thank you for keeping your poor anxious mammy going, for being honest and analytical. I'm glad I'm paying for that English degree now, it's been a useful investment! You've been brilliant.

To the rest of the gang, Charlie, Ruby and Lily – not to get too sentimental but your enthusiasm for my writing makes this mammy's heart so happy. And your tolerance of the benign neglect is also much appreciated. Ruby, best plot-bouncing buddy – that's two for two now.

And Dan, while you'll never make a living as a book reviewer, your proofing skills should win awards. Also, thank you for picking up the slack and making sure that benign neglect doesn't wander too far into the territory of actual neglect.

To my entire family, immediate and extended, who have been just the best support, I have been so, so touched. To my brother Dara in particular, who has gone over and above in helping me in my writing endeavours. I promise I'll freeze a book in a block of ice one day.

Thanks to Trevor O'Sullivan who unknowingly introduced me to Moore Hall – the inspiration for the fictional Butler Hall – by posting a breathtaking picture of it on Facebook. I was immediately fascinated by this ruin in the woods. Who wouldn't want to be murdered there?

To Cadbury's and my local Costa, without whom this book would never have been written.

To all my friends, for your enthusiasm and support. I cannot overstate how much it means to me. How much it keeps me going. You are the jet engines beneath my wings!

And lastly, because they were so delighted to be included last time, to my cats Bob, Maggie and Zuzu, without whom my writing day would have been a little lonelier. (I am getting you a cat-flap though. Seriously, make up your minds...)